BRIGHT FUTURES

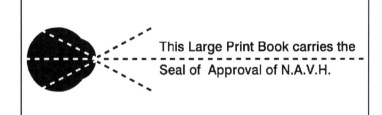

This Large Print Book carries the
Seal of Approval of N.A.V.H.

A LEW FONESCA MYSTERY

BRIGHT FUTURES

STUART M. KAMINSKY

THORNDIKE PRESS

A part of Gale, Cengage Learning

LT
M

GALE
CENGAGE Learning

Detroit • New York • San Francisco • New Haven, Conn • Waterville, Maine • London

GALE
CENGAGE Learning

Thorndike Press® Large Print Mystery.
The text of this Large Print edition is unabridged.
Other aspects of the book may vary from the original edition.
Set in 16 pt. Plantin.
Printed on permanent paper.

LIBRARY OF CONGRESS CATALOGING-IN-PUBLICATION DATA

Kaminsky, Stuart M.
   Bright futures : a Lew Fonesca mystery / by Stuart M. Kaminsky.
    p. cm. — (Thorndike Press large print mystery)
   ISBN-13: 978-1-4104-1424-3 (alk. paper)
   ISBN-10: 1-4104-1424-8 (alk. paper)
   1. Fonesca, Lew (Fictitious character)—Fiction. 2. Private investigators—Florida—Sarasota—Fiction. 3. Eccentrics and eccentricities—Fiction. 4. Singers—Fiction. 5. Sarasota (Fla.)—Fiction. 6. Large type books. I. Title.
PS3561.A43B75 2009b
813'.54—dc22   2009000221

Published in 2009 by arrangement with Tom Doherty Association, LLC.

Printed in the United States of America
1 2 3 4 5 6 7 13 12 11 10 09

To Natasha Melisa "the Perll"
Kaminsky,
from Dad with love.
And thanks for the idea.

PROLOGUE

Twelve hundred years before I drove my dying car into the parking lot of the Dairy Queen on 301 in Sarasota, saber-tooth tigers, mastodons, giant armadillos, and camels roamed what are now the high-end malls that house Saks, Nieman-Marcus, Lord & Taylor, and twenty-screen movie theaters.

The land that is now the Florida Keys was part of a single landmass double the size of the present state.

People who inhabited Florida twelve hundred centuries ago were hunters and gatherers who lived on nuts, plants, small animals, and shellfish. There was a steady clean water supply, good stones on the ground for toolmaking, and more firewood than they needed. Complex cultures developed with temple mounds and villages. These villages traded with one another and developed cultivated agriculture.

As ocean waters wore away land, the peninsula shrank.

Juan Ponce de León landed in 1513 in what became St. Augustine. He called the area "La Florida," in honor of Pascua florida — the feast of flowers. In 1539 Hernando de Soto arrived, and a short time later, in quick succession, came settlers, slaves, and hurricanes. The natives were gone, though remnants of natives and runaway slaves created the Seminole tribes. By this time the peninsula had already long since shrunk to its present size.

Soon came the railroads, the airplanes, and the almost endless stream of cars on I-75 and I-95 carrying snowbird Canadians and retirees from Illinois, Minnesota, New York, Michigan, and even California. The few remaining Seminoles were herded into casinos, which they fought over and operated at a profit.

Towering buildings rose, blocking out view and sun. The more that were built, the more they cost and the greater the crowds.

Then my wife was killed by a hit-and-run driver on the Outer Drive in Chicago. With a Chicago Cubs cap on my head and in need of a shave, I came 1,044 miles looking for the end of the world and settled in an office at the rear of the Dairy Queen parking lot in Sarasota when my car broke down forever.

Now the DQ is gone, replaced by a bank. The less-than-shabby, concrete block two-story office building I live and work in will be torn down in a few days.

There are twenty-nine banks and numerous branches in Sarasota County, and only one DQ remains.

There are more than 360,000 people in the county. Florida progress.

My name is Lewis Fonesca. I find people.

■ ■ ■ ■

I
PLAYING WITH CHILDREN

■ ■ ■ ■

1

"There's a man sleeping in the corner of your office," the boy said.

"I know."

"He's Chinese," the kid said. "You want to know how I know?"

"He looks Chinese," I said.

"But he could be Japanese or Korean," the kid said, looking at Victor Woo, who was lying faceup on his bedroll with his eyes closed.

"He's not."

"Pale skin, small eyes, and his . . ."

The boy was seventeen, a student at Pine View School for the Gifted. His name was Greg Legerman. He was short, nervous and unable to sit still or be quiet. Next to him sat a tall, thin boy with tousled white hair and rimless glasses. Winston Churchill Graeme, also seventeen, was tall, calm, and sat still, looking at whomever was talking.

"Am I right? Winn, am I right?" Greg said

to his friend with a laugh as he punched the other boy in the arm, punched him hard.

Winn Graeme didn't answer. Greg didn't care.

"You're moving," Greg said.

"How could you tell?" I asked.

"The six cardboard boxes over there near the Chinese man."

"I'm moving," I said.

It had taken me less than an hour to pack. I lived in the adjacent room, a small office space, and I owned almost nothing. We were sitting in the reception room, which had a desk, three chairs, and four small paintings on the wall. That was it. My friend Ames McKinney would be by later to pick up the desk, the boxes, the TV with the built-in video player, and the knee-high bookcase.

"They're tearing this building down," said Greg. He grinned.

He was easily amused. He punched Winn Graeme in the arm again.

"Why do you keep punching him?" I asked.

"We're kidding. He punches me sometimes."

Winn gave a halfhearted tap to the arm of Greg Legerman.

"Am I right? They're tearing the building down?"

14

"Yes."

"You have another place for your office?" asked Greg.

"Yes."

"The Dairy Queen used to be right out there," said Greg.

"Yes," I said.

"They should tear down banks and put up DQs," Greg said.

I agreed but didn't say so. He didn't seem to need anyone agreeing with him about anything.

Victor Woo stirred in the corner and rolled toward the wall.

"Mind my asking who that is?" asked Greg.

"Victor Woo."

"And what's he doing sleeping on the floor of your office?"

"He walked in one afternoon," I said.

"Why?"

"He killed my wife in Chicago. He feels guilty and depressed."

"You're kidding, right?" asked Greg.

"No," I said.

"Wow," said Greg.

I called out, "Don't punch him."

Greg hesitated, shrugged and let his hands fall into his lap for a few seconds before they started to roam again.

15

"Let's go," Winn said, starting to rise.

Winston Graeme had the remnants of a Russell Crowe accent.

"No wait," said Greg. "I like this guy. I like you, Mr. Fonesca. You come highly recommended."

"By who and for what?"

"By a Pine View student."

"Who is nameless?"

"No, the student has a name," he said with a laugh.

I couldn't open my mouth fast enough to stop him from punching his friend.

"I'm a process server," I said.

"You find people. You help people."

I didn't respond. He hadn't really asked a question. I make enough money to live by serving papers for lawyers. I didn't want more work. I didn't want money in the bank. I wanted to be able to pick up my duffle bag, which was always partially packed, add a few things, and walk out the door.

"We can pay," said Greg. "What's your fee?"

Victor got up on his elbows and looked over at us. He was wearing a red sweatshirt that had a Chicago Bulls logo and the word "Bulls" on the front. The sleeves on the sweatshirt had been roughly cut off.

16

Something in my face told the two boys that I wasn't interested.

"You can listen," said Greg, starting to rise, changing his mind and sitting again. "Ten minutes."

"Five minutes. What's your problem?" I asked.

"Ronnie Gerall is in jail, juvenile. He's seventeen. They say he murdered a crazy old man. He didn't. The police aren't even looking for anyone else."

Winn Graeme adjusted his glasses again and glanced at Victor.

"Okay," said Greg. "We want you to find someone — the person who killed Philip Horvecki."

I had read about the murder of Philip Horvecki in the *Herald-Tribune* a few days before. He had been beaten to death in his home. Horvecki was one of the Sarasota superrich. Semiretired, he had earned his money in land development when the market was hot. He was involved in local politics and had run without success for everything from property appraiser and tax collector to city council, and his causes were many.

His latest cause was something called Bright Futures, a program to provide financial aid to high school students going to a Florida college or university. Horvecki

17

wanted the program abolished. He didn't want to pay for people's college education. The argument that the program was paid for by the Florida lottery made no difference to Horvecki.

His second most recent and continuing cause involved Pine View School for the Gifted, a public school for high-IQ and high-achievement students who could test their way in. Pine View was consistently ranked in the top ten high schools in the United States. That didn't matter to Horvecki, who thought taxpayers shouldn't have to pay for elitist education. He wanted to turn Pine View into an open-admissions high school like the others in the county. For this position he had a lot of support.

All of this was in the article I had read. I remembered having the feeling that more was going on.

"Ronnie didn't do it," said Greg, looking around the room as if he had lost something or someone.

"He was found over the body covered in blood," I said.

"Circumstantial," said Greg.

"He was there to fight with Horvecki about his Pine View and Bright Futures positions," I said.

"Ronnie's got a temper I admit," said

Greg. "But he's not a killer."

I looked at Winn whose accent was more pronounced now as he said, "Ronnie's not a killer."

"Winn's from Australia," Greg said with something that sounded like pride at having an exotic trophy at his side.

"He was Australian thirteen-and-under golf champ before he moved here with his mom two years ago. Winn's a state runner-up in golf. Winn's also on the soccer and basketball teams at Sarasota High. Pine View doesn't have sports teams. Tell him."

I wasn't sure how Winn Graeme's athletic achievements qualified him to determine that Ronnie Gerall was not a killer.

"We have a rowing team," Winn said. "And cross-country."

Greg started to laugh again. He held up his fist and was stopped by the hoarse morning voice of Victor Woo saying, "Do not punch him again."

"Victor doesn't like violence," I said.

"How did he kill your wife?" asked Greg.

"Hit-and-run," I said.

"Tapping each other's just a joke with my friend," said Greg to Victor. "It's a joke. Don't be lame."

Victor was on his knees now, palms on his thighs. He was wearing purple Northwest-

19

ern University sweatpants. They didn't come close to being compatible with his Bulls shirt.

"Nonviolent hit-and-run Buddhist, right?" asked Greg. "Do you know there are an estimated seven million Buddhists in China?"

Victor was on his bare feet now, touching his face to find out if he could go another day without shaving. He didn't answer Greg Legerman, who turned to me and said, "Well, will you take the job?"

"You haven't told me who you want to find."

"Horvecki's daughter," said Winn. "She was a witness. Ronnie says she was there when he died. Now she's missing. Or find who killed Horvecki, or both. Charge double."

"No," I said.

"You haven't heard what happened," said Greg.

"I don't care. I'm sorry."

Greg looked at me, stood up, went behind his chair, and rocked it slightly. He was a short, reasonably solid kid.

"You don't look sorry," Greg said.

"I don't need the work," I said.

"We need the help," Greg said.

Nothing he said had turned it for me, but

something happened that made me open the door at least a little.

"Let's go, Greg," said Winn. "The man has integrity. I like him."

Greg was shaking his head "no." Victor walked behind the two boys and headed out the front door. He was almost certainly headed to the washroom at the end of the outdoor second-floor concrete landing. Either that or he was headed back to Chicago barefoot. It would not have surprised me.

"Wait," Greg said, shrugging off the hand that his friend had put around his bicep.

In style and size, the two boys were a study in contrast. Greg was short, compact, and slightly plump; Winn tall, lean, and muscular.

Earlier that morning, I had bicycled over, shaved, and washed at the Downtown YMCA on Main Street. I had brushed my teeth, too, and looked at my sad, clearly Italian face.

"How old is Horvecki's daughter?" I asked.

"I don't know," Greg said, looking at his friend for the answer, but Winn didn't know either.

"What's her name?"

"Rachel," said Winn.

"You have a car?" I asked.

"Yeah," said Greg.

"You know where Sarasota News and Books is?"

"Yes."

"We drive over there, you get me two coffees and two biscotti to go, and I listen to your story."

"Fair enough," said Greg. "What about Victor?"

"He knows I'll be back. I need to know who told you about me. I don't have a private investigator's license."

"Viviase," said Winn.

"Ettiene Viviase, the policeman?"

"No," said Greg. "Elisabeth Viviase, the freshman daughter of the policeman."

Sarasota News and Books wasn't crowded, but there were people dawdling over coffee at four of the six tables on the coffeehouse side of the shop. A few others roamed the shelves of firmly packed rows of books and circled around the tables piled with new arrivals.

We sat at a table near the window facing Main Street. The television mounted in the corner silently played one of the business channels. I wasn't tempted to watch.

"I've got to tell you," said Greg. "I am not

filled with confidence about you."

"Why?" I asked.

"Well, no offense, but you're a little bald guy in jeans and a frayed short-sleeved yellow shirt. You've got a baseball cap on your head and you look like someone just shot your faithful dog."

"I'm not offended. What do you have to tell me?"

"What? Oh."

Greg grinned and punched his friend's arm again.

"You really are funny."

"I wasn't trying to be," I said.

"I think that woman on television is talking about aliens," said Greg.

"No," said his friend.

"I don't mean illegal aliens. I mean the kind from outer space. Wishu-Wishuu-ooooo."

"That sounds like an Ivy League football cheer," said Winn.

"Get out," said Greg.

"Hit him and I walk," I said.

Greg, fist cocked, looked hurt, but he didn't deliver the punch. Instead, he said, "I did one of my blogs about so-called alien visitors. There aren't any. Aliens with two eyes and two legs aren't coming millions of miles to pluck people out of their beds to probe their rectums with metal rods."

A woman who had been talking to a younger woman at the table next to us looked over at the last comment.

"No aliens," I said.

"No, they're humanoids from the future, maybe hundreds of thousands of years in the future. They're archaeologists or anthropologists or whatever those sciences will be like. They appear and disappear so fast because they zip in and out of time. The shapes of the craft differ because they come from different times in the future."

"Why didn't the ones from farther in the future go back and visit the ones from more recently and coordinate?" I said.

Greg had finished something filled with caffeine over ice and topped with whipped cream. Just what he needed to calm him down. Winn had an iced tea. I played with my coffee and looked at the two extra cups of Colombia Supremo Deep Jungle Roast and the two biscotti to go.

I learned that Ronnie Gerall had come to Sarasota in his junior year, that he was a natural leader, passionate about protecting the school from politicians and social gadflies, particularly Philip Horvecki.

"Everyone likes Ronnie," said Greg. "Particularly the girls."

Greg considered a punch, but his eyes met mine and he dropped his hand to his lap.

"What about his parents?" I asked.

Greg and Winn looked at each other before Greg said, "His mother's dead. His father travels. We've never met Ronnie's father."

"I don't think his father makes much money," said Winn. "He drives a twenty-year-old Toyota."

The ride over and the two biscotti and coffee was the price I had to pay for the information. I listened.

"Did you know that, in their duel, Alexander Hamilton fired at Aaron Burr first, and that Hamilton had been undermining Burr, who at the time was Vice President of the United States?"

"What has this to do with the murdered man and your friend in jail?"

"Nothing," said Winn, adjusting his glasses. "Greg is a master of non sequiturs."

"A connection will occur," said Greg with enthusiasm. "String theory."

"Any other connections between Ronnie Gerall and Philip Horvecki?"

"No," said Greg, squirming in his seat.

The woman at the next table was trying not to listen for more talk about rods being applied to orifices. She was failing.

25

"Who else would want Horvecki dead?"

"Everybody," said Greg.

"I didn't want Horvecki dead," I said.

"You didn't know him," said Greg.

"Lots of people are happy that Horvecki is dead," said Winn.

"Can we narrow that down a little?"

"Horvecki had legal trouble with people," said Winn.

"Like?"

"We don't know for sure," said Greg. "It was all kept quiet, but everybody knew. Okay, okay, you didn't know."

"Just talk to Ronnie, please," said Winn.

"Start there. What do you charge?"

"Eleven thousand dollars a week, but in your case I'll give you a discount because I was recommended by Ettiene Viviase's daughter."

"Eleven thou . . . ," Greg began.

"He's joking," said Winn.

"I'm not good at jokes. I'm making a point. What would you pay for your friend to be found innocent?"

"Five hundred dollars a week plus expenses," said Greg. "We can get lots of people to contribute. My grandfather could write a check for four thousand and not miss it."

"That's comforting," I said.

26

"It is to Ronnie," said Greg. "I've got cash."

I let the bills he took out of his pocket rest on the edge of the desk.

"It goes back to you after I talk to your friend," I said, "if I'm not happy with his answers to my questions."

"Then you'll find the killer?"

"Then I'll try to find Rachel Horvecki."

"And the killer," said Greg.

"And the killer," I agreed.

I got a paper brown paper bag from the counter and carefully placed coffees and biscotti inside and then neatly folded the top over before cradling it against my chest. The heat was lulling. I had told the two boys that I wanted to be alone to think and that I'd make it back to my place on my own. Greg wanted to say a lot more. Winn guided him out of the News and Books.

Normally, I would have turned the possible job down with thanks for the refreshments, but I could use the money. I was moving. It didn't cost much but there were things I needed and my bike wanted repair. The number of court papers to serve for my lawyer clients was down for the summer. The snowbirds who came down to their condos, homes, and rentals wouldn't be back to engage in and be the victims of

27

crime for at least three months. There were fewer criminals being brought to justice or just being hauled before a judge for not paying child support. I didn't need much, didn't want much, but now I had Victor Woo to feed and a weekly dinner out with Sally Porovsky and her two kids at Honey Crust Pizza, which would eventually present a challenge even if Sally and I split the bill. And though I was a project for my therapist, Ann Hurwitz, I still had to pay something each time I saw her, even if it was only ten dollars.

When this meeting of the minds was over, I walked down the block to Gulf Stream Boulevard, across from the Bay, to get to my appointment with Ann.

I stepped through the inner door of Ann's office and held out my ritual offering of coffee and biscotti. She looked up from her blue armchair, and I sat in its duplicate across from her as she removed the lid from the cup and dipped an almond biscotti into it. I took off my Cubs cap and placed it on my lap.

"Make me smile," she said.

Ann is over eighty years old. I'm not sure how much over. I do know she doesn't like it when people say she is "eighty years young."

"I am by no stretch of the imagination young unless I have morphed into a tortoise. I've earned my years. It is the end of them I regret and not their number which I savor."

She had said that to me once when I told her I wasn't interested in growing old. Now she wanted a joke. For almost a year now, I had not only been responsible for refreshments but also for telling a joke. I do not smile. I do not laugh. When my wife Catherine was hit and killed by Victor Woo's car, I had lost my ability to consider happiness. Ann worked to have me lose my hard-earned depression, and I struggled to hold onto it. A joke delivered was a concession. It took research on my part.

" 'I have of late, but wherefore know I not, lost all my mirth,' " I said. " 'This goodly frame seems to me a sterile promontory.' "

"Shakespeare," she said.

"Yes, and *Hair.* Catherine liked *Hair.* We saw it four times."

"You liked it?"

"No."

"But you remember it."

"Yes."

"A joke, Fonesca. It is time to pay the toll."

Ann was well groomed, wore colorful tailored dresses, and had her white hair neatly trimmed short. She always wore a necklace and a wide bracelet. She had dozens of baubles of jewelry either made by her husband, a long-retired investment broker, or chosen by them during one of their frequent travels all over the world.

She skillfully managed to get the soaked end of her biscotti from cup to mouth without dripping — a skill I admired.

"A psychologist's receptionist says, 'Doctor, I have a man out here who thinks he's invisible.' And the psychologist answers, 'Tell him I can't see him now.' "

"I'm sufficiently amused," Ann said. "You think this joke is funny?"

"No."

"But you understand why others might?"

"Yes."

"Progress. Tell me about your houseguest," she said finishing the last moist bite of biscotti.

"Tell you what?"

"Whatever you wish to tell me. Does he like biscotti?"

She took a sip of coffee, looking at me over the top of her cup.

"I don't know. He killed my wife."

"Catherine."

"Catherine."

"And now he lives on the floor of your office and is going to live with you in your new office?"

"I think so."

"Why?"

"Why do I think so?"

"No, why is he going to live with you?"

"He doesn't say."

"No, I meant, why are you letting him live with you?"

This struck me as a good question.

"I don't know." ·

"Think about it and give me the best answer you can in your next office visit."

"No joke?"

"When you laugh and mean it, you can stop bringing me jokes."

"I'll bring you a joke."

She finished her coffee, examined the bottom of the cup, daintily reached in with her little finger to retrieve a biscotti crumb, and deposited it on her tongue.

"Some boys want me to help their friend get out of jail."

She looked up, definitely interested.

"What did this boy do?"

"They say he did nothing. He's accused of killing a man named Philip Horvecki."

She shook her head and said, "So I have read. He has a daughter?"

"She's missing," I said. "She may have

31

witnessed the murder."

"From what I have heard and read about him, Horvecki was an angry man, a very angry man, and proud of it. He could have used intensive therapy."

"He was angry about Pine View School."

She smiled. "And many other things," she said. "Taxes, landfill, religion, the price of gasoline."

"But mostly Pine View and Bright Futures."

"So I understand."

"You know something more about him, don't you?" I asked.

"Nothing I can talk to you about."

"He's dead."

"And you wouldn't mind my talking about our sessions if you were to die?"

That gave me pause.

"I wouldn't like it."

"He was a patient of yours?"

"No," she said.

"His daughter?"

I was about to push the issue when Ann rose from her chair with a bounce. I got up. "There's someone in the waiting room who is here to see me. Do you mind going out the other way."

"The other way" was through a door that opened into the offices of a Hispanic real estate and law office. I went through the door. A young woman, pretty and dark, was at one of the two desks in the outer office. She was on the phone and speaking in Spanish. I nodded as I went out onto Main Street, turned left, and then left again down Gulf Stream. My plan had been to walk back to my office.

But before I had gone five steps, someone offered me a ride.

2

He was smiling. He was one of those people who wore a perpetual smile. It didn't mean he was happy or amused. He walked at my side, a few inches taller than me, a few pounds heavier, a few years older, and much better dressed. His dark hair was brushed back. His dark eyes were moist.

"You want a ride," he said, his voice almost Robert Preston musical.

"No, thanks," I said.

"It wasn't a question," he said, keeping pace with me. "I was letting you know that your fondest wish at the moment was a ride in an almost-new red Buick LeSabre. The car was washed this morning and sprayed inside with the scent of a forest. You're not allergic to scented sprays, are you?"

"No," I said, continuing to walk.

"Good, very good. I'm new to Sarasota," he said. "Been here a few weeks. I like what I've seen so far. Air smells good, fresh.

Know what I mean?"

"Yes."

He looked to our right, beyond the manicured bushes and well spaced trees, toward the bay.

"And the birds, magnificent," he said. "I'm from L.A. . . ."

We were just passing a high-rise apartment building on our left.

"We have to turn around," he said. "I'm parked back there."

"I'd rather walk," I said.

He reached over and flicked the brim of my Cubs cap.

His smile remained, but his voice changed. We weren't just chatting anymore.

"Too hot to walk."

"No."

"It's not open for discussion."

I recognized him now, but I couldn't place him. He had the tough look of a television heavy. He caught me looking. His smile got a little broader. He put his left hand on my shoulder to stop me and turn me toward him.

An old woman with a small, fuzzy white dog leading the way on a leash came out of the apartment building. She glanced at us, moved past, and started across the street.

"She wasn't carrying a plastic bag," he

35

said, watching the woman and the eager dog pulling at the leash. "She doesn't plan to clean up after the dog."

"She's old," I said.

"Then she shouldn't have a dog."

"Maybe that's all she's got," I said. "Jeff Augustine."

"Son of a gun. You not only recognize me, you know my name. I'm impressed, flattered."

"I used to watch a lot of old television shows. Rockford, Harry O."

"I want you to meet a guy," he said seriously.

"Mike Mazurki as Moose Malloy in *Farewell My Lovely*," I said.

"Right, but it's also Jeff Augustine on a street in Sarasota. I really have someone who wants to meet you."

"And if I don't want to be met?"

He shrugged and said, "Suit yourself, but I think it would be a good idea if you met this fella. Besides, he'd be very disappointed in me if I didn't deliver you."

"What happened to your career?" I asked.

He shook his head and watched the old lady and the little dog, which was now making a deposit under a small palm tree.

"Twenty-five years waiting for checks so I could pay my phone bills and my rent and eat reasonably. Toward the end I was sing-ing second banana in dinner theaters. My biggest role was Judd Frye in *Oklahoma,* in Knoxville. When Judd Frye died that last time, I said good-bye to my career."

"Now you . . . ?"

"Yes, I work out, wear nice clothes, and persuade people to do things. It pays well and some people like the idea of having a guy with a familiar face getting things done for them."

"Is Steven Seagal really tough?" I asked.

"You remember."

"He threw you through a factory window and you fell four floors to your doom."

"Doom?"

"It's been nice talking to you," I said. "Now I'm walking home. I've got packing to do."

"You haven't been listening closely . . . Look at that. She's just leaving it there."

This was all said calmly, more with regret than anger.

"You want an appointment," I said, "give me a call or just drop by my new office. I'll give you the address."

"No, now," he said, his smile even more friendly.

"I don't think so," I said.

He opened his jacket to show a holstered gun.

"You're going to shoot me on the street because I don't want to get in your car?"

"The car smells like a forest, and I've got a small cooler with bottles of water," he said. "And yes, I could shoot you a little bit."

"No," I said, turning to walk away.

"You're a real phenomenon. You're not afraid, are you?"

"Worst you could do is kill me. This isn't a bad place, and it's a nice day for dying."

"You're a little crazy," he said.

"You caught up with me just when I ended a session with my shrink. You know any good jokes?"

"Jokes?" He looked puzzled now.

"Jokes," I repeated.

"Yes, lots. I did stand-up for a while. The good jokes weren't in my act, but I remember them from Larry the Cable Guy and Diane Ford."

"I'll go with you if you tell me five good jokes," I said.

The old woman with the dog was no longer in sight, but a shirtless black man with sagging slacks, unlaced shoes, and no socks was advancing on us, scratching his belly. I recognized him, had given him coffee and an occasional biscotti. He said his name was Clark, or maybe Cleric, and he claimed that he wasn't homeless. His home, he said, was under the second bench in Bayfront Park, not far from where the dog had just relieved himself or herself.

"Five good jokes?"

"Five."

"Deal."

"This way."

Clark was headed right for us.

"A friend of yours?"

"I don't know," I said as Clark lifted his chin, reached into his pants to adjust his testicles, and said, "Too many midgets. Too many."

"It's a problem," I agreed.

Clark looked at Augustine and pointed a finger.

"You shot ol' Kurt Russell. Some soldier movie."

I gave Clark two quarters and said to Augustine, "The scent of the forest in a Buick LeSabre?"

"That's right," said Augustine. "Let's go."

"The Cubs," said Clark, looking at my cap as if he had suddenly realized it was there. "Andy Pafko."

"Who?" asked Augustine.

"Never mind," I said. "Tell me jokes on

the way."

The LeSabre did smell like a pine forest. I turned down the offer of Evian water. Augustine drank one as he drove.

"Five jokes," I said, index cards and pen in hand.

"Okay," he said.

He told the jokes. I wrote them down. I didn't laugh or smile.

"You don't think they're funny?" he asked as we headed north on Tamiami Trail.

"They're funny," I said, tucking the cards into my appointment book.

"I like you," he said. "Do people generally like you?"

"Yes."

"Why? I mean, I like you, but I'm not sure why."

"It's my curse," I said.

"That people like you?"

"They expect to be liked back."

"And you can't?"

"I don't want to," I said. "The cost is too high, and people die."

He looked at me, one hand on the wheel, one grasping a bottle of water, which he squeezed, making a cracking sound.

"So you have no friends?"

"Too many," I said.

The big two-story gray stone house was right on a cul-de-sac on the water a few blocks south of the Ringling Museum. The house had a front lawn that looked as if it had been manicured with a pair of very small scissors. At the top of the house was a turret which probably had a great view across the water to Longboat Key. A blue Porsche was parked in the driveway in front of a three-car garage. The street had no curb. There was no sidewalk.

Augustine led the way. I followed up the redbrick path to the front door. Gulls were complaining out over the water, and waves flopped against the shore.

Augustine pushed a white button in the wooden paneling next to the door. I heard chimes inside, deep and calm. He rang only once, stood back, clasped his hands in front of him, and rocked on his heels waiting.

"The hat," he said.

I took off my Cubs cap folded it over and shoved it in my back pocket. The door opened. The woman who strode out was in a hurry. She was dark and beautiful and maybe in her forties. She wore a gray business suit over a black blouse and the necklace she wore was a string of large, colorful stones. She walked past us as if we didn't exist, her heels clacking on the red bricks.

Augustine and I watched her get into the blue Porsche and pull smoothly away.

I didn't know who she was. I didn't know who I was about to see. Augustine was no help. We went through the open door that the woman had not closed behind her.

We were in a white-tiled entryway with an open glass elevator, which was on its way down. A large man in it was wearing a pair of tan shorts, a matching polo shirt and sandals over bare feet. He had a full head of brown and white hair and a white-toothed smile of what looked like real teeth that were carefully tended. He was a well-kept sixty-five or seventy year old. I knew his name before the elevator door opened and he stepped out.

"Mr. Fonesca," he said, extending his hand. "Thanks for coming."

I took it. His grip was firm, but he wasn't trying to win any macho hand-squeezing contest.

"You're welcome," I said as he held out a hand, palm up, in invitation for us to follow him.

He ushered us off to the right. He smelled like something slightly sweet and musky and displayed the redness of someone fresh out of the shower.

We went through a large kitchen that

42

opened into a family room and library.

"Please sit," he said, sitting on a yellow leather chair.

Augustine and I sat on a matching yellow leather sofa.

He poured three glasses of something dark brown from a pitcher full of ice on a low, ornately carved table with inlays of white stones. It could have been from India or Serbia. It could have been Wal-Mart.

The drink was strong iced tea. The three of us drank.

"You know who I am," he said.

"Yes, D. Elliot Corkle."

"And?"

"You sell gadgets on television."

The tea was good and strong. I could have used a biscotti.

"Used to. Household aids," he corrected, chewing on an ice cube. "For nineteen-ninety-nine, your kitchen fantasies can come true. Our products are all made of the finest durable Oriental plastics and South American metals."

"My favorite's the steamer chopper," I said.

"You have one?"

"No, I watch infomercials. Insomnia. I don't get cable."

"Want to know why I asked Mr. Augustine

to invite you here?"

"No. I just want a ride back to my place. I've got packing to do."

"It's taken care of. Right, Jeffrey?"

"It's taken care of," said Augustine. "Mr. Fonesca is fully moved."

"There," said Corkle. "Now we can have a brief but leisurely few minutes."

"That should be pleasant."

"D. Elliot Corkle will see that it is," said Corkle. "I would appreciate your doing something for me."

I nodded and drank some more tea.

"After your hospitality, how could I refuse?"

"D. Elliot Corkle would like you to politely return whatever money may have been advanced to you this morning by Gregory Legerman. I will give you a check for double the amount plus a ten-percent bonus if you decide right away. I'm a gambler."

"If I act right away, you pay shipping costs," I said.

"And I throw in a set of four eternally sharp cutting knives with handles made from the hulls of salvaged ships — a forty-nine-dollar value."

He laughed. He was having fun. I didn't laugh.

"Why?"

"Why do I want you to return the money and go about your business?" he asked, looking at Augustine, who smiled attentively. "Greg is my grandson. He is smart, full of energy and vigor, and inclined to do things without thinking that might get him in trouble."

"Like hire me?"

"Like trying to prove his friend didn't murder Phil Horvecki. I think it's possible; even likely, that there are people who are not unhappy that Horvecki is dead, people who might have killed him, people who do not have the conscience of an orange beetle or a lovebug. Horvecki was not a nice human being."

He leaned toward me and lowered his voice.

"And if such a person or persons were responsible for the demise of Philip Horvecki they would not be happy to know that you are trying to help that young man in jail, a young man who, I might add, is not the most socially acceptable of characters. They would prefer that young Mr. Gerall go to a juvenile facility for the crime."

"Got it," I said.

"Do you? Good. Take it from me. D. Elliot Corkle loves his grandson. Word has already gone out that D. Elliot Corkle will

45

be seeing to it that his grandson is no longer pursuing this inquiry."

"No," I said.

"No?" said Corkle.

"I took your grandson's money and told him I would at least talk to Ronnie Gerall and look around, and that I fully intend to do."

"Randolph Scott in *Comanche Station*," said Augustine.

Corkle looked at the ex-actor with something less than approval. Augustine shrugged.

"My grandson could be hurt," Corkle said, smiling no more.

"Your grandson could hire someone else if I walked away."

"Perhaps someone not quite so stubborn."

"This could wind up costing a lot," I said.

"I can afford it. You know how many Power Pocket Entertainment Centers I sold last year?"

"No."

"Three million."

"I'm impressed."

"You're damn right you are," he said, plunking his almost empty glass on the table. The remaining ice cubes clinked musically.

"I'd like to go now," I said.

"Who is stopping you?" asked Corkle.

I put down my glass, which didn't clink as musically as Corkle's, and stood. So did Augustine and Corkle, who wiped his hands on his shorts.

Corkle silently led the way back through the kitchen and to the front door, where we paused while he made a stop at a closet and came up with a white box about the size of a large book. He placed the box in my hand.

"Forty-two songs on three CDs," he said. "Best of the original jazz crooners. Bing Crosby, Dick Powell, Russ Columbo."

"I don't have a CD player," I said.

"Not in your car?"

"I don't own a car."

He shook his head and said, "Wait."

I looked at Augustine as Corkle disappeared back in the closet and came up with a white box even smaller than the one with the CDs. He placed it in my free hand.

"Big seller in its day," he said. "Nine ninety-five. Thirty-dollar value. Great little CD player."

"Thanks," I said.

"Think about my offer," said Corkle. "D. Elliot Corkle is as good as his word. You a poker player, Fonesca?"

"Used to be."

When Catherine and I were first married,

I played poker twice a month with two cops, an assistant district attorney and another investigator who, like me, worked for the state attorney's office. Well, he wasn't quite like me. He was in prison now, for murder.

"I host a weekly Wednesday game in my card room. If you like, I can let you know when we have an open seat. You can join us, see how you like it, how we like you."

"Game?"

"Five card stud. That's it."

"Stakes?"

"Ten, twenty-five, fifty for the first hour," said Corkle. "Last hour, one to two in the morning, we go up to twenty-five, fifty, and a hundred. We start at nine at night. I know where you can get the money to play. Think about it."

He started to close the door as Augustine and I stepped out and said, "If I can't get you to say 'no' to Greg, can I hire you?"

"To do what?"

"Exactly what my grandson hired you to do, with one exception."

"Yes?"

"I don't care if you find evidence to clear Ronnie Gerall or get him locked up till he is ready for Social Security."

"I'll think about it," I said.

"D. Elliot Corkle doesn't work that way.

The offer is going fast. Just fifteen seconds to decide. I'll make it a cash offer, payable right here on my doorstep. Two thousand dollars."

"Your grandson is still my client."

"Now you've got two clients. You just have to report to me and keep a protective eye on Greg."

I looked at Augustine, who gave me no help, and then back at Corkle.

"Why not?" I said.

Corkle reached into his pocket and came out with an envelope and folded sheet of paper.

"Two thousand in hundreds and fifties in the envelope. Just sign the receipt. It's made out 'for consulting fees.'"

"You were sure I'd agree."

"Reasonably," he said. "D. Elliot Corkle could always put the cash away and tear up the unsigned receipt. One should always be prepared for contingencies."

I took the envelope without checking the contents and said, "I can't sign this receipt."

Corkle smiled in understanding.

"I'm a process server, not a consultant."

"Then," said Corkle, "we'll just have to trust each other. Call when you have information."

He closed the door behind us as Augustine

and I walked down the path.

"I think he likes you," said Augustine. "He's never invited me in on that poker game, not that I could afford it."

"I'm glad," I said, putting the envelope in my pocket.

"He's a good guy. You don't know him."

"And you do?" I asked.

"He sells gadgets, has millions of dollars, and refers to himself in the third person," said Augustine. "Also, he loves his grandson and he never leaves the house."

"Never?"

"For the last four years at least, I've been told. I don't know what his reasons are."

I shifted my gifts and got in the car.

"Corkle produced the only movie I ever starred in."

Shoot-out On a Silent Street," I said, closing the car door. "You and Tim Holt."

He started the car. I put on my Cubs cap.

"Who was the woman who ran out of the house?" I asked.

"Alana Legerman."

"Greg's . . . ?"

"Mother. D. Elliot's daughter. If you ask me . . ."

I never found out what he wanted me to ask him. The front window exploded. Glass shot toward my face. I covered up. Augus-

50

tine lost control. We spun around three times, skidded onto the freshly cut lawn of a large ranch-style house and came to a stop against a row of trimmed bushes.

I looked at Augustine. He was silent. Blood dripped like a red tear from the corner of his right eye and made its way down his nose. I was fascinated. Then I passed out.

Ames McKinney looked down at me. He was tall, lean, a little over seventy years old with tousled gray hair and an accent that came from the West. He always wore jeans with a big buckled belt and a flannel shirt, even when the temperature hit a humid one hundred. He never sweated. Ames was the closest thing I had to a best friend.

"You're lookin' tempered," he said.

My face was scratched in four or five places, and my shirt was torn. Nothing was broken.

"I feel fine," I said trying to stand. "Augustine?"

"Other fella in the car? He's a bit chiseled down but he'll survive."

"Envelope? Money?"

"Right here," said Ames, holding up the bulging envelope.

I tried to stand.

My legs didn't cooperate. I started to sink back on the bed. I had been taken to Sarasota Memorial Hospital by ambulance, treated and asked if there was anyone I wanted the people in the ER to call. I came up with Ames, who I knew would be at the Texas Bar, where he worked as a handyman, cleanup man, occasional short-order cook, and bartender. Big Ed, who owned the place, had been taking more time off to visit his children and grandchildren back in New Jersey. The only person Ed trusted was Ames.

Ames and I had met four years ago when I tried to stop him from having a shoot-out on Lido Beach with his ex-partner, who had gathered every dime in their company and run off to Sarasota to change his name and spend his way into what passed for society on the Gulf Coast. Ames had done some jail time, but not much, since I had testified that the partner had shot first.

"Steady, partner," Ames said, grabbing my arm and easing me back when I tried to rise again.

"What happened?" I said.

"Don't know."

"How long was I out?"

"Four hours," Ames said. "Besides those cuts on your face, you have yourself a concussion."

The room tilted at a slight angle and then tilted back the other way. I closed my eyes.

"Augustine?" I said.

I passed out again.

When I next opened my eyes, Detective Ettiene Viviase of the Sarasota Police Department was standing next to Ames.

"You all right?" he asked.

He was a burly man of about fifty who pretended to be world weary. We had experienced a number of close encounters of the third kind.

"Fine and dandy," I said.

Augustine would have known I was quoting Earl Holliman in *The Rainmaker.*

"You were serving papers?" he asked.

I didn't answer.

"Lewis is confused," said Ames. "Trauma."

Viviase nodded and said, "What's it all about?"

"How is Augustine?" I asked.

"He'll live," said Viviase. "Maybe they can save his sight. He had a .177 caliber pellet lodged in his right eye."

"A pellet? Someone shot Augustine with Ralphie's Red Ryder you'll-shoot-your-eye-out BB gun?" I asked.

"And came close to shooting his eye out.

Something like that," said Viviase. "Any idea who shot at you?"

"Me? What makes you think they were shooting at me?" I said. "They could have been shooting at Augustine, or maybe it was just kids shooting at a car."

"Ronnie Gerall," Viviase said.

I closed my eyes and started to lean back, and then I remembered. I touched the top of my head. The hair was definitely thinner with each passing crime. Ames reached back into his pocket and came up with my Cubs cap. He handed it to me. I clutched it like a teddy bear.

"You had Gerall's name and the words Greg and Winn in your notebook."

He held up my notebook and handed it to Ames.

"Think it might have something to do with your getting shot at?"

"No."

"Doc says you can go when you're up to it," said Ames.

"In a minute," said Viviase, eyes fixed on me. "Are you getting involved with the Philip Horvecki murder?"

"I promised a friend I'd drop in and see Gerall, talk to him."

"Need I remind you that you don't have a private investigator's license?"

"I tell people that all the time. I'm just doing a friend a favor," I said.

"The Gerall kid did it," said Viviase. "Caught inside the victim's house kneeling by the corpse. Kid had motive. Kid's a hothead. Only thing the kid said when he was arrested was, and I quote, 'I'm glad the son-of-a-bitch is dead.' Who's the friend who asked you to stop in and see Gerall?"

I hesitated. Viviase's daughter Elisabeth had told Greg and Winn about me. A few more questions and I'd have to lie or tell her father that she was the one who got me involved.

"I'd like to talk to Augustine," I said.

"Jeff Augustine, onetime actor, minor arrests in California, looks tough, maybe. I know he's working for D. Elliot Corkle. It's not clear in what capacity, and he is too narcotized to explain or talk to you. You happen to know what he does for Corkle?"

"I think he's a kind of companion," I said.

"We talked to Corkle," Viviase said.

"What did Corkle tell you?" I asked Viviase, making another effort to get up. Ames reached for my arm.

"Lie down, partner," he said.

I did. The thin pillow felt just right behind my head, and I wanted to go to sleep. I was sure I had been given something to ease the pain.

"Corkle had nothing much to say," said Viviase. "He did refer to himself in the third person and compared life to a game of poker twice. He tried to give me a box with a Wonder Chopper inside. I told him I couldn't take it. Your mini CD player and the CDs are being held as possible evidence."

"Of what?" Ames asked.

"I don't know," said Viviase. "I have a headache and I don't know. Just answer the questions, Fonesca, and don't ask any. I have places to go and things to do, and my wife promised me that she would have chicken in duck sauce for dinner tonight. I plan to be there for it."

I nodded. Ames stood straight and silent.

"You moved to a new place," Viviase said.

"Yes. Had to. DQ is gone. My office building goes down tomorrow. I'm right around the corner, off of Laurel."

"Life goes on," Viviase said.

"Even when we don't care."

"The Chinese guy?" said Viviase.

"He's moving with me, I think."

"You're nuts," said Viviase.

"No . . . Maybe. It doesn't matter."

"Get better. Come and see me," he said

taking a deep breath. Then he turned his head toward Ames and added, "Take care of him."

"I aim to," said Ames.

When Viviase was gone, I stood again, this time without Ames's help.

"We going to look for whoever took the shot?" he asked.

"We are," I said. "Either that or I buy a car and head out of town forever."

"That won't work."

"I guess."

"Where do we start?"

"In juvenile detention," I said, adjusting my Cubs cap and noticing that it had a slight but real tear on the right side. "First we talk to Augustine."

I didn't fall on my face as we moved to the elevator to go up to the private fourth floor room where Jeff Augustine was lying on his back. He wore a white hospital gown with a thin white blanket pulled up to his chest. An IV was going. His left eye was closed. His right eye was covered by a taped-down gauze pad. His hands were folded in front of him. He looked like a one-eyed saint.

"Jeff?" I tried.

Augustine made a sound but didn't open his eye. I tried again.

"Augustine."

This time his left eye popped open and he let out a pained groan as he reached up with his right hand to touch the injured eye.

"Hurts," he said.

"I know," I said.

"How would you know?"

"I have a natural empathy. Besides I got caught by flying glass."

"We get a medal or something?" Augustine asked, closing his eye again and explaining, "Hurts less when both eyes are closed. I may lose the eye."

"Maybe so," said Ames.

"Who is he?" Augustine said, being careful not to turn his head.

"My friend," I said. "Ames McKinney."

"Weren't we both in an episode of *The Yellow Rose*?"

"Not an actor," said Ames.

"I could have sworn, but . . . Damn, what if this killed me? My obit would make a single line in *Variety,* 'Bit Player Killed by BB Gun.' Bitter irony."

Alana Legerman walked in. She wafted perfume and looked sleek, dark, and beautiful.

"What happened?" she asked, moving to the side of the bed next to Augustine.

She was as tranquil as her offspring Greg

was wired.

"Someone shot BBs at us," said Augustine. "Hit me in the eye."

"Who did it?" she asked.

No one had an answer, but Alana Legerman had a question. She looked at Augustine and said, "Are you all right? Are you going to lose your eye?"

She tried to say it nice, but it was as if she were asking if the dime dropped on the floor was his. I couldn't be sure if she was just saying the right thing or if she had shown concern to her father's employee beyond that of an heiress.

"I'm all right," Augustine said. "I've still got one twenty-twenty eye."

"I'm all right too," I said.

There was no way even a casual glance would have failed to reveal the scratches on my face and neck.

"I'm sorry," said Alana Legerman. "How are you, Mr. . . ."

"Fonesca," Ames supplied. "Mr. Lewis Fonesca. And my name's Ames McKinney."

"And what have you got to do with my father and Jeff?"

"Your father has asked me to look into the murder of Philip Horvecki."

"You're a private investigator?"

"No, a process server."

She was unimpressed.

"You think my son's friend killed Horvecki?"

"The police think so. The television stations, the newspaper and most of the people in Sarasota probably think so."

"Why don't you just ask Ronnie Gerall what happened?" she asked.

Jeff Augustine's left eye was open wide and looking at Alana Legerman. I moved toward the door, Ames at my side.

"I think we'll do that," I said.

3

The problem was immediately clear after we talked to Ronnie Gerall across a table in the visitors' room in the county jail. I got the impression that he worked at being independent, superior, and unlikable, but I could have been wrong. He could simply and naturally be what my uncle called a *Merdu,* which roughly translated from the Italian means "dickhead."

Ronnie was about six feet tall and had the build of an athlete, the drawn-back, almost blond hair of a teen movie idol, blue eyes, and a look of total boredom. He could easily have passed for twenty-one, which I was sure he did when it suited him.

It had started badly. Gerall had been ushered in. He wore a loose-fitting orange jail suit and a look that said, "Look at what those jerks sent me." He didn't offer his hand to Ames and me or ask or say anything at first; he just sat in the wooden chair with his right leg extended and half turned as if he planned to escape at the first sign of ennui.

Ames and I took seats. The full-bellied, uniformed guard, who looked almost as bored as Ronnie Gerall, stood with his back to the door, arms folded. The room was large enough that the guard wouldn't hear us if we whispered. Ronnie had no intention of whispering.

"Greg Legerman told me you were coming," he said.

That required no answer so I just kept sitting and watching him.

"Please do me a favor before we have anything that resembles conversation," he said.

"Yes."

"Would you mind taking off that dopey baseball cap."

"Yes, I would."

"I watched you and an old man drive up on a motor scooter," he said, ignoring my answer.

"And . . . ?"

"You can't afford a car?"

"Don't want the responsibility," I said.

"How did Greg Legerman find you?" he asked shaking his head and looking first at Ames and then at me.

"Luck," I said.

We sat in silence for about a minute, during which he found his fingernails fascinating and the palms of his hands, particularly the right one, profound.

"I did not kill Philip Horvecki," he said, looking up.

"Tell us what happened."

"Why not? I've got time. It was Thursday night. He called, said he would meet with me. Horvecki said he wanted to talk."

"You sure it was Horvecki?" I asked.

"Old men all sound alike, either like sick hummingbirds or gravel pits. This was gravel pits. Pure Horvecki."

He looked at Ames, who could have been number five on Mount Rushmore.

"Go on," I prompted.

"I went to his house."

"Right away?"

"Yes."

"You told someone you were going?"

"No. Can I go on?"

"Yes."

"I rang the bell. No answer. I tried the door. Open." I went in. The place is a nightmare. Black wood, black tile floors, white walls. Even the paintings are almost all black and white. No wonder someone killed him."

63

"I don't think you should say that," I said.

"You don't think so?" Ronnie said with a smile.

"He doesn't think so," said Ames. "And you'd best heed what Mr. Fonesca tells you."

"Or what, old man?"

"Or I reach across this table and slap you three or four times. And you won't stop me, because even though I just warned you, you won't be able to," said Ames, eyes fixed on Ronnie Gerall's face.

"He'll do it, too," I said.

"Then he'll be in here with me," said Ronnie.

"Is that where you want him? Respect means a great deal to Mr. McKinney."

The uniformed guard slouched a little more. He wasn't interested in what we had to say.

"You found Horvecki," I said.

"On the floor in the hallway. Definitely dead. Lots of blood on his face and shirt. Mouth open. I thought I saw someone in an open doorway on the right. Then I saw someone go out the window."

"And you followed him," said Ames.

"No. I mean yes. I went out the front door looking for him. Whoever it was was gone."

"You saw nobody?" I asked.

"No . . . wait. There was a man in a pickup truck, but it wasn't the one who was in the house. The guy in the pickup was there when I got to Horvecki's. I thought he was waiting for somebody."

"Could he have seen the man who jumped out of the window?" I asked.

"Could have? He would have had to," said Ronnie.

"Can you describe the man or the truck?" I asked.

"It was a small pickup, not old, not new. Guy in the truck had on a baseball cap. Couldn't see his face. I think he was black. Maybe. Couldn't tell you how . . . Wait, I had the feeling he wasn't an old guy like Stokes over here."

Ames did not take kindly to the remark, but he held his tongue.

"And I don't know how tall he was," Ronnie went on. "He never got out of the truck. I only saw him for a few seconds."

"Did he look at you?" I asked.

"Yes."

"We'll find him," I said.

I must not have filled the room with my infectious optimism, because Ronnie said, "You don't believe me."

"No matter if we believe you," said Ames. "It matters if we find him."

"What did you do after you went outside and didn't see him?" I asked.

"I went back in the house to be sure Horvecki was dead. Before I could call 911, I heard the door to the house open. Then a voice saying, 'Throw your gun toward the door and stand up slowly with your hands high and your palms showing.'

"I did. I was read my rights and arrested."

"Did you tell them about the person in the doorway and the man in the truck?" I asked.

"I did. They didn't believe me, either. I'm glad Horvecki's dead, but I didn't kill him."

"You have a lawyer?" I asked.

"You're not a lawyer?"

"No," I said.

"Goddamn it!" he shouted loud enough to make the guard almost slump to the floor. "I'll kill Greg when I get my hands on him."

"You really know the right things to say," I said.

"What the hell are you then?"

"A process server," I said. "And someone who finds missing people."

"Who the fuck is missing here?"

"The person who shot Philip Horvecki," said Ames, "provided that person is not you."

"And," I added, "whoever might have been standing in the open doorway when you went into Horvecki's house."

"Guard, get these two out of here," said Ronnie. Then he turned to me and said, "I'll get my own lawyer."

"Suits me," said Ames rising.

I got up, too. The guard was alert now.

We got to the door. Then Ronnie Gerall said, "Wait."

I turned as the guard moved toward the prisoner.

"I think the person in the doorway was a woman."

"Horvecki's daughter?" I asked.

He shrugged. "I don't know."

"Whoever it was might have seen the person who went through the window kill Horvecki," I said.

"Or might have been the person who killed Horvecki," said Ames.

"I've got no money, but I don't want a public defender," Ronnie said. It sounded like a challenge.

"I'll see what I can do," I said.

Ames and I went past the guard and into the corridor.

"He's scared," Ames said.

"He's scared," I agreed as we walked toward the thick metal door.

67

"Full of hate," Ames said.

"Full of hate," I agreed.

"You gonna help him?" Ames asked as we got to the door.

"It's why I get the big bucks," I said.

"Philip Horvecki," I said.

There were twenty-two wooden steps leading up to the three rooms under a pitched roof into which I had moved. This was on Laurel, around the corner and about half a block from the departed Dairy Queen. The steps had once been white. The railing, which shook if you put a hand on it, had once been green. I couldn't call it an apartment. You had to move carefully under the ceiling or you would bump your head. The first room was a big, blank square with a bathroom across from the front door. The second room, about the size of a prison cell, looked as if it had originally been installed by indifferent Seminoles and recently painted white by someone who wanted to set the record for speed painting. There was a third room, a little bigger than one of Superman's phone booths. With luck you might be able to get a rocking chair into it.

The walls of the big room were white painted plaster board under which the smell of sad and ancient wood managed to persist.

The big and little rooms were connected by a varnished wooden door. There were no overhead lights, but Flo Zink, who had found the place, had not only painted it but put two bright floor lamps in each room. I had met Flo shortly after I came to Sarasota. I had found her husband, Gus, who was dying from too many diseases to count. Gus had been kidnapped to keep him from voting on a land issue in the City Council. Ames and I had gotten him to the meeting, where his last act on earth was to cast the deciding vote. He left Flo with enough money to sustain five widows comfortably for a lifetime. Flo felt responsible for me. Finding my new home was just one of the ways she had shown it over the last four years.

There were three small windows in the big room and one in each of the other two rooms. Ames had already moved the air conditioner from my last place overlooking the defunct DQ to a window in the big room. It was already clear that the air conditioner wouldn't be able to adequately cool one room let alone two or three. There was more space than I needed.

As Augustine had said, my boxes and furniture had been moved. My meager furniture looked sad and frightened in these rooms.

The first thing Victor Woo had done was put up my Stig Dalstrom prints, including a recent painting Flo had given to me as a housewarming present. Victor had pinned the Dalstroms to the wall in about the same places they had been in my former space.

"Philip Horvecki," I repeated into the cell phone which I now reluctantly owned.

The phone was another housewarming present. It was from Adele, who was just about to become a freshman at New College in Sarasota. She could have gotten into dozens of colleges, but she wanted to continue to live with her baby, Catherine, in Flo's house. No dorm experience for Adele, but she wouldn't regret it. Adele's father had sold her to a pimp when she was fourteen. Getting her away from Dad and pimp had had its complications, but when Flo took her in, Adele blossomed, turned her life around, became an A student in high school, and was now going to college. There had been one major speed bump in the path. Adele had gotten pregnant by an older man who was now doing time in prison for murder. Adele had named the baby Catherine in honor of my dead wife.

"Horvecki. Did he have a criminal

record?" I asked.

"I'll check," said Viviase. "The county might have something. If that doesn't work, I've got another place you can look."

I had walked back out to get better reception.

Victor Woo had followed me out and sat next to me on the top step. The Serita sisters, friends of Flo, lived in the bottom two floors of the brightly painted white and green wooden house. They owned the building, so I'd be paying rent to them, the same rent I had been paying behind the DQ.

From my seat on the top step, I could look past the freshly painted house across the street and into a yard where the edge of a screen-enclosed pool was visible. I stared at the water of the pool flecked with light from the setting sun and decided that I needed a shower.

"Check with Sergeant Yoder in the Sheriff's Office," added Viviase.

"Thanks," I said.

The sun seemed to be dropping quickly now. I heard something below.

"Fonesca, you are one hard dog to find."

It was Darrell Caton, which usually meant it must be Saturday, but I knew it wasn't Saturday. Darrell was the fourteen-year-old that Sally Porovsky had conned me into being a big brother for. She was a county children and family services social worker I had been seeing socially and seeking in ways I didn't understand.

Darrell was lean and black, wearing baggy jeans and a T-shirt that had something printed on the front. I couldn't make out the word from twenty-two steps up.

"It's not Saturday," I called.

"I know that," said Viviase on the phone. "You losing it, Fonesca?"

"Darrell just showed up," I said.

"It's not Saturday," said Viviase, who knew of my weekly commitment to Darrell.

"I know," I said.

Darrell had grown in the time he had been trailing me once a week. He looked forward to being with me because, as he said, "Man, something's always happening with you. Guns, dead people, and shit. You are an education, Fonesca."

I did not want to be an education, but I had grown used to seeing Darrell.

Darrell started up the steps. Victor started to move over so Darrell could sit.

"One more question," I said into the phone.

"Yeah."

"Why are you helping me?"

The pause was long. He was considering

telling me something.

"He may not be guilty, and it's not really my case, but if you're looking into it . . ."

Darrell was almost in front of me now. He had bounded up the steps. He wasn't panting. I remember once, when I was fourteen, lying in my bed and praying to God to let me live through Saturday because I had a soccer game on Saturday. We lost the game to Lane Tech, and I missed an easy goal. God did let me live, but it didn't look as if he were about to do the same for Darrell.

I could now clearly see what was printed on the front of Darrell's T-shirt. It read, in black block letters, "Pope John Paul II Girl's Volleyball Team Kicks Ass."

There was a crack in the air, a sudden sharp pinging sound from somewhere on the side of the house with the pool. Darrell lifted his head toward the sky as if he were startled by the sudden appearance of a UFO. Then he arched his back, groped over his left shoulder blade as if he had a sudden itch.

He was about to tumble backward down the stairs.

I dropped the phone and reached for him. His right hand almost touched mine and he bent over backward. Victor Woo was up, behind Darrell now, stopping his fall, setting him gently on the small landing in front of my door. Victor was holding the rickety handrail and taking the steps two at a time.

I knelt next to Darrell and groped for the phone.

"Fonesca, what the hell is going on?" asked Viviase.

"Someone shot Darrell. Send an ambulance."

Victor hit the ground running like a sprinter. If he was lucky, he would catch up with the shooter. If he wasn't lucky, he would catch up with the shooter. Victor was armed with nothing.

"I'm on the way," Viviase said and ended the connection.

Darrell was groaning. A good sign.

"What the fuck, Fonesca? Oh. I like the action, but I don't want to be the victim. You know what I'm saying?"

I rolled him gently onto his side.

"This isn't for real," he whimpered. "Why'd anyone want to shoot me?"

"I think they were trying to shoot me," I said. "You got in the way."

"I took a bullet for you?"

"Yes, but I'm guessing it was a pellet, not a bullet."

"Hurts like a bullet."

"You've been shot before?"

"Hell no," he said and then gasped. "Life's funnier than shit. You know what I'm saying? My mother's going to be all over your ass, Fonesca. Jesus, it hurts. Am I going to die?"

"Yes, but so am I. You're not going to die for a while."

"You know how to make Christmas come early, don't you Fonesca?"

"Ambulance is on the way," I said.

"You ever been shot at, Fonesca?"

"Yes."

"When?"

"A few times."

"Last time?"

"This morning." An actor took that pellet in the eye.

There was no doubt where the pellet had entered Darrell, just below the left shoulder blade. The hole was small, the T-shirt was definitely ruined. There was blood dripping from the wound, but it didn't look as if anything vital had been hit.

Police headquarters was, at maximum, a five-minute drive from where Darrell lay bleeding. Viviase made it in three, and somewhere in the distance an ambulance siren cut through the twilight.

4

The emergency room triage nurse, a wiry thin woman with wiry thin straw-colored hair, looked up at me and said, "You're back, Mr. . . ."

"Fonesca."

"Are you . . . ?"

"I'm fine. I'm here about Darrell Caton. He was brought in here by ambulance a few minutes ago."

"What's your relationship to him?"

"I'm his big brother," I said. "It's complicated."

She looked from me to Ames to Victor and said, "He's being taken care of by a doctor. His mother is on the way. Just have a seat."

We had a seat.

That was when Victor told his story.

"I took your bicycle from under the stairs," he said.

"Okay."

"I went after the shooter, who I saw running from behind the house across the street. He was carrying a rifle."

"What were you planning to do?" asked Ames.

"I don't know."

In a seat across from us, a drunk cradled a limp arm with his good arm like a baby. He snorted in half sleep.

"You chased him," I said, getting Victor back on track.

"He ran down Laurel. When I turned the corner onto the street . . ."

"Laurel," I said.

Victor knew almost nothing about Sarasota geography. He had spent most of his time in town squatting in my two former rooms.

"What'd he look like?" Ames asked.

"I don't know, it was starting to get dark. He was a block away. He opened a car door, threw the rifle inside, climbed in, and started to drive away when I was about forty yards from him."

"He got away," said Ames with a touch of disapproval.

"He drove west. I followed him. I don't know where we went. North, I think, then west again. He ran a light on Oxbay . . ."

"Osprey," said Ames.

Victor nodded.

"Ran a light and then went way over the speed limit. I would have caught him on Fruit Street."

"Fruitville," I said.

"He went right through without stopping, almost hit a couple," said Victor. "I stopped."

"Why?" asked Ames.

I knew. Victor had killed my wife in a hit-and-run accident. He didn't want to be the cause of another hit-and-run.

"You get a license plate number?" I asked.

The drunk across from us snorted louder than he had the first time. He was definitely asleep when he grunted, "Can there be any doubt in the mind of the jurors?"

Then he slumped over on his left side.

"No," said Victor. "I think it was a dark-colored Nissan. Late model. As he crossed Fruitville, he went under a streetlight. I'm sure he gave me the finger."

"When we find him," said Ames evenly, "I shoot him."

"Ames . . ." I began.

"He shot the boy," said Ames. "Could have killed him if Victor here didn't keep him from tumbling down the stairs."

"He was aiming for me."

"More's the reason," said Ames.

"No," said Victor. "No killing."

"I'll not kill him," said Ames. "I'll just give him some sense of what it feels like to get shot in the eye or the back."

"No," said Victor.

The drunk roused himself, blinked his eyes, rubbed his chin, and tried unsuccessfully to flatten his bushy hair. Then he looked at us and said with a cough, "You're just puttin' on an act for me, right? I like the story, but it lacks romance. You know what I'm talkin' about?"

That was when Darrell's mother came through the emergency room doors, looked around, saw us, and moved in front of me. She was a dry, tired brown stick of a woman who had touches of good looks left over from only a few years earlier.

"You were supposed to look after him," she said.

"Yes," I agreed.

"You got him shot."

"Yes. I'm sorry."

She stood, looked around the waiting room, and saw the drunk, who either bowed in his seat or was about to fall over again.

"I want to be angry at you, but I can't do it. You're a crazy man, but a good one," she said. "Darrell thinks you . . . I've got to go see him."

She turned and hurried to the desk where

the wiry triage nurse came around and led her through the double doors to the treatment area.

"I'm sorry I didn't catch the shooter," said Victor.

"You probably saved Darrell's life," I said. "A fall down those stairs might have killed him. I'll settle for that."

"I am the click-clack man who never made it to Oz. I am the bold deceiver who winks to those who understand, who winks only to himself in the mirror, a store window, the dark screen of a computer. I am the truth, which is a lie. I'm looking down at everyone from a spot reserved for me in the asshole of a serial killer with the blood of children in the webbing between his fingers."

He had called about ten minutes after Victor, Ames, and I got back to my new rooms, which would always smell like decaying wood. He didn't announce himself, just began talking with a muffled, high-pitched Latino accent that was more Billy Crystal than Ricardo Montalban.

"You're the click-clack man," I said. "You almost killed a 14-year-old. I've got that much."

"Stop looking. Visualize yourself in dark glasses looking only straight ahead," he said.

"I'd fall."

Ames was reaching for the phone in my hand. He was not to be denied. Victor sat against the wall on his open bedroll.

"Someone here wants to say hello," I managed as Ames took the phone from my hand and put it to his ear.

Ames looked very calm. I'd learned that Ames always looked calm when he was angry — dangerous and determined. I knew, given enough time, that Ames would find the shooter as Ames had found his former partner when he came to Sarasota. He had found him on the Lido Key Beach. There had been a shoot-out. The partner, a plaster pillar of the community who had cheated Ames out of a small fortune, had not survived the volley.

"Where did you get blunt-force .22 bullets?" asked Ames.

"What?" the caller said.

"The ones you used to shoot out that man's eye, and to shoot the boy. We can trace them."

"No, you can't," said the caller.

"Here," said Ames handing me back the phone and moving back to lean against the wall with his arms folded.

"My friend is angry," I told the caller.

His voice betrayed a quiver and went a

little higher when he said, "I didn't intend to kill him or even shoot him."

"You wanted to shoot me?"

"Yes. And I will if you don't stop."

"Stop what?"

"You know."

Ann Hurwitz would say I should stop fighting my emergence from depression over my wife's bloody death against the grille of the car Victor Woo had driven down Lake Shore Drive. It had happened as Catherine was crossing at the light. I think we were going to have steak for dinner. Or was it chili?

"Fonesca?" said the caller. "You listening?"

"Not really. Why are you calling?"

"Stop looking," he repeated with some frustration.

"Or you'll try to shoot me again with a pellet gun?"

"I have a real rifle," he said.

"Having it and using it are different things," I said, looking at Victor, who was gently bouncing his head against the wall as he sat.

"I don't want to kill you," he said.

"Then don't."

"But you might make me."

"Then do. You want to tell me now what

I'm supposed to stop doing?"

"Whatever you're doing," he said.

"I'm talking to a frightened person on the telephone," I said.

"Looking for the person who killed Horvecki," he said.

Ames was looking at me. I met his eyes.

"You killed him?"

"Yes, I did. The police have the wrong person in jail. Ronnie didn't do it. They have to let him out. You've got to stop looking."

"This doesn't make much sense," I tried. "Ronnie didn't do it, but you don't want me to look for who did."

The pause was long. I could hear breathing.

"What can I do to convince you?"

"Stop shooting at me, that would make a nice start," I said.

"Lewis," Ames said firmly.

"What's your favorite movie?" I asked.

"What?"

"Your favorite movie. Mine's *The Third Man,* or *Mildred Pierce,* or *The List of Adrian Messenger,* or *On the Waterfront,* or *The Seven Samurai,* or *Once Upon A Time in America,* or *Comanche Station . . .*"

"You're crazy," he said.

83

"Deeply neurotic," I corrected. "You have a favorite movie?"

"Gone With The Wind."

"And?"

"Wuthering Heights. From Here to Eternity."

"You didn't kill Horvecki," I interrupted.

"I did."

"Let's meet for coffee."

"I don't drink coffee," he said. "I hate the stuff."

"Tea?"

"Tastes like water someone pissed in."

"A cheeseburger."

"You'll arrest me. That other guy, the old one. He'll shoot me or break my face."

"I'll persuade him not to. And I'm not a cop, I can't arrest you," I said.

"Citizen's arrest."

"You have something to tell me, don't you?"

"I'll think about it."

"You almost killed that boy on the steps."

"I'm sorry. I'll let you know about meeting you."

He hung up.

"He didn't do it," said Ames.

The phone rang again. I pushed the button and put it to my ear. The phone was a gift to keep me in touch with the world. I did not wish to keep in touch with the world.

"Philip Horvecki was a murderer," came the voice of the person who had just hung up. "He deserved to die."

The connection clicked, and the line went dead. I pushed the button and handed the phone to Ames, who wanted no more to do with it than I did. Ames handed it to Victor, who put it in his pocket.

"The shots at you were pellets and that business about blunt-force .22 bullets was a small pile of cow chips," said Ames.

"I know," I said.

The next call came that night, from Sally Porovsky.

"Lewis," she said wearily.

"Sally," I said.

"Darrell's mother doesn't want him to see you again," she said.

"He's all right?"

"Whatever it was he was shot with didn't go very deep," she said.

I had been going with Sally for about two years. We didn't see each other much because she was a child services worker who regularly put in ten-hour days and spent whatever hours she had left with her two children. I was at the fringe of her schedule, which I understood. It was fine with me.

We had never slept together, though we had come close a few times. I had to admit that it was less and less out of a commitment to the memory of Catherine and more an unwillingness on my part to take the symbolic and real action.

I wanted to hold onto the belief that at any moment I could simply fill my duffle bag, get on a Greyhound bus, and head somewhere, anywhere, where no one expected anything of me and I could nurture my depression. I was increasingly aware that my belief that I could do that was becoming an illusion. Ames, Flo, Adele, Darrell, and Sally — I knew I could not easily ride away from them. I'd need a major blow to let me escape.

"Darrell's fine," she said. "He's weirdly proud that he took a bullet —"

"Pellet," I corrected.

". . . that he took a pellet meant for you," she said.

"I don't like Ronnie Gerall," I said.

"He takes some getting used to."

"You know him?" I asked.

"I handled his transition when he came from San Antonio to Sarasota."

There was something in her voice, an unfamiliar impatience or something I couldn't quite grasp.

"His friends are paying me to prove he didn't kill Philip Horvecki," I said.

"I've got to go."

"Meet me tomorrow?"

"We'll see. Call me in the morning," she said. "We can set a time when I can come and see your new . . ."

"Lodgings," I said.

"I'll talk to Darrell's mother," she said. "I'll make her love you again."

"You can do that?"

"No," she said. "I can't."

"Thanks."

"Take care of yourself, Lewis Fonesca."

"Yes," I said. "And you too, Sally Porovsky."

I had not been doing a good job of taking care of myself since Catherine had been struck and killed by the man sitting on the floor, against the wall. Ann Hurwitz said progress was being made.

The last time she had told me that, I suggested that maybe we needed either another hundred thousand troops in Iraq or a small team of psychologists to speed my progress.

"We'll talk in the morning," Sally said.

She didn't seem to want to end the call.

"Something wrong?" I asked.

"Nothing."

"Okay," I said.

What I really wanted to say was, "I'll see you if I'm alive. I'll see you if I don't run away. I'll see you if I don't curl into a ball on the floor next to Victor, hugging my knees."

I turned off the phone and looked at Victor.

Ames walked in from the other room and said, "Beer, Dunkin' Donuts, or ice cream?"

Victor shrugged. He didn't care.

"Make it doughnuts," I said.

Ames left, and I picked up the phone.

I called the number Greg Legerman had given me. A woman answered after three rings. I said I wanted to talk to Greg. She politely said she would get him. About thirty seconds later he came on the phone with a wary, "Yes?"

"Do your Cheech Marin for me again," I said. "It's bad, but probably a little funny for anyone who has a sense of humor."

"What are you talking about?"

"You called me," I said. "Told me to stop looking for whoever killed Horvecki. Meet me at the Waffle Shop at eight tomorrow morning."

Silence.

"You're at a loss for words?" I said.

"I didn't call you," he finally said.

"I think I'll just give your money back and continue to try to locate a reasonably sane world."

"Tomorrow at eight. Waffle Shop on 301," he said. "I'll be there."

I made one more call, to Dixie Cruise, and told her what I needed and what I would pay.

"I'll work on it tonight," she said. "Call me after ten tomorrow."

"Tomorrow," I repeated and turned off the phone.

Dixie was a waitress. She had just moved to the Appleby's on Fruitville near I-75. Dixie was pert, energetic, in her thirties, and working online toward a business degree from the University of South Florida. Dixie was also a first-rate computer hacker with a small apartment in a 1920s apartment building on Ringling Boulevard.

When Ames returned, Victor took one plain, Ames had a double chocolate, and I had a strawberry iced. We ate, drank decaf coffee, and said nothing for the rest of the evening.

There was nothing to say.

5

The Waffle Shop is on Washington, also known as State Road 301 or just 301 to the locals. The shop is just before the point where 301 meets Tamiami Trail, known as 41 to the locals. It's across from a car dealership, half a block from a McDonald's, and another block from Sarasota High School. It was also a five-minute walk from where I now resided. It didn't feel right yet for me to say I "lived" there. It probably never would.

The Waffle Shop is semi-famous. Elvis once stopped there. The sign outside says so. There's a big poster of The King on the wall inside. He was a frequent topic of conversation.

There were regulars at the shop, which looked like it belonged in the 1950s without trying to create the illusion. There was a wraparound counter with red leatherette-covered stools. There were tables against the walls by the windows where morning cops, hearse drivers, car salesmen, high school teachers, truckers and deliverymen, and all kinds of people just hung out.

I sat on a stool and got a coffee from one of Gwen's daughters, who served as hostesses, waitresses, and owners of the landmark.

For an instant, as I looked at Elvis, I felt like a regular. I did not want to be a regular anywhere, but such things happen.

"Carrots are bullshit," said the old man who climbed up on the stool next to me.

I knew him. He was a regular. His name was Tim — Tim from Steubenville. Tim said he was sixty, but he was closer to eighty and looked it. He lived in an assisted living home a short walk away at the end of Brother Geenen Way. He spent as much time as he could at Gwen's, reading the newspaper, shaking his head, and trying to lure people into conversations about eliminating the income tax. Almost everything he said about income tax, abolishing drug laws, and eliminating gun laws ended with the punctuation, "damn government."

He always had a newspaper and commented on stories ranging from war and devastation around the world to cats and dogs waiting, hoping to be adopted before they had to be urged to pass away, making room for others to wait their turn.

"Do animals have souls?" Tim asked, the blue veins undulating over his thin bones.

"I don't know."

"What about carrots?"

"Carrots don't have souls," I said.

"What's the matter with your Cubs?" Tim asked in one of his familiar dancing changes of subject.

"They're cursed," I said as he was served his coffee and a slice of pineapple upside down cake.

"I'll drink to that," he said, lifting his coffee mug and bringing it to his lips.

"No," I said.

"I won't drink to that?"

"No," I said. "Animals don't have souls."

The coffee was hot. I could see the steam rising, feel the heat with my fingers through the porcelain mug. I hadn't drunk any yet, even after adding milk from the miniature aluminum pitcher. My grizzled counter partner took no such precautions. He sipped, made an "uhh" sound to indicate he had made a mistake, and put the coffee down.

"You do that all the time," I said.

"I do what?"

"Add the milk and then remember that

you don't like it with milk."

"My problem," he said. "Just like Jesse always said when she was living — that I don't learn from my mistakes. I'm just doomed to keep repeating them. What about people? They have souls?"

"I don't think so," I said.

"Cubs, here's to you."

He raised his mug and drank more cautiously this time after having cooled down his coffee with the milk I had passed to him. He called me "Cubs" because of the Chicago Cubs cap I wore. I wore the cap for several reasons. First, it was a memento of my affection for the Cubs. Catherine had bought it at Wrigley Field one afternoon when she and I had taken the day off to catch a game with the Pirates. The Cubs had won 4-1. Catherine had bought it for me. I had put it on her head. She looked cute in it. It made her smile. Now she was dead and I wore the cap. Second, it covered my increasing baldness. It was not a receding hairline. It was a steady retreat. Vanity? Maybe. I didn't take time to analyze it. Old bald men look younger in hats. They don't necessarily look better. Men my age who wear baseball caps either look tough or would like to be thought of as athletic.

Greg Legerman showed up. He was alone.

I couldn't tell if he was any more nervous than he always was, but he was sufficiently nervous to make the patrons uncomfortable. He wore jeans and a short-sleeved buttoned shirt with a collar. The shirt was green with yellow lines. He sat on the open stool to my right.

The old man leaned forward to get a better look at Greg and said, "Young man, you think people have souls?"

"Good question," said Greg, avoiding my eyes.

I thought serving this permanently wired kid coffee would not improve the coming conversation, but I was too late. Gwen's daughter, the one with two kids, including a teenage boy who sometimes worked in the shop after school, put a mug of hot liquid in front of Greg and said, "Decaf. Breakfast?"

"Waffles," Greg said.

She nodded and moved off. You ordered waffles here. You got waffles, butter, maple syrup. You didn't get built-in blueberries or bananas or bacon bits. You didn't get wheat or bran waffles. You got the old-fashioned kind. Just the way Elvis had eaten them half a century ago.

"I can explain," Greg said.

"I'm sure you can," I said.

"I was just joking," he said. "I do things like that for no reason. I get excited . . ."

"Carrots are bullshit and so are you," I said. "How did you know someone had shot at me?"

"Everybody knew," he said.

"Everybody? The King of Jordan knew? Brad Pitt knew?"

"Oh come on," he said. "I mean . . ."

"First you hire me to help Ronnie Gerall. Then you call me to warn me off. You think he did it."

"No, it's just that I . . . it's too dangerous."

"For who?"

"I gave you five hundred dollars to find the real killer. I'll give you five hundred dollars to stop looking."

He reached into his pocket and came up with a roll of bills wrapped in a thick rubber band, which he placed in front of me. I pushed it back and added to it the money he had given me the day before.

"My teeth need fixing," the old man said. "If neither one of you want that money . . ."

Greg Legerman and I ignored him and looked at the money.

"Leave it there," said Gwen's daughter as she placed the plate of waffles in front of Greg, "and it'll be the biggest tip anyone ever left here."

"What about Elvis?" I asked.

"His tip is legendary," she said moving on.

"Someone shot at me in a car and probably blinded the man with me," I said. "Then someone shot a pellet into the back of a fourteen-year-old I'm responsible for. He could have died if he tumbled down my steps. It seems pretty likely that someone was trying to shoot me. I'm getting interested in finding out who killed Philip Horvecki."

"Why'd they shoot at you?" asked the old man.

"To scare me off."

"Please stop," Greg said. "You could get killed."

"My therapist says I'm suicidal, only I'd never kill myself. I wouldn't, however, object to someone else doing it for me."

"Why are you suicidal?" asked the old man with interest.

"Because my wife was murdered and the killer was never arrested."

"Then go look for him, Cubs," said Tim.

"I know where he is."

"Where?"

"Sleeping on the floor of the place I'm living in."

96

"You are a strange duck, Cubs. Kid, you think people have souls?" he asked again.

This ignited Greg. "No definitive evidence," he said. "Though research at universities in France, Germany, England, and the United States, including Princeton, is inconclusive, there seems to be evidence that electrical impulses . . ."

"Greg," I interrupted.

"He's just getting started," said the old man.

"I know. Who are you trying to protect?"

Greg shook his head no.

"Winn doesn't know what you did, does he?"

Greg shook his head again.

"No. You're not going to tell me, are you?"

"You don't even like Ronnie," he said. "No one does."

"He hasn't been arrested because people don't like him. He has been arrested for killing Philip Horvecki."

"Lots of people wanted to kill Horvecki," Greg said, looking at his waffle.

"Put the butter and syrup on 'em kid," said the old man, "and whale away while they're still hot."

There was an early morning breakfast hubbub in the Waffle Shop. All the stools and all the tables were full. Men in suits laughed at each other's jokes. Men in work clothes talked softly and tended to concentrate on eating. The smell of waffles wafted, and Gwen's daughters bustled. I put enough on the counter to cover my coffee and a tip and said, "I have work to do."

"Please," said Greg. "Take the money. Stop looking."

He looked as if he were about to cry.

"Don't be a dumb shit, Fonesca. Take the money."

Greg nodded. I moved toward the door as the old man sidled over to sit next to Greg.

I didn't listen to find out if they were talking about the existence of the human soul, teeth in need of repair, or Elvis. I did have work to do.

No one shot at me as I stepped out of the Waffle Shop. So far, it was a good day.

I had the papers in the back pocket of my jeans. They stood up, scratched my lower back, and reminded me it was time for them to be served.

My bicycle, which Ames had named "Steadfast," was locked in a storage bin under my twenty-two stairs. I had a key. That made two keys in my pocket. One for my front door and one for the locker. Two keys too many.

I rolled Steadfast into the street, adjusted

my Cubs cap, pedaled to Laurel, and then made a right toward Pineapple. On Pineapple I turned left, went through downtown, and walked Steadfast across Fruitville Avenue when the light turned green. From there it was three minutes to the house I was looking for.

It was, as all the houses in the neighborhood were, a small one-story cement-block building with long-dead orange siding. The slightly slanted roof was almost completely covered with leaves and pine cones from a big tree which looked as if its roots went right under the house. Grass, or what passes for it in Southern Florida, still fought a losing battle to live in the stony rubble of the front yard. A severely rusted pickup truck of unknown vintage stood next to the house.

I walked up the narrow and cracked concrete path to the door. The day was already hot. I didn't mind. The heat didn't bother me. I didn't sweat. Even the coldest mornings of winter in Chicago hadn't affected me very much. When I was fifteen I had a mild case of frostbite from being out too long in subzero weather. I hadn't felt cold, but even now I get occasional tingling at the top of my ears.

I looked for a bell button. There was one. There was a badly rusted small door knocker. I decided against using it lest it fall off. I knocked.

"Coming," the high, almost child's voice inside called.

The door opened.

Below me, head only about thigh high, stood a small black man of no clear age in jeans, a blue T-shirt, and a Cubs cap, though a more expensive one than mine.

"Zo Hirsch?"

"That's right."

I handed him the folded order for him to appear at a divorce settlement hearing in the office of my lawyer client. I never deliver court orders or summonses in an envelope. I was supposed to deliver papers, and that I did.

"Shit. Shit. Shit."

He muttered, looked at the papers I had just handed him, and shook his head.

"Do I look like I can pay six hundred dollars a month?"

"No," I said.

"Want a beer?" he asked.

"No, thanks."

"Dr Pepper, Mountain Dew, Diet Pepsi?"

"Diet Pepsi."

"Come in."

He stepped back. Had I reached down, I could have rested the palm of my hand on his head. I resisted the urge to do so.

"This way," he said.

A few things struck me as we moved past the living room on the left and another room on the right, which must have been a dining room at one point, but was now a library filled with shelves and books. A desk stood near the front window which, if he had been sitting there, meant he would have seen me coming. Another thing that struck me was that everything looked immaculately clean. The furniture looked Arts & Crafts and the many framed photos on the walls were crisp, clear, and signed by Major League Baseball players. The other thing that struck me was that not one piece of furniture was a concession to Zo Hirsch's size.

"Sit or look around," he said pointing to the living room.

I examined some of the photographs while Zo Hirsch moved down the short corridor.

There were photographs of Bobby Bonds, Deon Sanders, Andre Dawson, and even Sammy Sosa. All of the players on Zo Hirsch's walls were black. He returned quickly with a can of Diet Pepsi in one hand and an Amstel Light in the other. He handed me the Pepsi. We sat.

"You meet my wife?" he asked, after taking a long drink.

"No."

He reached into his pocket awkwardly, took out his wallet, flipped it open, and handed it to me. The woman in the photograph looked of normal size, darkly Hispanic, and quite pretty. She was smiling. Her left arm was draped over the shoulder of Zo Hirsch, who was also smiling.

"Pretty," I said, handing back the wallet.

"Fucking beautiful," he said, accepting the wallet and stuffing it back in his pocket.

"Cubs fan?" I said.

He seemed puzzled and then got it. He touched the brim of his cap and pointed to mine.

"Not especially," he said. "Billy Williams gave me this one."

"Vintage," I said.

He shrugged and drank some more.

"What happened to your face?" he asked.

"Flying glass. Someone shot at me."

"Why?"

"I'll ask when I find him. Nice collection," I said looking around.

"I make my living writing about baseball," he said. "Mostly for Spanish language newspapers, magazines, and websites. My mother is Haitian. My father was a Jew from Cuba, a fisherman. He's gone. They were both normal-sized, if you were wondering."

I had been wondering, but I said, "No."

He looked at the photos on the wall and said, "I'd rather be playing right field anywhere for half of what Emilio Vezquez is getting."

"Emilio Vezquez?"

"The Double-D level pitcher my wife walked off with who will never, never make it to the majors. You want to know why?"

He finished his beer and looked at the empty bottle as if it had betrayed him.

"His fastball never hits ninety and he is scared shitless of line drives."

He sat back and took off his cap, a look of satisfaction on his face. He looked around the room at the photos of the men whose photographs surrounded him as if they had just applauded his observation.

"I've got to go," I said, rising and placing my empty can on a coaster on the table between us. The coaster had a Cincinnati Reds logo on it.

"Think you might forget I was home?" he said, holding up the papers I had served him. "I'll have a check from a Dominican newspaper coming in a few days and I'll be able to hire a lawyer."

"I don't —" I began, but was cut off by the ringing of Zo Hirsch's phone.

103

"Hold on," he said and moved to the library, where I heard him pick up the phone and say, "Yeah. Okay. Hold on."

He came back into the living room carrying a black phone, which he handed to me.

"It's for you," he said.

I took the phone and moved to the window, being careful that someone parked and watching wouldn't be able to see me. No one knew I was at Zo Hirsch's, not even the lawyer I was serving papers for. Conclusion: I had been followed here.

"Fonesca," I said.

"You're supposed to be working on the Horvecki murder."

The car parked across the street was familiar — a red Buick LeSabre. The window blown out by the BB had been replaced, but the left fender definitely needed work and the left front headlight was missing. Jeff Augustine's right eye wasn't missing but it sported a black eye patch. He held a cell phone to his ear.

"You should be in bed," I said.

Zo Hirsch held up his empty beer bottle, inviting me to join him in a morning brew. I shook my head no. He shrugged and got another beer. Maybe a steady diet of bottled beer had contributed to the departure of Zo's wife.

"I can't afford to be in bed," Augustine said in that musical Robert Preston voice.

"You ever play the Music Man?" I asked.

"Yes, dinner theater. You want me to sing 'Seventy-Six Trombones'?"

"Maybe later."

"How's the investigation going? Corkle wants to know."

"I'm working on it."

"I know. You're in the home of one of Philip Horvecki's few friends."

I looked at Zo who, with pursed lips, appeared to be deciding if a burp were in order.

"My eye aches," said Augustine.

"I'm sorry. You should take something for it."

"I am. I've got a container of painkillers that begin with the letter B. Make my life easier. Tell Corkle you can't find anything so I can go back to simply taking care of his nuttiness. I'm in pain and may never have three-dimensional vision again. I'm in desperate need of a Corkle Pocket Fishing Machine."

"You are?"

"No, but I still seem to have something resembling a sense of humor."

"I don't have a sense of humor," I said.

"It's my turn to be sorry. Do we understand each other? Do we share the common language of English? Corkle wants to protect his grandson from anyone who might be unhappy about his paying you to look for an alternative to jolly Ronnie Gerall. We've been over this."

"We have. Can I buy you a cup of coffee or a sandwich?" I asked. "The Hob Nob is five minutes away. Great sandwiches."

"I'm supposed to be threatening you," Augustine said. "I can't do it if you feel sorry for me and offer me coffee and sandwiches. Tell the little man I'm sorry."

"For what?" I asked.

"Playing the role," he said.

Augustine turned off his phone before I could ask him what he meant. I turned back to Zo Hirsch. It couldn't have been more than ten seconds later that a rock came through the window, showering the room with glass. I turned to the window again and watched Augustine drive out of sight to the metallic clank of a piece of dragging undercarriage.

I handed the phone back to the stunned Zo Hirsch who seemed to be baffled by the gift. Then he hung it up.

"What did he do that for?" Zo asked.

"His job," I said. "Sorry."

"His job is to throw . . . forget it. It's just

another piece of crap thrown at me."

"Want another beer?" Hirsch asked, looking at the rock near his feet.

"No thanks, but I do have a question."

"Ask."

"You were a friend of Philip Horvecki?" I said.

"Phil the Pill, Phil the Eel," he said, sitting down in what appeared to be his favorite chair. "Much beloved by all who knew him. He was almost a saint."

He looked at me and waited.

"I'm lying," he said.

"I know," I said.

"Phil Horvecki was an asshole."

"You weren't friends?"

"He was on the bowling team I manage," said Zo. "Zo's Foes. Phil Horvecki was a man of many alibis, always ready to criticize the play of others. He will be easily replaced. I wish he had had a funeral so I could stand up and say it. Rest in peace you A-number-one asshole. I did have an occasional beer with him and some of the other bowlers. Small group got together at Bennigan's on Monday nights after our league games."

"Was he friendly with any of the bowlers?"

Zo was smiling now.

"The cost of further information is your forgetting to deliver your papers till the end of the week."

"What papers?" I said.

"Just me," said Zo. "But I wouldn't call the relationship friendly. We shmoozled."

"Shmoozled?"

"Talked."

"About?"

"Who knows? We have a deal?"

"Not yet," I said.

"He told me about people he had cheated out of property. He didn't think it was cheating. He went after old people, mostly."

"Old people who might want to kill him?"

"Old people who have sons or daughters who might be mad enough to do some killing. Phil the Pill had a restraining order against two such offspring who threatened to kill him."

"You know their names?"

"No," he said. "I've been dreaming about my wife. Bad dreams."

I moved toward the door.

"Ever meet Horvecki's daughter?" I asked.

"Once," he said. "She stopped by the bowling alley and just sat there watching. Skinny thing. Big scared eyes. I didn't talk to her. Horvecki didn't even introduce her, just said, 'My daughter,' once when he saw me looking."

"How did he say it?"

"Say what? 'My daughter'? I don't know. Almost as if he were apologizing or something."

I had no response, so he continued as I opened the door.

"I've been thinking about killing Vezquez, but there are too many damned Vesquezes out there and too much killing."

"The phone book probably has a couple of columns of Vezquezes," I said.

"I don't mean people named . . . forget it. Leave me with my thoughts of Roberto Clemente."

I offered to help him clean up the mess, but Zo just looked at it and said, "I'll take care of it."

"Can I . . . ?"

"No one can," he said.

I left him. I had another appointment, maybe another client.

I sat on my bike and called Dixie Cruise at the coffee bar on Main Street where she served espresso and kept the Internet-connected patrons happy and their electronics running. Dixie was slim and trim, with very black hair in a short style. Dixie lived in a two-room apartment in a slightly run-down twelve-flat apartment building on Ringling Boulevard, a block from the main post office. The apartment was almost laboratory clean, neat, and filled with computers and electronic gear.

"Working on it, Mr. L.F.," Dixie said in her down-home Florida accent. "Lady knows her stuff. Horvecki's daughter Rachel seems to have migrated to an alternate universe. Since her father's murder, she hasn't used a credit card, written a check, flown on an airplane, booked a room at a motel or hotel, or rented a car, at least not in her own name. She's running on cash and another name. Every Sarasota business, from dry cleaners to Red Lobster, has no record of her having been there."

"Keep looking," I said.

"You keep paying in cash, I keep looking. I've got bills to pay and things to buy for my wedding."

"You're getting married?"

"Didn't I tell you?"

"No."

"Wedding'll be in June. First Baptist. Reception after at Cafe Bacci. You and the cowboy are invited. You'll get an invitation."

"New address," I said, and gave her the address.

"My beau's name is Dan Rosenfeld. He's an airplane mechanic at Dolphin."

"Congratulations," I said.

"Thanks. I'll keep looking for her. Today,

I check on unidentified bodies found from
North Carolina to Key West."

6

I would have forgotten about the appointment if I hadn't written it on one of the three-by-five index cards I carried in my back pocket. The call had come in early the day before. With everything going on, I had almost forgotten about it. The index cards got dog-eared quickly from my sitting on them, but I wrote my notes to myself in clear block letters and had no trouble reading them.

At the age of forty-three, I was having trouble remembering simple things like why I was going to the refrigerator or what I was planning to do when I opened the medicine cabinet in my bathroom.

The card read:

Bee Ridge Park softball field. 11 a.m. Monday. Ferris Berrigan

The bike ride to Bee Ridge Park was long. It was made longer by my expecting that someone might pull alongside me, roll down a window, and take a few shots, or that someone would run me into oncoming traffic on Beneva Road. It would be fitting, to die the same way Catherine had, but I wasn't really ready for that. Progress, Ann would say. I no longer welcomed accidental death.

Traffic wasn't too heavy, but a pickup truck did pass by when I crossed Bee Ridge, and the passenger did throw something out the window in my general direction. The sight of a somewhat lean man in a Chicago Cubs cap riding a bicycle seemed to bring out the redneck in some people. Actually, this was better than the panic that the sight of me brought to ancient drivers who often came near losing control and running me down.

I made it to Bee Ridge Park just before 11 a.m. I was familiar with the place. There were two softball fields. No one was playing on or standing by the nearest field, the one next to Wilkinson Road. But on the more distant field, a group of men were playing ball. As I rode across the parking lot and down the narrow road that marked the west side of the park, I heard the cool aluminum-on-ball clack followed by the shouting of men.

"Take two, Hugo!"

"Take three! What do you mean, two?"

"Dick is coaching at first."

"He took second easy, you dumb cluck."

"Grow up, John."

I parked my bike in a bike rack next to the field. I could see now that the players were all wearing uniforms, white ones with the words "Roberts Realty" on one and "Dunkin' Donuts" on the other. All the players were men who looked like they were in their sixties or seventies or eighties.

A few of the players glanced in my direction. There was a lone spectator, a man in a black cloth on a dark wood folding director's chair. Next to him there was an identical chair. I moved toward the man in the chair. He was sitting forward with his elbows on his knees and his chin in his hands. The pose of a bad boy who has been caught.

The man in the chair was even leaner than I am and a little older, maybe fifty. He wore brown slacks and a matching short-sleeve pullover shirt with what looked like a guitar etched on the lone pocket over his heart.

He sat back, waiting, and removed his glasses. He was clean shaven and nervous.

The empty chair next to him had *"Blue"* written on it in fading white paint.

I sat and looked at the game. Hugo scored.

"What's the score?" I asked.

"The score?"

"What inning is it?"

"I don't know. I don't really understand baseball."

"This is softball," I said.

"That ball doesn't look soft."

"It isn't," I said.

Another ball was hit with that pleasant bat-kissing-ball sound.

"You know who I am, don't you?"

"Ferris Berrigan?"

"Yes, but who else?" he asked.

"Who else are you?"

"Do you have any children?"

"No."

"Still," he said. "You should know who I am."

"You're the man who wants me to find out who is blackmailing him," I said.

"Something like that. You know what he said he would do?"

"No," I said.

"He'd go to the newspapers and television with a lie. You sure you don't know who I am?"

"No. Did you lose your memory?"

He looked puzzled and reassessed whatever positive feelings he had drawn from a first impression of me.

"No, I did not lose my memory. Someone wants to take it from me."

My fond wish at that moment was that whoever the good guys were out on the field full of battling voices and hoarse calls would win and go home.

"Okay, who are you and who is trying to take your memory?"

"Actually, it's all my memories they wish to take. You are positive you don't know who I am?"

"You're King Solomon, Master of all the Aegeans."

"If you can't take this seriously . . ."

"I'll take it seriously," I promised.

"I'm Blue."

"I'm sorry. I know how it feels."

"No, I'm Blue Berrigan, Blue the Man for You, Blue with Songs Ever New. Blue. The one on television. Fourteen years on television. I'm syndicated all over the world. Two generations of children have grown up singing my songs. Go to YouTube. One-year-olds dancing to Mitchell and Snitchel, The Great Big Blue Starfish, Empty Bottles of Juice."

"I've heard of —"

A clack, a shout of "Look Out!", and a yellow softball whizzed past Blue's head.

"You aren't in a safe place," the first baseman said as he ran after the ball.

"You're telling me," Blue said. "What was I saying?"

"Television."

"Television," he repeated, sitting back. "You want some walnuts?"

"No, thanks."

"Suit yourself. I'm semiretired. I don't need the money anymore, but it's my money and I'm not giving it away to fake blackmailers."

"They aren't really blackmailers?"

"Extortionists. They have photographs of me in bed."

"Yes."

"With two naked people."

"It happens," I said.

"One of the naked people is a man; the other is a woman, a very young woman who could pass for sixteen or even fifteen, but she's twenty-four and reasonably well known. Since you didn't recognize me, you probably wouldn't recognize her."

"Show business," I said.

"I work with kids. TV, tabloids, newspapers, magazines, blogs, they'll all show it and say I'd been in bed with a minor. I'll have to say it's a lie and no one will believe me. Even the suggestion will end my career. I don't want to end my career, but I can

117

live with it. What I can't live with is what it will do to my reputation, my reruns, as unsuccessful as they've been everywhere but Guam and Uganda. You know why I asked you to meet me here with the softball players rather than the playground where kids are playing? A man in his forties, alone. Pedophile. You get it?"

"We could have met someplace else."

"I live right over there, across the street, on Wilkinson. This is convenient and, dammit, I don't want to hide."

Long pause. A skinny guy who couldn't have weighed more than Ames's broom hit a line drive out to shortstop.

"Come on," said Berrigan.

The teams changed positions while we folded up the director's chairs.

"I'll take those," he said.

I followed him to the road and a parked Mazda SUV. He opened it to put the chairs inside.

"What do you want me to do?" I asked.

"Find the blackmailers, expose them, tell me who they are, kill them, break their legs, feed them to the stingrays at Mote Marine Park. Find a way to blackmail them back."

He reached into his pocket and with difficulty came up with a CD. He handed it to me. "Take the job. Don't take the job. The

CD is still yours."

"Thanks," I said, putting the CD into my back pocket.

"I signed it with a Magic Marker."

"One more perk and you'll have me."

He slammed down the door.

"Do you have a note? A recorded message? How did they contact you?"

"A young woman came to the door of my house and told me they, whoever they were, had the photographs. She gave me some of the pictures, said there were more. She was perky, bright, pretty, dark, possibly Hispanic. She said they would call and would expect me to have an initial payment of fifteen thousand dollars ready when they did. She wished me a nice day and bounced away like a teen in a toilet bowl commercial.

"Did you do those things, the things in the photographs?"

"Does it make a difference? Consenting adults."

"I think you should go to the police."

"I think I should not. I live there."

He pointed across the field and to the street a good hundred yards away.

"The yellow house. They put those photographs on the internet and I won't work again, and then I'll find pickets outside my house demanding that I move away from the playground."

"None of the photographs were of you with underage children?"

"Not one," he said. "Two generations. Two generations of people who grew up and are growing up with my music will have a childhood dream broken, a friend lost, a trust betrayed."

"We don't want to do that," I said.

"We do not. So?"

"I'll look into it. I'll take the photographs and talk to some people. If you're contacted, call me."

"What will it cost?" he asked.

"Two hundred dollars flat fee for two days of work to see what I can find."

He took out his wallet and paid the money in twenty-dollar bills.

"Want a receipt?"

"No," he said.

I wrote my number on an index card and handed it to him.

"Call me when they get in touch with you again."

"I will," he said. "Want to put your bike in back and I'll drive you home?"

"No, thanks," I said.

"Looks like rain."

"Let's hope," I said.

"Let's hope," he said.

He had lied. Not everything, but a lot of it. He was a nervous look-away liar, his act semirehearsed, his voice low. Lying didn't mean he was guilty of what the blackmailer claimed. People lie for many reasons — because they are ashamed, because they like to seem to be more or less than they are, because they want to protect themselves or others, or because lying was automatic. I didn't know what kind of liar Blue Berrigan was.

Throughout the ride home I was sitting on the CD in my back pocket and hearing its plastic cover crack. I took it out and drove with it in my hand. The photographs were tucked inside my shirt. It did rain, not hard at first but coming down in a heated, pelting shower by the time I hit Tamiami Trail and Webber.

No one tried to kill me, either intentionally or inadvertently.

When I hit Laurel, I did not look at the building that had replaced the Dairy Queen where, had it still been there, I would have stopped for a chocolate-cherry Blizzard and a few minutes of conversation with Dave, who had owned the place, about the call of the Gulf as we sat under a red and white umbrella. No more. Dave had been forced out by what passed for progress. Dave had also made over a million on the DQ's death.

I felt wet and was not filled with a sense of merriment as I went up the steps to my new rooms. My pants clung heavily to my legs and, not for the first time, I considered buying a cheap car, leaving a cheap note, and going to Key West to sit for a decade and look toward Cuba as I cheaply lived out my life.

When I opened the door, Flo and Adele were there with Catherine in Adele's arms. Ames was there, too, and by the sound of the toilet flushing I figured Victor would soon make an appearance. The people in front of me were all reasons why I wanted to leave. They were also reasons I wanted to stay.

"Nice place you have here, Lewis," said Flo, her silver earrings tinkling if you listened quietly.

"We've got a ride to take, Lewis," Ames said.

Adele put Catherine down so I could see that she could now stand on her own with arms outstretched. I looked at Ames.

"Darrell," he said. "Doing poorly. You'd best put on something dry."

Catherine took a lone baby step toward me.

"Ain't that something?" asked Flo in her

best Western drawl, which decades ago had replaced the twang of Brooklyn.

Victor appeared and looked at Catherine, who looked up at him and smiled. Victor knew the baby was named for my dead wife, the woman he had run down while he was drunk. Victor tried to smile back.

"Lewis," Ames said, "we'd best go."

Darrell's mother, dark and angry, came out of the intensive care unit at Sarasota Memorial Hospital. She said nothing to me or Ames. She didn't have to.

"I'm sorry," I said.

For an instant, her anger seemed about to turn to fury. I waited for the outburst. I would welcome it. But just before the anticipated attack, something changed. The tightness in the lean woman let go and her shoulders dropped. The anger turned to pure sorrow.

"You didn't do it," she said. "I know that. Fault's mine for letting Ms. Porovsky talk me into letting Darrell spend time with you. I should have known what kind of business you were into. I should have asked. And then Darrell started liking you, talking 'bout you, changing, gettin' better in school and such. You find the man who shot my only boy. You find him and shoot him back before you give him up to the police. You hear?"

"I hear," I said, acknowledging that there was nothing wrong with my hearing but not that I was agreeing with her order for me to commit murder. I owned no gun and wanted none. As long as Ames was nearby, I wouldn't need one.

"How is he?" asked Ames.

"Poorly," she said. "Poorly. That BB or whatever it was infected him. Poorly."

Victor had driven Ames and me to the hospital. It was not the car he had driven when he had killed my wife, but he was the driver. Once again I searched for anger. Ann Hurwitz had urged me to find the anger, to purge it, to deal with it. Though she couldn't tell me, I had the distinct impression that she would have considered it a step forward if I suddenly attacked Victor in a bitter rage. It wasn't in me. The hate button in my psyche didn't seem to exist. I had witnessed much in my life that would put others into squinting anger. I should probably have felt that way about whoever had shot Darrell. Nothing came except a sad determination to confront the person who had put Darrell in that hospital bed.

It was still raining. Flo, Adele, and Catherine went home, and I promised to stop by the house and report.

Darrell's mother went back into the intensive care unit with us. Darrell lay on his side, knees up near his chest, hands under his face on the pillow, eyes closed. Curled up, he looked like a dark, peaceful baby. The usual machines were blinking and beeping in the darkened room.

"She's right," Ames whispered. "We should shoot him when we catch up with him."

Darrell's mother couldn't hear the whisper, and I chose not to respond.

The rain was down to a steady shower with a full bright sun shining round, red-orange, and happy when we got back to the place I was now expected to call home. Victor parked on the gravel path next to the stairs.

All three of us got out slowly, ignoring the rain. A clump of small white and yellow flowers yielded to rain drops and then popped up again for another gentle assault. Before I hit the first step, I heard her.

Parked on the street was a familiar car. When the window rolled down I saw Sally Porovsky looking at me. She didn't call out or wave. She just looked at me.

"You've got work to do," Ames said.

"I know."

Victor stood silently, a thin trail of rain

wending its way down his nose. Ames nodded at me and said no more. My door was open. Ames knew it. He led Victor upward, their shoes clapping on each wooden step.

I went to the street and moved around Sally's car to the passenger door. It was open. I got in and sat.

"You're wet," she said.

I nodded.

"There's a beach towel in the trunk. You want to get it?"

"No."

Her hands were tight on the steering wheel as if she were about to peel into a drag race. She looked forward. The shadow of rain rolling down the front window danced against her face. She looked pretty. She was pretty. Her skin was clear and pale, her hair dark and cut short. She was slightly plump and normally totally in control of herself, but not at this moment.

"I was going to call you," I said.

"I remember," she said. "I decided not to wait. How is Darrell?"

"I don't really know."

"His mother won't answer my calls."

I didn't know what to say.

She went on. "I think she blames me for getting Darrell involved with you."

"She does."

"She told you that?"

"Yes."

We went silent for about half a minute and then she said, "Let's go someplace where we can talk."

I could have said, "What's wrong with right here," but I sensed that she wanted to talk about something other than Darrell.

"FourGees?"

FourGees is a coffee shop, a decent place for lunch and late-night live music, at Beneva and Webber. It was dark in the daytime, with amber shadows and places to talk quietly.

"I can't stay long," she said as she drove. "I have to go back to the office."

The office was children's services, about ten minutes from FourGees.

I nodded. She drove. I like company when I drive alone. I'll listen to conservative talk shows, ball games, religious evangelists, but not music. I want no music. I want company. When I'm with other people in a car, I like to listen to them talk, which they seem to do whether or not I'm doing the driving.

Look at your watch or the time on your cell phone and count off a minute, then two, then three. Minutes become interminable when you count them. Silences become an anticipation of bad news.

We said not a word as Sally drove to Four-Gees and found a space directly in front of the shop.

The rain had stopped.

Silently, we got out of the car and went inside. Only two of the tables in the front room were occupied, one by a man and a small boy, and the other by three older women. The boy was playing with the straw in his drink. The women were eating slices of cake and drinking coffee. They seemed happy with one another's company.

Sally and I marched solemnly past the counter near the rear, where a tattooed girl in her twenties said, "I'll be right with you."

The second room was empty. Sally hesitated as if this wasn't what she had had in mind, and then she decided to sit on a wooden chair as far from the window as she could get. I sat too. I sat, and I waited.

"I have to tell you something, Lewis."

She leaned over and put a hand on mine.

"Your husband isn't dead," I guessed.

"He's still dead," she said.

"You have cancer."

"No. I think you should stop guessing."

The girl with the tattoos appeared and asked if we had made up our minds. I ordered a plain black coffee and a slice of the same kind of cake the women in the other room were having.

"Nothing for me," Sally said. "No, wait. Tea. Hot. Mint if you have it."

"We have it," the girl said. "Two forks for the cake? It's big."

"Sure," Sally said.

When she was gone, Sally looked down and said, "Lewis, I'm moving."

"I'll help."

"No, I'm moving to Montpelier."

"France?"

"Vermont."

This time, the silence almost insisted that no one break it.

"For good?" I asked.

"For good."

"People move here from Montpelier. They don't move from Florida to Vermont. Why?"

"My family, cousins, brother, people I've known all my life, people I went to school with. Besides, I have a good job offer at a hospital as social services director. Double my present salary."

"And?"

"And," she said, "I've been doing what I do for more than twenty years. I'm burned out, Lewis. I can't stand getting up in the morning and facing children who keep getting sent back to drug-addicted parents, kids who are hurt, abused, ignored, and dumped on the system, on me, with no resources other than whatever we can get by with off the books and paperwork. I don't want to think about the pile of cases on my desk that keeps growing. I want to be with my kids more, come home without feeling the footsteps of those kids behind me, silently calling for attention."

"I understand."

All the things she said were true, but I felt that something was missing, another reason that haunted her, a reason she didn't want to share.

"Do you? Do you understand without just feeling sorry for yourself because you're going to have to deal with another loss?"

"I don't know," I said.

Music started. It came down from a speaker mounted high on the wall. Lilly Allen was singing one of those songs that sways gently but carries lyrics as sharp as the edge of a sheet of newspaper.

"Lewis, how many times in the more than two years we've known each other have we made love or even had sex?"

"None," I said.

"I've respected your memory of Catherine with you, but we both have to move on. How many times have we kissed, really kissed?"

"Seventeen."

"I make it twenty, but you're almost certainly right. You never forget anything."

"My curse," I said.

"It's the way you want it," she said.

"When are you leaving?"

"As soon as the school year ends, so the kids won't be too disrupted."

"Seven weeks," I said.

"Seven weeks," she repeated.

The girl with the tattoos came back and placed the drinks in front of us and the cake between.

"Two forks. Enjoy."

I would not cry, but not because of pride. It just wasn't in me, but I would feel it. I would feel it, alone, sitting on the toilet, lying on my bed, listening to someone speak or Rush Limbaugh rant. I would feel it.

"I'm sorry," Sally said.

I handed her a fork and answered without saying that I was sorry, too.

"It's banana-chocolate," I said.

7

"Seven weeks," Ann Hurwitz said, dunking one of the two biscotti I had brought her into the cappuccino I had also brought to her office. A bribe.

"Seven weeks," I said.

"How do you feel about it?"

"Helpless. Relieved. I'm thinking of buying a cheap car and leaving."

"Again."

"Again," I said. "This time maybe I'll go west till I hit the Pacific Coast somewhere."

"And you'll look out toward Japan but see nothing but water."

"Maybe it will be clean."

"Pollution is everywhere."

"Sally's leaving me. Someone is trying to kill me or at least frighten me. I have a new client I don't like and another client who lied to me and may be a child molester."

"Lied about what?"

"I don't know, but I know he lied. Lies

are heavy, dark, deep behind too much sincerity. And there are people depending on me, Ames, Flo, Adele. And Victor."

"Your houseguest from Chicago."

"Yes. And I don't like my new rooms. Too big. I like things, and places, small."

"Cubicles," she said, leaning forward to ensnare the moist end of a biscotti with her teeth. "What else are small places?"

"Boxes, caskets, car trunks, jail cells, monks' cells, closets."

"You can hide in all of them," she said. "You can even die in them. All both protect and threaten."

"I guess. You're supposed to tell me that people can't run from their problems, that nothing is solved by running away."

"No," said Ann. "You got these biscotti at News and Books?"

"Yes. I always do."

"They taste different. Very good. Sometimes things are solved by running away."

"I should run away?"

"If you feel that you must," Ann said, wiping her chocolate-tipped fingers with a napkin and then discarding it in her almost empty wastebasket. "I would miss you. You would miss Ames, Flo, Adele, and the baby."

"Her name is Catherine," I said.

"I know. I wanted you to say it."

"Because she was named for my wife, and it ties me to Sarasota."

"It ties you to people," she said. "You're not going to run away."

"I suppose not."

I leaned forward, my head between my legs.

"Are you all right? Are you going to be sick?"

"No," I said. "I'm trying to find a box to hide in."

"Have you been having nightmares again?" she asked.

"Yes."

"Tell me."

My head still down, I said, "I'm in New York City, at a hotel. I look out the window, across the street, at another hotel. On the seventh floor of that hotel, there's an open window. A child, about two, is about to climb out the window. It's New York during the day. The distance and the city noise let me know it would do no good to yell."

"So what do you do?"

"Nothing. I stand there, looking, hoping, praying. I can't move away. I can't close my eyes. I'm crying, muttering."

"Muttering what?"

"Oh, no. God, no. Jesus, no."

"Does the child fall?"

"The child looks over at me and smiles over the chasm, the canyon of buildings and streets. I try to wave her back, but she just smiles and waves back at me. I push my hands forward. I'm afraid to scream or make a frightened and frightening face for fear she will fall."

"She?"

"Did I say she?"

"Yes."

"So what do you think?"

"The child is Catherine or the baby we never had. She is about to die and there's nothing I can do about it."

"What does the child look like?"

"Dark curly hair. Wide eyes, brown eyes. Even at this distance I know they are brown."

"And," said Ann, "Catherine's hair was curly?"

"No."

"Not even as a child?"

"No," I said.

"And her eyes were wide and brown?"

"No, her eyes were blue."

"Who is the baby?"

"Me," I said. "She looks just like my baby pictures."

"Breakthrough," Ann said, sitting up in her well-padded swivel chair.

"But why is it a girl?" I asked.

"We save that for another time, to give you something to think about between now and then. Time for one more quick dream."

Knowing I would stare into the eyes of that baby who was me, looking for answers, I said, "Thalidomide man."

"Thalidomide man?"

"You know. About fifty years ago in Chicago a lot of women who were given thalidomide and had deformed babies, withered arms or legs or both. In my dream I see a man with a deformed right hand advancing toward me in slow motion. He's smiling and holding out his hand to shake my hand. I don't want to shake his three-fingered stump of a hand, but I extend mine to him. I always wake up then, and almost always it's 4:13 in the morning."

"How did you know about thalidomide?" Ann asked.

"I'm not sure. I think my mother and father talked about it, or I ran across it in a newspaper or magazine."

Ann looked puzzled, as if there were something she was trying to recall.

"Lewis, think."

I thought. Nothing came.

"The man with the withered right arm?" she prompted.

136

Nothing.

"The boy whose parents abandoned him."

I remembered. "I forgot."

"You never forget anything," said Ann.

"That's what Sally said."

"The boy?"

"His name was David Bryce O'Brien. I met him when I was investigating a homicide for the Cook County State Attorney's Office. You know this."

"Tell me again," she said. "I'm ancient and often forget what I move from one room to the next for."

"His father was a suspect."

"And?"

"His father was the murderer. He killed his dry cleaner. Then he killed his wife and son."

"David Bryce O'Brien."

"Then he killed himself."

"And what did he do to the body of his son?"

"No," I said.

Ann went silent. So did I. A waiting game. I could get up and leave, but I didn't. Then I said, "He cut off his son's withered arm and left a note saying, 'I'm sorry.' It's the most common suicide note in the world."

"Biblical," she said.

"Biblical?"

"If my right hand offends . . . ," she said.

"It wasn't his right hand."

"How old was David Bryce O'Brien?"

"Almost two years old."

"About the same age as the child in the window in New York?"

"Yes."

"That feels true?"

"Yes. You want me to think about it?"

"Yes, but not consciously. Let it go. When the time comes to talk about it, you will. You forgot to bring me something, Lewis."

I looked at the empty white bag that had held coffee and biscotti. The pungent smell of coffee and pastry hung lazily. She shook her head.

"I have a joke."

"Good, but you were supposed to bring something else. You were supposed to bring me the first line of a book. Do you have one?"

" 'And he shall turn the heart of the fathers to the children, and the heart of the children to their fathers, lest I come and smite the earth with a curse.' "

"And that is the first line of what?" Ann asked.

"It's the last line of the Old Testament. The only line I remember."

"Come back next time with first lines,"

she said. "Who told you the joke?"

"A man with one eye I met outside your office the last time I was here."

"The joke," she said.

"Actually, he gave me five of them."

I took out my index cards.

"One will be enough."

"Treat each day as if it's your last. One day you'll be right."

"That's a joke?"

"Yes."

"You think it's funny?"

"No."

"Next time, first lines," she said.

Augustine was waiting for me outside of Ann's office again, but this was a very different Augustine from the one who was there the last time I emerged into sun and heavy, moist air.

"Need a ride?"

"Yes," I said.

"I put your bike in my trunk. I'll buy you a new lock."

"Thanks," I said.

He walked us slowly to the corner and made a right turn onto Main. He was silent. So was I. I was trying not to think about what Ann and I had talked about, but I was doing a bad job.

"How is your eye?" I asked.

His hand reached up to be sure the patch was still there.

"Hurts," he said.

"I'm sorry," I said, and I was.

"Corkle fired me."

"What for?"

"Failure to get rid of you."

We hit the first corner and I was tempted to invite him across the street to News and Books, but I had had enough darkness for one day.

"Get rid of me? He just hired me."

"He wants to scare you away from the job. He's nuts. I'm glad I'm no longer in his employ. He gave me a check for five thousand dollars and an instant electric machine that both cores and peels apples, pears, and even peaches and plums."

"How will you get it on a plane?"

"I don't know."

"Why does he want to scare me away?"

"Don't know. Ask him."

"And you're telling me this because . . . ?" I asked.

"I like you," he said. "And I don't like loose ends."

His car, a gray two-door Mazda rental, was parked halfway up the block. Parking space downtown was always at a premium.

I didn't consider telling him he was lucky. He had almost lost an eye. It could have been much worse.

"I think the kid shot at us," he said when we were driving.

He was one of those people who instantly turns on music when you get into their car. It made intimate conversation difficult. The music was '40s and '50s pop. Rosemary Clooney was singing "Come On To My House." She bounced.

"The kid?"

"Corkle's grandson, Gregory Legerman."

"Why?"

"Because Corkle thinks the kid killed Philip Horvecki."

"And then hired me to find himself?"

"Go figure," he said, making a turn on Orange and heading south. "We're talking about crazy people here."

"Corkle's daughter, too?"

"Why not?"

We drove silently for a few minutes, and then he said, "I'm not supposed to drive till I get another driving test. Hell, I can drive better with one eye than all these old farts with two."

"Someday you may be an old fart," I said.

"Great, an old fart with one eye."

He went to Laurel and turned left. A

minute later he parked in front of my new home, the one with rooms too big and visitors too many.

"I'm cashing Corkle's check and heading for the Tampa airport," he said. "I'll work in commercials if I'm lucky, dinner theater, wherever a one-eyed character actor is wanted. Who knows? This . . . ," he said, pointing to his patched eye, "may be the opening of new career opportunities."

"Who knows?"

"We both do," he said with a smile as bitter as orange peel.

I got out of the car.

"Watch yourself, Cub fan," he said.

I touched the brim of my cap in a gesture of good-bye. He tore down the street with a drag racer's abandon. The tires weren't his. The car wasn't his. It was too bad the Dairy Queen two blocks down was closed and torn down. He could have had a Blizzard to ease the rush hour trip to Tampa.

"Let's go," Ames said when I went through the door.

He was standing to my left, near the wall. Victor, in his Chicago Bulls sweatshirt with the sleeves cut off, was seated on the floor, his bedroll wrapped neatly in the corner. Ames was wearing black corduroy pants, a red-dominated, plaid shirt, and boots.

"Where this time?" I asked.

"To see a man," said Ames. "Brought you this."

He held up a wooden plank about the size of a rolled up newspaper. Burned into its dark, grainy surface were the words LEWIS FONESCA.

"So people will know you're here," said Ames. "I can mount it outside somewhere."

"I don't want any more people to know I'm here," I said.

"Suit yourself," he said, placing the plank faceup on my desk. "Let's go. Victor'll drive us."

In response, Victor Woo got up from the floor.

"Where are we going and why?" I asked.

"I found a man who knows all about Philip Horvecki."

Victor chauffeured. Ames and I sat in back. Ames gave Victor directions. They weren't easy. We drove up I-75 to the University Parkway exit and headed east. Ames gave clipped driving directions like, "Next right," and Victor drove without speaking.

"Fella came into the Texas a few hours ago," said Ames. "Heard him talking. Sheriff's Deputy. Talking about the murder. Told

143

another fella that the detectives should ask Pertwee about it. I asked him who this Pertwee was. He told me."

Ames went silent. Long speeches were not his medium.

After telling Victor to go down a narrow dirt road, Ames went on.

"Seems Pertwee knows a lot about old crimes in the county," said Ames.

Silence again, except for the bumping tires and the *rat-tat* of pebbles against the undercarriage of the car.

"How do you know where to —" I started.

"Came out here on my scooter when the deputy gave me directions," Ames interrupted.

We had gone almost twenty miles from my apartment. On a scooter, going over this road, one would have to be very determined.

"Look out on the right over ahead. Hardly see it, but there's a low wooden fence and an open gate."

Victor turned into a rutted path even narrower than the dirt road. Ahead of us about fifty yards was a mobile home with a small addition. It was a house of aluminum waiting for a hurricane to wash it away.

The closer we got the better it looked. The place was recently painted white. A small, umbrella-covered metal table with three wrought iron chairs sat in front of the mobile home's door.

Victor parked. We got out as a man lumbered through the door and held the sides of the doorway to keep from slipping on the two steps to the ground. He was short, with a sagging belly. He wore jeans with suspenders over a blue striped polo shirt that was sucked into the folds of his neck. He was about sixty years old.

He looked at the three of us with amusement.

"A visit from a formidable trio," he said. "A cowboy, a chink, and a gingerbread man. What brings you, and would you like a beer?"

We all said no. Pertwee shrugged and said, "So be it. What brings you here?"

"Deputy I met said you know a lot about Philip Horvecki," said Ames.

"That I do," said Pertwee. "And who did you say you were?"

"My name is Lewis Fonesca and I —"

"Lewis Fonesca," he said. "Formerly an investigator in the state attorney's office in Cook County, Illinois. You came here four years back after your wife was killed in a hit-and-run on Lake Shore Drive in Chicago. The driver of the red convertible that killed her was an Asian man who has yet to be found by the police."

"This is the man," I said, nodding toward Victor.

Pertwee bent forward and looked up at Victor. Not much could happen that would surprise him.

"And this is Ames McKinney," I went on.

"Four years ago, beach at Lido," said Pertwee. "You shot your ex-partner. Fonesca was there. You did a little time. I sit out here, keep track. Retired detective, Cincinnati Police. Come on in."

We followed the wobbling Pertwee into his house. The living room was larger than I had expected. It had the musty but not unpleasant odor of dried leaves. Family portraits hung on the walls, and the sofa and matching chair were each covered with a bright blue knitted blanket. Beyond the living room and down a step into the one-room addition to the home was an office lined with file drawers. A computer with a large screen sat next to a printer and a fax machine. There was a duplicate of the sofa in the other room complete with knitted blanket, only this blanket was brown.

"Wife's in town at a photography class at Selby Gardens," Pertwee said. "Won't be back for a long while. She'll have a portfolio full of photographs of flowers and trees when she walks through the door."

He nodded toward the wall over the sofa. Color photographs were mounted one after another, all around the room. All the photographs were of flowers or bright fish in a pond.

Pertwee sat in front of the computer and pressed the power button. While the machine was firing up, he rose and waddled to a file cabinet, opened it, rummaged in a lower drawer, and came up with a manila file folder.

"Cold cases," he explained as the image of a red flower appeared on his computer screen. "Sheriff's office lets me see what I can find. Won't find stuff like this on the Internet."

"Horvecki was involved in a cold case?" I asked.

Victor had sat on the sofa. Ames stood at my side looking at the screen. Pertwee's face was red with the reflected color of the flower before him.

"Two cold cases," said Pertwee, opening the file folder and placing it on the table next to him. "First case was back in 1968. Young Horvecki was but a stripling. "Two fourteen- and sixteen-year-old black girls were raped and beaten. They were found wandering the byways. Both girls identified

Horvecki as the attacker. Both later changed their minds. Case still open. Both girls are grandmas now. One's a great grandma. One has a son who is not fond of Mr. Horvecki and has been known to speak ill of the now deceased. Son's name is Williams, Essau Williams. Detective in the Venice Police Department. Detective Williams has been given disciplinary warnings because Horvecki claimed Williams has been stalking him for years."

"And the other case?" I asked.

Pertwee said, "Ah" and flipped pages until he found what he was looking for.

"Here 'tis, 1988, same year Cynthia and I arrived in the State of Florida and purchased this little bit of heaven. Costs almost as much to get an Internet hookup and dish TV as it cost to buy Buddenbrooks."

"Buddenbrooks?" I asked.

"The abode in which we sit, away from civilization in a field of rattlesnakes, raccoons, and seldom-seen rodents of unusual size and appetite. I can shoot them at my ease from one of those chairs under the umbrella. My principal physical exercise."

"Sounds like fun," Ames said.

"Yes, 'tis. However, all in all, I'd rather be back in Cincinnati. Cynthia, however, longed for Paradise, and we wound up here.

I'm not complaining."

"The second case in your files," I reminded him.

He turned the page of the stapled sheets in the folder and said, "One Jack Pepper, sophomore at Riverview High School. Attacked from behind while crossing an orange grove on his way home from school. Assailant told him to pull down his pants or die. Assailant proceeded to attempt anal intercourse. Failed. Boy stepped out of his pants and drawers and ran. Pepper turned and saw the attacker coming after him. Pepper ran faster, covered himself with a damp, dirty newspaper and entered a gas station. Pepper identified Horvecki but Horvecki had the best lawyers money can buy and some friends in the right places. That was nineteen years ago. Jack Pepper is now thirty-six years old and living in relative tranquility in Cortez Village. Thrice Jack Pepper confronted our Mr. Horvecki in public places, broke his nose and cheekbone with a well-placed and probably knuckle-hurting punch, and kicked him into unconsciousness. Attempted murder, but . . ."

"Horvecki did not press charges," I said.

"He did not. No other incident involving the two of them in the last nineteen years."

"You have Pepper's address?" I asked.

"That I have. I'll give you both his and Essau Williams's address," said Pertwee. "And I shall print some possibly pertinent information for you."

"Cost?" asked Ames.

"Close those two cold cases and find out who killed Horvecki," said Pertwee. "These cases of open files challenge and mock me. The fewer there are, the lighter my burden, even though I know others will come to fill the drawers."

We started back to the car, and Pertwee called out, "A sweet fella like Horvecki probably had lots of people who didn't much care for him besides Williams and Pepper."

We kept walking. One of the people who didn't like Horvecki was Ronnie Gerall, sitting in juvenile lockup for killing a man everyone seemed to hate.

Cell phones are wondrous things. They keep people connected regardless of where they are. Going to be late for an appointment? Call. Have an accident on the road and need AAA? Call. Lapse into drunkenness at the side of the road and need AA? Call. Supposed to meet someone and they don't show up? Call. Cell phones are wondrous things. They take photographs and videos,

150

tell you the temperature and baseball scores, let you order pickup at Appleby's, tell you what time it is and where you are if you get lost, and play music you like.

People can find you no matter where you are.

The problem is that I don't want to be connected, don't want to order braised chicken to be picked up at Appleby's, don't want to take photographs or videos, and am in no hurry to get baseball scores.

But the machines give us no choice.

The young don't have wristwatches.

Phone booths are dying out.

Good-bye to all that.

Still, I had a cell phone in my pocket, a birthday present from Flo Zink. Adele had programmed in a ringtone version of "Help!" that was now playing.

"L.F., unless her body is enriching a wood or bog, Rachel Horvecki is not dead. And she is still not leaving her footprint on the sands of time. I can tell you stuff about her. Got time to hear?"

"Yes."

"She is twenty-seven years old, went to Sarasota Christian High School where she was on the yearbook committee, Spanish Club, Poetry Club, Chess Club, Drama Club, cross-country team; did three years at

Manatee Community College, where she was on no club, went to a small school called Plain River College in a small town in West Texas. Her major was English Lit. No extracurricular interests or clubs. Plain River College registrar records show she dropped out. Reason stated: Getting Married. Sarasota Memorial Hospital records show she had an appendectomy when she was seventeen and came into the ER once, when she was fourteen, for a broken arm and bruised ribs. Hospital reported possible abuse, but Rachel insisted she had fallen down some stairs. Want me to keep looking?"

"Yes. See if you can find out who, if anyone, she married."

"Will do."

We hung up. I called Winn Graeme's cell phone and told him I wanted to talk to him without Greg at his side pummeling him. He had something to do at school but would call me when he could get away.

I called the home of D. Elliot Corkle and left a message when he didn't pick up. Since he said he never left the house, I wondered where he was. Maybe he was taking a shower or a swim or just didn't feel like being connected to someone beyond his front door. I gave my number to the machine and said, "Please call me soon. What's the 'D' in your name for?"

I called Sally. She answered. I said nothing.

"Lew?"

Cell phone. Caller ID. She knew who was calling.

"Yes."

"What is it?"

"Nothing," I said. "I hoped that words would come when I heard your voice, but they're not coming."

"We can talk later," she said. "I'm with a client now."

"How is Darrell?"

"Better, much better. I'll call you later. Promise."

She ended the call, and I tried to think of other people to call. I wanted to wear out the charge in my phone so it would go silent, but I couldn't bring myself to do it.

I was tempted to launch into baseball metaphors.

Victor drove me to the Fruitville Library, where I got my bike out of his trunk.

"I can come back for you," said Victor.

"No, thanks," I said.

Ames said nothing, just looked at me and nodded. I nodded back. They drove off. The sun was high, the air filled with moist heaviness and the smell of watermelons from a truck vending them on Fruitville, just beyond the parking lot.

I chained my bike to a lamppost and went inside.

The cool air struck and chilled for an instant.

Two minutes later I had an oversize book of World War II airplanes open on my lap. I didn't want to look at it. I wasn't interested. It was a prop to keep a vigilant librarian from making a citizen's arrest for vagrancy.

No more than five maybe six, minutes later, Blue Berrigan sat down across from me.

8

"You just happened to see me hiding here behind the fiction," I whispered.

He was wearing a pair of dark corduroy slacks and a short-sleeved green and white striped polo shirt.

"I . . . I followed you."

"From where?"

"You're going to get angry," he said. "It can't be helped. We're talking about my life here."

He looked over his shoulder and out the window and gently bit his lower lip.

"You're talking," I said. "I'm listening."

"I put an electronic tracer under the rear fender of your bicycle," he said. "I removed it before I came in. They're really cheap now. You can get them online."

He held up both hands in a gesture designed to stop me from rising in indignation. I didn't rise. I wasn't indignant.

"I was afraid you didn't believe me when

we talked in the park."

"I didn't," I said.

"I do lie a lot. People always say you should tell kids the truth; you shouldn't lie to them. But there are truths you want to keep from children. There are truths they are better off without. What are you reading?"

A thin woman with wild hair came down the aisle perpendicular to us carrying a load of books she wouldn't be able to read in a generation. The books at the top and in the middle of the pile threatened to fall. Blue Berrigan was silent until the woman rounded the corner, went up the next aisle, pulled out two more books, and balanced them on top of her heap. Then she went out of sight.

"I'm looking at pictures of old airplanes," I said.

"Good."

I wasn't sure why he might think that was good.

"You're not being blackmailed," I said.

"No."

"Then . . ."

"I'm being paid to distract you," he said with a great sigh.

"From what?"

"Whatever you're working on."

"Who's paying you?"

"A man who called me, said he knew my work, knew I was down on my luck. I'm supposed to keep bothering you, sending you on wild grouse hunts, tell you someone tried to kill me. Improvise."

"How much is he paying you?"

"Five thousand dollars in advance. I've got it back in my room."

"But you've decided . . ."

"The guy sounds nuts, is what I'm saying. I'm keeping the money, packing up, and moving west. I'm only renting a room here. He's got someone keeping an eye on me. I'll have to lose whoever it is."

I was tempted to say I'd join him in his getaway, but it wasn't temptation enough.

"Don't go yet," I said.

"Don't go?"

"He calls you?"

"Yes."

"Tell him you have me looking for grouse."

"Ah, I see," he said.

"What's a grouse?" I asked.

Neither of us knew for certain.

"Let's leave separately," I said. "He might have followed you. I'll get back to you."

He got up without certainty and said, "I'm really very good with kids. I just, you know, got lost."

"I know," I said.

"You don't live near here."

"No. I come here when I want to be alone, where no one can find me unless they plant tracking devices on my bicycle. You want to give me a ride home?"

"No, can't," he said standing quickly. "I've got to go."

He strode away quickly. I waited about ten seconds and then followed him to the glass doors at the entrance to the library. I stayed against a wall inside, watching him find his car in the lot and leave. It was a well-used Jeep of uncertain vintage. I got the first three letters of his tag before he turned left. That's when whoever was in the backseat sat up. I couldn't see who it was.

"Embarrassing, demeaning, humiliating, abasing," Darrell said. "It brings me down. Know what I mean?"

He was out of intensive care and propped up on a couple of pillows. There was an IV in his right arm and a look of exasperation on his face. He was out of danger, but not out of flaunt.

"Almost killed by a BB in my back," he said with a single shake of his head. "How do I explain that? How do I strut that? 'Hey

158

man, I got shot.' 'Yeah, with what?' 'A BB gun.' "

"It almost killed you," I said.

"That makes no difference on my street. Take that back. Shot with a BB gun? That's below a misdemeanor on my street."

"Sorry. Maybe you'll be lucky next time and get shot with a machine gun."

"Not funny. I was lucky. Bad lucky," said Darrell. "Hey, do me a favor and get the shooter. Then let old Ames shotgun blast him a second asshole."

I nodded. He was still hooked up to the machine with the green screen that painted white mountains and valleys to the sound of a low *beep-beep-beep.*

"I'll find him," I said. "You want my hat?"

"Your Cubs hat? I'm touched, Fonesca. I know what that hat means to you but a, it's your sweat in there, and b, I'm not a Cubs fan."

I nodded again.

"My mom still mad at you?"

"Sort of."

"Ms. Porovsky?"

Sally was more than Darrell's caseworker. She was someone who cared. Sally knew she couldn't save the children of the world one abuse at a time, but she couldn't help trying.

"She's fine," I said.

"You?"

"I'm fine."

"Why don't you look fine? I don't look fine," said Darrell.

"Nurse says you can go home in a few days," I said.

"From almost dead to back to school in three or four days," he said.

"It happens."

"But not much," he said. "Old Chinese Victor saved my butt from going down the stairs."

He made a tumbling motion with his free hand.

"I decided something," he said, licking his lips.

I poured him water from a pitcher into a plastic cup on a table near his bed. He took it and, with my help, drank.

"Don't laugh. Don't even smile, and don't tell anyone, not even my mom."

"I won't."

"I know," said Darrell. "I'm going to try out for the play at Booker."

Booker High, I knew, had a big annual musical production. I'd been told by Sally and Flo that they were very nearly professional.

"You sing?" I asked.

160

"That's what I like about you, Fonesca. You are dribbling down with emotion. I can sing. I can act."

"What have you done?"

"Nothing yet," he said. "I just know I'm good. I'll tell them on the street that I'm going to be the next Will Smith or Denzel or Cuba. Maybe they'll buy it, you know?"

We went silent and I listened to and watched the green mountain-and-valley machine.

"Get the guy who shot me, Fonesca."

"I'll get him," I said. "Darrell, he was trying to shoot me."

"I know that. It didn't hurt less because of that. I'm tired."

"I'll be back," I said.

"I might be out of here first," he said so softly I could barely hear him.

Darrell's eyes were closed. He was asleep.

I had people to see and a bicycle parked outside. I made a decision.

There were only two cars parked in the small driveway of the EZ Economy Car Rental. The EZ was a converted gas station, a half-block north of the now-demolished DQ on 301. It wouldn't last much longer. The banks were moving like relentless giant Japanese movie monsters gobbling up small businesses and looking for more along the strip of 301 from Tamiami Trail to Main Street.

This didn't matter to Alan, the formerly jovial partner of Fred, who was now dead with one heart attack too many. Alan had been the more likely candidate for heart trouble. In his late forties, Alan was twenty years younger than Fred but fifty pounds heavier. Alan was addicted to strong coffee. Alan had lost the sense of sardonic humor he and Fred had shared. It had kept them both sane between infrequent customers.

"Fonesca, the man from whom there are no secrets," Alan said when I walked through the door.

He was seated at his wooden swivel chair behind the counter with a cup of coffee in his hand, a cluttered desk drawer lying in front of him. The coffee was in a black thermos. The suit and tie he usually wore had been replaced with slacks and a wrinkled white dress shirt with an open collar.

"You came at the right moment," he said. "Today is the third and final day of liquidation. No more rentals. Two cars out there to sell. Take your pick."

"I don't want to own a car," I said. "I want to rent one."

"You don't want to own anything," he said. "And until Fred went to automobile nirvana, I wanted to own everything. The price is right. Both cars will be gone by tonight even if I have to give them to Goodwill."

"How much for the Saturn?" I asked.

I had rented the gray 1996 Saturn before. There had been a little over 110,000 miles on the odometer when last we met. In its favor, it had behaved, though hollow clanks echoed under the glove box. The last car I had owned was the one I escaped from Chicago in and managed to get as far as the DQ parking lot. Cars and I are not friends. One of them had killed my wife. One of my many fears was that I might one day accidentally hit someone and spend the rest of my life like Victor Woo. Perpetual apology. Perpetual shock.

"What do you have in your wallet?" Alan asked after another sip of coffee followed by a face that suggested the coffee or life or both were bitter.

"I'm flush. Two clients."

"Okay, how does sixty-six dollars sound to you?" he asked.

"For the Saturn? Reasonable."

"You just bought a car. Congratulations. Enjoy. No, wait. You don't enjoy anything."

He picked up a pair of keys on a small metal hoop and threw them in my direction. They arced through the air, tinkling as they flew. I caught them.

"I've got the papers right here," he said, shifting his considerable bulk so that he could dig into the exposed desk drawer.

I took out my wallet, extracted the sixty-six dollars and placed it on the counter. Alan shifted out of the chair, which let out a weary squeak. He placed the papers on the counter, signed them, asked me to sign, and said, "You want another car?"

"No."

"Gift for a friend?"

"No."

"We're having a two-for-one sale."

"No."

"You are a tough customer."

He held out his hand. We shook.

"Are you all right?" I asked.

"Decidedly not," he said, "but I am solvent. Fred and I owned this business and the land on which it sits. I have a generous offer, which I have accepted. Fred's widow and I will share right down the middle. Want to know how much we're getting?"

"No."

"A million six. I'm heading back to Grosse Pointe as soon as the papers are signed and the check is in my hand."

"Good luck," I said. "All right if I leave the car here for an hour?"

He shrugged, a good shrug that shook his expansive body, and said, "Till the wrecking ball descends."

Outside, I used the cell phone, called Ames, and asked if he could meet me. I told him where. He said he could and would be right over. I walked across the street and into the Crisp Dollar Bill, where Sammy Davis, Jr., was singing "There's a Slow Boat Sailing for New York." The familiar smell of beer reminded me of Mac's bar, back in Chicago, when I was a kid.

I made out the shape of four people at the bar to my left. No one was in any of the booths across from the bar. I sat in a booth where I could watch the door, looked over at Billy the bartender and owner, and nodded. He knew what I wanted.

Some say that good things come to those who wait. Bad things come, too.

The comedian Steven Wright says, "When worse comes to worse, we're screwed."

Blue Berrigan came through the door and sat across from me.

"I followed you again," he said.

"I figured that out."

Billy placed an Amstel and a mug in front of me.

"You want a beer?" I asked Blue.

"A beer?" He didn't seem to understand.

"A beer, to drink."

"Blue doesn't drink alcohol. Dr Pepper."

Billy nodded and moved off. Sammy Davis, Jr., had moved on to "What Kind of Fool Am I."

"You ready to tell me who hired you?"

"No. Well, maybe."

Blue was fidgeting, whispering, casting glances at the people at the bar who were not looking in his direction. Billy turned on the television set mounted up near the ceiling. He changed channels until he found what looked like a rerun of a high school football game. He turned off the sound. Blue had watched Billy.

"I think I know who it was," I said. "I think it was a man who hides in the backseats of Jeeps."

He started to slide out of the booth, but before he could, Ames sat next to him, blocking his exit.

"Blue Berrigan, this is Ames McKinney. Ames has done time for killing his former partner. Ames is a man of honor who has a fondness for weapons, usually of an older vintage."

166

Ames was wearing his very old, very well cared-for tan leather Western jacket. He held it open so Blue could see something against Ames's waist. I couldn't see it from where I sat. I didn't have to.

Berrigan looked frightened, very frightened, and said, "Wait, I have evidence that Ronnie Gerall didn't kill Horvecki."

"What evidence?" I asked.

"I've got it at my place."

"Let's get it," Ames said.

Billy appeared with a bottle of beer for Ames and said, "Burger'll be up in a few minutes. One for you?"

"No thanks. Ate at the Texas."

"Blue Berrigan," Ames went on when Billy left. "Kids' singer?"

"Yes," Blue said, moving farther into the corner.

" 'How Many Bunnies in the Hole'?"

"Yes."

"You believe in coincidence?" Ames asked.

"Yes," Blue said, growing smaller.

"I just bought a CD of yours for Catherine and Adele."

"Coincidence," Blue said. "This whole thing has gone too far."

"It went too far when someone murdered Philip Horvecki," I said.

The burger came. It was big. I knew it

had grilled onions and tomato on a soft bun.

"I told you the truth. About distracting you, I mean. Listen, Blue needs the bathroom. He needs it bad, real bad," Blue said.

" '*The Potty Is Your Friend,*' " Ames said, looking at me.

"Let him out," I said.

Ames sidled out of the booth, letting Blue get out and hurry toward the bathrooms at the rear. Ames got up and followed him. Then I heard Ames say, "He locked it."

Two of the bar patrons looked toward the bathrooms. One was a shaky woman who kept blinking, the other a skinny man who tried to keep his elbows from slipping off the bar.

There was a window in the men's room. It was high on the wall and narrow, but it was definitely possible for a man to squeeze through. I left my burger and called out for Billy to open the men's room with a key. He got the urgency in the situation and moved quickly. So did I, but not toward the bathroom. I went past the bar and onto the street.

The red Jeep was parked half a block down, to my left. Blue Berrigan was racing for it and moving fast, fast enough to get into the car, make a U-turn, and be on his way before I got twenty steps, but not fast enough to keep me from seeing something move in the backseat of the Jeep.

Ames appeared at my side.

"Gone?" he asked.

"Gone," I said.

"Know where?" asked Ames.

"I think so."

We went back inside. I paid Billy, who said, "Always a pleasure having you. You bring a touch of chaos into an otherwise tranquil bar."

I had the feeling he meant it.

I took my burger and led the way out the door and to my Saturn.

"Nice car," he said.

"I bought it."

"Needs help."

"We all do."

We got in, and I ate while I drove.

I came to three conclusions:

The Saturn would definitely not qualify for the Indy 500.

There was no radio in the car.

I still didn't like driving.

Ames sat silently, jostled by what might be a weeping loose axle.

This was my kind of car.

Traffic wasn't bad. It wasn't snowbird weather, but as I tried to pick up speed I did pass three kids in a pickup truck wearing baseball caps. The kid in the middle had his cap turned around.

"Why do they wear their caps backward?" I asked Ames, who wasn't likely to know but was the only other person in the car.

"Insecurity," said Ames. "Want to look like millions of other kids."

"Insecurity," I said as I considered trying my Cubs cap backward. I decided not to. I already knew what a fool looked like.

"Only catchers behind the plate should wear their caps backward, to accommodate their masks," I said.

I was in the right lane, going south on Beneva. The pickup pulled next to me. The kid in the window gave me a one-finger salute. Ames leaned over me and showed his long-barreled gun. The kids pulled away fast.

I tried for fast, too, and failed as the Saturn let me know that quick turns to the right were subject to grinding. We were on Wilkinson now. When we got in sight of the park I looked down the block at the parked red Jeep. I pulled in behind it and got out quickly, Ames right behind me as I hurried toward the yellow house after checking to be sure there was no one hunched down in the back of the Jeep.

I knocked at the front door of the yellow

house. Ames was still behind me, his hand under his jacket. I knocked. There was a wheezing sound behind the door, which then opened.

The old woman who opened the door in an orange robe and slippers carried a yellow cup of steaming something.

"Blue Berrigan," I said.

"Are you those paparazzi people?"

"No," I said. "We're fans."

Ames gently pushed the door open and stepped in. I followed and closed the door.

"Don't, for Jesus' sake, sing me one of his songs, especially that one about the rabbits."

"We won't," I said. "We just . . ."

"Mr. Nelson Berrigan isn't here and he doesn't give autographs or signed photographs to fans who seek him out. You'll have to wait till his next public appearance. Besides, he's not home."

"His car is parked outside," I said.

She looked at Ames with suspicion, took a sip of her brew, and leaned between us to look at the Jeep at the curb."

"He's still not here. No way he could get to his room without getting past me, no fucking way. Pardon my French."

"Could he have gone around the back?" I tried.

"Yes, but there's no way to get upstairs

171

back there. Doesn't the old guy talk?"

She wheezed mightily and fished an inhaler out of the pocket of her robe. A wad of tissues came with it and drifted to the floor. She caught them deftly without losing a drop of whatever she was drinking.

"Used to be a juggler," she said, putting the tissue wad back in her pocket and taking a deep puff of the inhaler. "Long time ago. I suppose that's how Nelson got the show business bug. His father was a tombstone carver."

"He's your son?" I asked.

"He is definitely not my son. He lived next door to us when he was a kid. Now I definitely want you the hell out of here. Good-bye."

She closed the door. We turned and walked to the curb. I looked through the window of the jeep. Nelson Blue Berrigan was slumped over on the floor, legs beneath the steering wheel, head and torso on the floor near the passenger door. He was not taking a nap. The deep reddish black oozing wound on the back of his head felt like death, but I made sure by opening the door and reaching over to see if there was a pulse. There wasn't.

We had been inside the house for no more than two minutes.

Maybe we should have gone back and told the old woman he was dead.

Maybe we should have called 911.

Maybe we should have looked for clues.

Maybe we should have looked for the killer. He couldn't have been more than a few minutes away, but a minute or two was enough if he had a car parked very close by.

I slid into the backseat and looked at the floor. There were splatters of blood. On top of one of the splatters were two little pieces of plastic, one white, one red. I knew what they were, but I needed to get the answer to a question before I could decide what to do.

"We've got to go back inside the house," I said. "Keep her busy."

Ames and I went back to the door. The old woman in the orange robe opened it a crack and said, "What the hell you want now?"

"I've got to call 911," I said. "Berrigan is in his car. I think he's dead."

"Dead?"

"Where were you the last half hour?" Ames asked as I slipped by her and went to Berrigan's room.

"Me? I didn't kill him."

I didn't call 911 right away. First, I looked around. I didn't see what I was looking for.

I tried the closet. It wasn't there. When I was satisfied, I called 911 and then went to get Ames.

The old woman was saying, ". . . a quiet man."

"Sorry ma'am," Ames said. "Can we get you anything?"

"You call the police?" she asked seeing me.

"Yes. I have one more question."

"Question?"

I asked her. The answer confirmed what I found, or failed to find, in Berrigan's room.

Ames and I moved to the door.

"You're not staying till the police get here?" the old woman asked.

"Can't," Ames said gently. "Police will be here in a minute."

She seemed bewildered as we opened the door. She looked out at Berrigan's jeep, pulled a pair of glasses from her pocket and put them on, saying, "You sure he's in there? I don't see him."

"He's there," I said.

We got in the Saturn and drove away, not quietly, but definitely away.

9

Half an hour later I was seated behind my desk, looking across the room at the Stig Dalstrom paintings on the wall. They were the only art I owned — four small paintings given to me by Flo Zink. They were of dark jungles and mountains at night with just a small touch of color, a single bird or flower, the distant moon.

Outside, Ames was working on the Saturn. He knew guns, machines, trucks, and automobiles, but it would take a lot of knowing to make the Saturn live again.

I half hoped he would fail. I felt uncomfortable owning anything larger than a DVD player.

My cell phone was on the otherwise empty desktop in front of me. I was waiting. On the way home I had told Ames that it would probably take an hour or less for the police to arrive, so he had better do as much as he could on the car before men in blue appeared bearing guns in the usually quiet street.

The old woman former juggler in an orange robe would describe us to the police. That would be enough.

"A tall old man wearing a coat in the heat and a not-too-tall, sad-looking fella wearing a Cubs baseball cap," Ames had said as we drove.

"Driving in a noisy old car," I added.

"Won't be hard," he said.

It was at that point that I called Detective Ettiene Viviase to tell him about the body in the jeep across from Bee Ridge Park. It was better to have a cop I knew around.

Viviase arrived thirty-five minutes into my longing for the comfort of dark jungles. It was just enough time for him to take a look at Berrigan's body, leave someone to take over the crime scene and get back to Ames and me.

I heard the footsteps on the wooden stairs and watched the door open. Ames was at Viviase's side.

Once, I had heard Viviase referred to as "Big Ed." He wasn't particularly big, maybe a little under six feet tall and weighing in at a little over two hundred and twenty pounds. He was wearing his usual uniform, a rumpled sports jacket, dark slacks, a tie with no personality and a weary look on his face.

"Got a little more to do on the car," said Ames. "Need a few parts. Should get it working within reason."

"I'm glad to hear it," said Viviase, stepping into the room and closing the door behind him. "Now tell me a story. Nonfiction preferred."

"Mind if I wash up my hands?" asked Ames.

"Please do," said Viviase moving to the desk and facing me across it.

Ames walked slowly through the bathroom door and closed it behind him. Then I heard the water start to flow.

"We didn't kill him," I said.

"I know that," said Viviase. "If you had, you probably wouldn't have walked up to his door asking for him after you crushed his skull."

"I definitely wouldn't have," I said.

"Talk," he said.

"Berrigan found me at the Crisp Dollar Bill," I said. "He said he wanted my help. He was nervous. When Ames showed up, Berrigan went to the bathroom and out the window. You can check with Billy the bartender and the customers who were there. When Berrigan went through the bathroom window, we followed him. He was frightened. I thought maybe we could help. I ran outside and saw him pull away in the jeep. There was someone in the car with him. I couldn't make out who. My car —"

"Your car?"

"I bought it this morning."

"The Saturn McKinney was working on?"

"Yes."

"It's a gem."

"Thanks. It moves at its own pace."

"Two questions," said Viviase. "First, what did Berrigan say he wanted?"

"He didn't have time to tell me."

"Thin, Fonesca. Very thin. Third question: Why did you leave the scene of a murder?"

"Because we didn't want to get involved."

"Then why did you call me?"

"I changed my mind."

"Civic duty, right?"

"I knew you'd find us."

Ames emerged from the bathroom and joined us.

"I'll talk to McKinney now," said Viviase. "Let's see if he remembers it the way you do."

Ames did. We had gone over the story as we clunked our way home. Ames got it down perfectly. He told it tersely.

"This have anything to do with the Horvecki murder you've been asking about?"

"Don't know," I said, and I didn't, though it was more than likely that the two were related.

"Since I'm here, would you like to tell me how you got involved in the Horvecki business?"

I didn't want to tell him for many reasons, not the least of which was that I had been recommended for the job by Viviase's own daughter, Elisabeth, but I had to tell him something.

"Two kids just came to me. Friends of Gerall."

"Why you?"

I shrugged and said, "Ask them."

"I will," he said. "Fix your car. Stop trying to get the Gerall kid off. Lighten up this room. I'll get back to you. You listening?"

"Yes," I said.

"But you won't back off, will you?"

"No."

"All right, give me the names of the two kids," he said. "And don't tell me it's confidential. You're not even a private investigator."

I gave him Greg and Winn's names. He wrote them down and said, "They visited Gerall in juvie," Viviase said putting the notebook away. "I knew who they were."

"Just trapping the coyote," said Ames.

"Very colorful," Viviase said.

"Anything new on the Horvecki daughter?" I asked.

"Nothing I plan to share."

Which, I concluded, meant that he had nothing more than what Dixie had given me and probably a lot less.

Viviase left.

Seconds after he was gone, the door to my bedroom opened and Victor Woo came out with a girl. She was no more than fifteen, dark, cute, still holding onto a little baby fat. She wore faded jeans and a white tucked-in short-sleeved blouse with a flower stitched over her left breast.

"Is my father gone?" she asked, standing back in case Viviase decided to return. His footsteps had clacked down the stairs and, unless he had taken off his shoes and tiptoed back up, he was gone, at least for now.

"He's gone," I said. "How did you find me?"

"Your name is in my father's address book. I went to where you were supposed to be, but there was no building."

Victor moved to the floor in the corner. Elisabeth Viviase glanced at him.

"I asked a sad fat man in the car rental place. He told me where you live. Why is that man sitting on the floor in the corner?"

She sat in one of the two chairs on the other side of my desk.

"Penance," I said, sitting.

"For what?"

"Ask him."

She turned to Victor and said, "Why are you doing penance?"

"Murder," he said softly.

With a veteran policeman as a father, the possibility of murder in close proximity was not confined to CSI on television.

"Why here?" she asked. "Why do penance here?"

"I killed his wife," Victor said flatly.

Elisabeth turned back to me, tried to figure out if this was some comic routine with her as the butt of the joke. Whatever she saw in my face, she decided to change the subject.

"Ronnie didn't kill Horvecki."

"How do you know?"

"Because he was with me," she said.

"When?"

"A week ago on Saturday," she said.

"What time?"

"From seven till midnight."

She sat with back straight and false sincerity masking her face.

"The murder took place after midnight," I said.

"Well, I may have left Ronnie's at one or later."

"I was just testing you," I said. "Horvecki was actually killed no later than noon."

"Well," she said, sliding back as far as she could go. "Now that I think of it, I was with Ronnie from seven to midnight on the day before the murder. On the day of the murder, I was with him as early as eleven in the morning, maybe earl . . . You're testing me again."

She looked away.

She returned to the self-certain statement of "Ronnie didn't do it."

"You didn't go to the police with your alibi for Gerall," I said.

"You kidding? My father would find out in five minutes. I wanted to tell you so you could find the real killer without telling my father about, you know, my coming here."

Victor suddenly stood, and asked, "Would you like a Coke?" The move reminded me of James Coburn when he tilted his hat back and suddenly stood erect, ready for a showdown with his knife against a gun.

"Diet Coke," she said.

Victor looked at me.

"Nothing for me," I said.

Victor left. Elisabeth and I listened to his footsteps on the stairs.

"Gerall's your boyfriend?"

"I wish," she said eyes looking upward.

"You told Greg Legerman and Winn Graeme about me."

"Yeah."

"Tell me about them."

"Greg is kind of electric-cute, super-smart, dancing around, adjusting his glasses, a walking public service ad for hyperactives anonymous."

"He get in a lot of fights?"

"No. He just talks, makes people nervous. Winn is his only friend. He takes a lot from Greg."

"But they stay friends?" I asked.

"Go figure," she said.

"Greg talks. What does he talk about?"

"You think I pay that much attention to Long-winded Legerman?"

"I think you pay attention to a lot of things."

She gave me a questioning look.

"That's a compliment," I said.

The quizzical look was replaced by a minimally appreciative smile.

The door opened. Victor and Ames entered together. Victor moved to my desk with an offering of Diet Coke for Elisabeth who said, "Thank you."

"It's warm," he said.

I knew a twelve-pack of Diet Coke was in the back of his car.

"That's okay," she said.

She popped the tab and drank from the can.

Victor went back to his bedroll and Ames leaned against the wall.

"Anything else you can tell me?" I asked.

"About what?" she said, looking over her shoulder at Ames and Victor.

"Greg, Winn, Ronnie, Horvecki. A man named Blue Berrigan."

"Blue Berrigan? I can tell you about him. I have his three CDs. Haven't listened to them in a long time. I was a big fan. I've still got my Blue Bunny night slippers, but if you tell anyone, I'll come back here and claim you raped me."

"I won't tell anyone," I said.

She took a big gulp from her Diet Coke.

"Hot Coke is gross. Am I through?" she asked, placing the can on the desk.

"How'd you get here?"

"Walked from school. I can catch a bus home."

"Victor can drive you home."

She looked at Victor who had returned to his place in the corner.

"No, thanks," she said, looking at the man who had called himself a murderer.

"Ames can give you a lift on the back of his scooter."

I looked at Ames. He had a strong avuncular feeling for children.

"Has he murdered anyone?" she asked.

"Not recently," I said.

"I'll take the scooter."

"Do you know the first line of a book, any book?"

" 'The event on which this fiction is founded has been supposed, by Dr. Darwin, and some of the physiological writers of German, as not of impossible occurrence.' "

I asked her to repeat it slowly. She did, while I wrote on a pad from my desk drawer.

"The book?" I asked.

Frankenstein," said Victor.

"That's right," said Elisabeth. "We had to memorize a paragraph from a novel on our reading list. I picked *Frankenstein.*"

"Because it's scary?" I tried.

"Because it was written by a woman," she said.

"You want to be a writer?"

"I want to be an FBI agent," she answered. "But don't —"

"Tell your father."

"He's not ready for it," she said. "And I

might change my mind."

I got up to show I had nothing more to ask or say. She stood and headed for Ames and the door. She paused at the door and said, "You won't tell my —"

"I won't tell," I said.

Ames and the girl left. I was making some assumptions. I assumed the timing was such that my investigation of the Horvecki killing, the bullet through the window of Augustine's car, the shooting of Darrell Caton, and the murder of Blue Berrigan were all tied together. What if I were wrong? I had two suspects I hadn't yet spoken to, Essau Williams, the cop in Venice, and Jack Pepper in Cortez Village — two people whose names were in files in a cabinet in the mobile home of an ex-Cincinnati cop named Pertwee. Both had sworn to make Philip Horvecki pay for what he had been accused of, the rape of Essau's mother and aunt when they were young girls and the attempted rape and beating of Pepper, whom Horvecki had tried to sodomize. Pepper lived north, just outside of Cortez Village, and Williams south, in Venice.

When night came, I lay in bed silently for I don't know how many minutes listening to traffic on 301, thinking of something I could say or do to induce Sally to stay.

I had nothing to offer. Armed with addresses that I had gotten from Pertwee's files, I got up just before six in the morning and asked Victor, who was cross-legged on his bedroll reading a book, to tell Ames I was going to Cortez Village and that I'd be back in a few hours.

There are no hills in Florida south of Ocala unless we're talking about man-made ones. Construction is constantly going on in Sarasota — streets torn up and widened, new streetlights, hotels, mansions, developments, high-rise apartments, new malls. From time to time a pile of dirt resembling a fifteen-foot hill will rise and occasionally a dazzled teen or preteen will climb up and be knocked down or even buried in a small dust-raising avalanche. The flat landscape of Sarasota County is paled over with nonnative palm trees and trees that thrive on enough water to drown most other fauna and with tall, sometimes fat condominium buildings that present a view of heavily trafficked roads and other condos.

I passed a mess of construction heading north on Tamiami Trail. Wooden yellow-and-black traffic horses and dingy red cones created a minor maze that slowed vehicles and made ancient drivers, pregnant mothers, and slightly drunken men mad with the challenge.

It took me almost an hour to make the trip to Cortez Village. Ames had installed a third-hand junkyard radio in the car. It worked just fine, so I was accompanied by the soothing voice of a man with a Southern accent. The voice wasn't strident; he was confident and sounded as if he were smiling as he spoke. I had been told when I called Jack Pepper's phone number that he was at the studio doing his show. The woman told me the address of the station's studio and number on the dial where WTLW could be found. I found it and listened as I drove.

"You know, friends," the man said, "the Jewish people are holy. They are the people chosen by God to redeem the land of Israel, the sacred land of our Lord Jesus Christ. We must support the Jewish people in their quest to survive against heathen hordes. Palestine does not belong to the Arab. Palestine comes from the Biblical word Philistine. The Philistines were neither Arab nor Semite. The Emperor Hadrian designated the land as Palestine. The Arabs can't even say the word. They call it 'Palethtine.' "

He almost sounded as if he were crying.

"We can't let the Jewish people be pushed into the sea. We cannot let the land of Israel once again go into the hands of those who would make of it an unholy land. If there need be another Crusade, we must march in it armed with truth."

And a lot of heavy firepower, I thought. Pepper was just getting warmed up.

"There will come a time," he said, "when our Savior returns and those who have believed in him will be saved and shall sit in the house of the Lord and bask in the warmth of Christ."

And what about the Jews? I thought, but Jack Pepper let it hang in the air.

Cortez Village, on the Gulf of Mexico, still has a few small fishing companies and some independent fishermen making a living pretty much as fishermen have been doing there for more than a century. The air was salty with the smell of fish.

The radio station was a little hard to find. It was about thirty yards down a narrow dirt street, at the rear of a small frame church on a white pebble-and-stone parking lot. Four cars were parked in the lot. A four-foot sign indicated that I was indeed not only in the parking lot of the Every Faith Evangelical Church but, that, if I followed the arrow pointing toward the rear of the church, I'd find radio station WTLW, THE LORD'S WORD.

There was a seven-foot-high mesh steel

fence with three strands of barbed wire surrounding the lot. Inside the fence there was a patch of crushed white stone and shell about the size of my office. About twenty yards beyond the enclosure was a three-story steel radio tower.

On the patch of grass on my side of the fence was the door with a freshly painted white cross about the size of an ATM machine. Next to the cross was a gate with a button and a speaker just above it. I pushed the button. The clear but speaker resonant voice of a woman said, "Who is it?"

"Lew Fonesca. I'm here to see Jack Pepper."

"Reverend Pepper," she reprimanded.

"Reverend Pepper," I said.

"Why?"

"Philip Horvecki," I said.

Long pause. Long, long pause.

"Why?"

This time it was a man's voice, the same voice I had just been listening to on the radio.

"Detective Viviase of the Sarasota Police suggested I talk to you," I lied.

Another long pause.

"I do not wish to testify," he said.

"Ronnie Gerall may not have done it," I said.

I could hear the man and woman talking, but I couldn't make out what they were saying. One of them must have put a hand over the microphone. I could tell that the woman sounded insistent and Pepper sounded resigned.

"Come in," said Pepper. "Close the gate behind you."

Something clicked and I pushed the gate open.

The door at the end of the path was painted a bright red. It looked as if a new coat of paint had been applied minutes earlier. The station's call letters were painted in black in the middle of the door with a foot-high brown cross under them.

"Come in," came the man's voice.

I opened the door.

"Take off the hat please," the man said. "This station is part of the House of the Lord."

I took off my Cubs cap, stuffed it in my back pocket, stepped in, and closed the door behind me.

The room was about the size of a handball court. There were three desks with chairs lined up side by side on the left, and on the right stood a narrow table with spindly black metal legs. The table was covered in plastic that was meant to look like wood, but it looked like plastic. On the table there sat a computer and printer and boxes of eight-by-ten flyers I couldn't read from where I stood. There were eight folding chairs leaning against the wall. Beyond all this, through a large rectangular window, I could see a studio barely big enough for two people. In fact, two people were in there. One had a guitar. One was a man. One was a woman. They were obviously singing. They were smiling. I couldn't hear them.

I looked over at an ample woman of no more than fifty whose dark hair was a study for one of those "before" pictures on early morning television.

"Speak," she said.

I looked at the man behind the second desk. He was gaunt and had red hair and an almost baby-like face. He could have been any age.

"You're Reverend Pepper?"

"I am," he said. "And you are?"

"An investigator hired to see if Ronnie Gerall killed Philip Horvecki. Want to go someplace more private?"

"Whatever you have to say to me can be said in front of Lilly."

"Philip Horvecki," I said. "He was not a good man."

Lilly closed her eyes and nodded her head.

"He wasn't punished for what he did to you," I said.

"It was my word against his. The police said that wasn't enough," Pepper replied.

"He wasn't punished," I said.

"Yes he was, but not by the law. His punishment was delayed, but the Lord was not in a hurry."

Lilly was slowly nodding her head to the rhythm of Pepper's voice and the eyes of Jack Pepper vibrated back and forth.

"Where were you Saturday night?"

"What time?"

"Evening, at about ten."

"In my home, my aunt's home where I live. She looks after me. Lilly was there too."

"I was," Lilly said.

"Lilly came to dinner and to talk about a tour I have been planning. I'm sorry. I have to get back in the studio. Gilbert and Jenny are almost finished with their song."

"And today, about eleven in the morning?" I asked.

"Another crime?"

I said nothing.

"I was here, doing the morning call-in show," he said.

Before I could question Lilly, the theory I had been putting together about recorded shows and lying alibis seemed to come apart. Maybe I had just seen *Laura* too many times.

Jack Pepper rose with the help of two aluminum forearm crutches. He leaned forward as he slowly came out from behind the desk.

He looked up at me with what may have been a touch of pain and said, "MS. Multiple Sclerosis. The Lord has chosen to touch me with this affliction. Would you like the name and number of my doctor to see if I'm telling the truth?"

"No," I said.

"Fonesca? Italian. You are a Catholic?" he asked.

Lilly was shaking her head yes. She was either answering for me or at the brilliance of Jack Pepper's observation.

"No," I said.

"Lapsed?"

"No. I'm a lapsed Episcopalian."

"We are all one in Christ," he said.

"Except for the Jews and a long list of others."

"They are welcome to join the faith and be embraced as brothers and sisters and be saved," he said.

"Amen," said Lilly softly.

"You believe that in spite of what God has let happen to you?"

"Because of what God has let happen to me."

"Philip Horvecki sodomized you," I said gently.

"No," he said with a smile. "He tried and failed. The Lord did not choose to let it happen."

I shut up and watched him make his painful way toward the door to the studio in which I could see that the two singers had wrapped up. Then he stopped and looked back at me.

"The Lord has allowed something bad to happen to you, too," he said. "You are filled with grief and sorrow."

That could have been said of just about everyone I knew or had ever known. But, it hit me. He opened the door to the studio a few seconds after the red light over the door had gone off.

"You have a favorite first line of a book?" I asked.

"Genesis one," he said.

"Something else."

He paused and said, " 'Ours is essentially a tragic age, so we refuse to take it tragically.' "

"What's that from?" I asked taking out my index cards and pen.

"Lady Chatterley's Lover," he said.

He entered, and the studio door closed behind him.

Never underestimate the ability of a human being to surprise.

"There are many roads to enlightenment and belief," Lilly said.

If there were that many roads, why wasn't I on one of them? I looked at her. She was beaming, her eyes fixed on the studio door.

"All are welcome to this church," she said.

"Then why the barbed-wire fence?" I asked.

"There are people on this earth who have been put here to challenge, vex, and destroy to keep us from spreading the faith."

"Vandals," I said.

"Minions of the devil," she said.

I thought I might save a little time, so I simply asked, "You didn't happen to kill Philip Horvecki and Blue Berrigan?"

"I don't know any Blue Berrigan and I don't believe in killing."

"You happen to have a favorite first line from a book?"

" 'It was a pleasure to burn. It was a special pleasure to see things eaten, to see things blackened and changed,' " she said.

"Fahrenheit 451."

With that, I went to the door.

"Feel free to come back," Lilly said.

I had no intention of doing so. When I got back into the car and turned on the radio, I was greeted by the voice of the Reverend Jack Pepper:

". . . a special prayer for the soul of Lewis Fonseca, one of our Lord's lost children."

"Fonesca," I said softly. "Not Fonseca."

I turned off the radio and drove amid the sound of silence.

10

Essau Williams was in the Venice telephone directory. I sat in the Saturn and punched in the number I had written on one of my index cards.

The phone rang three times before a man answered with a sleepy, "Williams."

"Fonesca," I said. "I'm from Sarasota. I'd like to talk to you about Philip Horvecki."

"He's dead."

"I know."

"I'm not sorry."

"I'm not surprised. Can I talk to you?"

"Who are you?" he asked sounding a little more awake. "A reporter?"

"No, a friend of the family."

"Whose family?"

"Ronnie Gerall."

"You want me to contribute to his defense fund? Put me down for an anonymous fifty dollars. No, make that a hundred dollars. Any killer of Horvecki is a friend of mine.

And since you're calling me, I think you know why I'm being generous."

"Can we meet?" I asked. "I'd like to gather information about Horvecki that might help justify what Gerall did."

"Where are you?"

"I'm in Venice," I said.

"Come over."

He gave me directions and we hung up without good-byes.

Essau Williams's house was not near the beach. It was in Trugate West, a development about three miles south of the hospital. What it was west of, I have no idea. His was a small ranch-style house, one of hundreds built in the 1950s to house the middle-class migrants who didn't have enough money to buy near the beach. They did have a little more money than the retirees who moved just outside of what was then the city limits into the mobile homes lying on tiny patches of grass that most of them tried to make homey with flowers and bright paint.

The green grass, really the weeds that passed for grass in Florida, was mowed short. The two trees, one a small palm, the other a tangelo, grew on opposite sides of the narrow concrete path that led to the front door.

I knocked. Essau Williams opened. He wasn't big, he was huge. He wore a pair of blue shorts and a gray T-shirt with the name ESSAU in red block letters across his chest and the number 8 under it. He had a yellow towel draped around his neck, and sweat was thick on his forehead, cheeks, and arms. He was all muscle and probably could have made a career with his body if he had a face to match. Essau Williams, light brown with a brooding brow, looked a little like my cousin Carmine, who was not the beauty of our family. Williams had the additional drawback of a raised horizontal white scar across his forehead.

"Go around back," he said and closed the door.

I walked through the grass to the back of the house where Williams was placing two tall glasses of what looked like lemonade on a wooden picnic table.

"Have a seat," he said.

I sat. It was hard to tell how big the yard was. It was dense with fruit trees, succulent bushes, flowers, and vines. The picnic table was on a round redbrick island that left no room for anything but the table.

"Nice," I said, looking around.

On a mat a few yards from the table was a plastic-covered bench. A series of bars and weights were lined up evenly next to the bench.

"Thanks. If you go that way, down the path . . . See it?"

"Yes."

The lemonade was cold with thin slices of lemon and clinking cubes.

"There's a fountain over there with a small waterfall. You should be able to hear it."

"I hear it," I said.

"Okay, maybe I can save us some time." He took a deep drink of lemonade and looked in the general direction of the running water. "Philip Horvecki raped my mother and aunt when they were kids and got away with it. Eight years ago Philip Horvecki came to my mother and my aunt's home, threatened them, and left them crying. He warned them not to tell anyone or he would come back and kill them."

I nodded. There was nothing else to do. He went on.

"My mother was sixty-four, my aunt sixty-six. I was on the force in Westin, Massachusetts. They didn't tell me what had happened till I came down for Thanksgiving. That was three months after the attack. I went to the sheriff's office and demanded that Horvecki be arrested. My mom and aunt filed criminal complaints. Only the word of my mom and aunt against Horvecki, who had the best lawyers money could buy. They tore at the reports, said they were filed by two sexually frustrated, old black women who changed their minds about selling the house for what he called 'a fair price.' He also said they were angry because he wouldn't accept their advances. His lawyers brought up medical histories, family history. We didn't have a chance."

"So . . ."

"Didn't even go to trial," he said, shaking his head. "He walked. Then I moved here, took a job with the Venice police and began watching everything Horvecki did or said. My mother and aunt moved back north. They've both been in therapy. They're recluses. They seldom go out, and they've got guns and know how to use them. They think Horvecki's going to make good on his promise to kill them."

"Didn't you feel like doing more than watching him?"

He was nodding now, considering. Then he leaned forward toward me.

"I wanted to kill him. I told him I would. I told him I'd pick my own time. I wanted to turn him into a pile of frightened jelly."

"Did it work?"

"No," he said. "After a while, he didn't believe me. The fact, which I'll deny, is that I had a date set, the anniversary of what he did to my mom and aunt, to beat the bastard to death. Three weeks from today. I'm glad someone beat me to it."

"Horvecki was rich," I said.

"Very. Worth about sixty or seventy million. Real estate. He made at least two million of that from my aunt and mother's house and property."

"You know who gets his money?"

"His daughter I guess. Who cares? My mother and my aunt are lost. You know what it's like to lose someone you love? You know what it's like to become obsessed with punishing him?"

"Yes," I said.

He looked at me long and hard over the rim of his lemonade and then said, "Maybe you do. When you see him dead in a funeral home, the feeling of vindication doesn't come. You just feel flat, empty."

"I know," I said. "Did you kill Horvecki?"

"What?"

"Did you kill Philip Horvecki?"

"No. I told you. I thought you were trying to find information that would justify what Gerall did, not come up with another suspect. Who do you work for?"

"Ronnie Gerall. I told you. He says he didn't do it."

"Surprise. A killer denies his crime. If you find out someone else did it, I'll give that hundred dollars to his defense. Now I think you better leave."

He stood up, but I didn't.

"I think there's something you're not telling me," I said.

His fists were clenched now. The scar across his forehead distended and turned a clean snow white.

"Get out," he said, kicking the bench.

"You've got a temper," I said. "How angry are you?"

"You want to find out?"

He was around the table now standing over me. I didn't want to find out.

"You lose your temper easily," I said.

"Maybe."

He had me by the front of my shirt, now, and pulled me to my feet.

"You are about to have an accident," he said. "A bad one."

"Don't think so," came a familiar voice from the corner of the house.

Ames stood there with a pistol in his hand.

"Best put him down and back away," Ames said.

"You have a license for that weapon?"

asked Williams.

"No, but if I shoot you dead, legality of the weapon won't mean much, will it?"

He still had my collar and was squeezing more tightly. I gagged.

"You won't shoot," Williams said.

"He will," I gagged. "He's done it before."

Williams lifted me farther. I felt myself passing out. Ames fired. He was a good shot, a very good shot. The bullet skidded between Williams's feet leaving a scratch in the bricks. Williams let me drop. I tumbled backward, fell over the bench, and landed on my back.

"You all right, Lewis?" he asked.

I had trouble answering. My back was a flash of pain, and my throat wouldn't allow words to come out. I made a sound like "Mmmm," which in the universal language of the beating victims of the world could mean no or yes.

Williams stood still, looking at Ames.

"One question," I rasped, getting to my knees.

"I didn't kill Horvecki," said Williams.

"Not my question," I said, making it to my feet. "Have you got a favorite first line from a book?"

Williams turned to look at me. "No," he said.

I staggered to Ames's side, and he said, "Let's get my scooter in your trunk and get out of here."

I didn't argue. Ames kept his weapon trained on Williams, who was now ignoring us and sitting on the bench again. He had poured himself another large lemonade.

On the way home, Ames explained how he had found me. He knew the names of the two suspects I was out looking for. The files Pertwee had given me were on my desk. He used the same telephone directory I had and made his way to the house in Venice.

"He kill Horvecki?" Ames asked as I drove.

"I don't think so," I said.

"The other fella, Pepper?"

"I don't think so."

"Where do we go now?"

"You have a favorite first line from a book?"

"Yes."

Ames is the best read person I have ever known. His room across from the kitchen and near the rear door of the Texas Bar and Grill was jammed with books neatly arranged on wall-to-ceiling shelves Ames had built. He always carried a book in his pocket or in the compartment of his scooter. The last book I saw him reading was *Dead Souls.*

"What is it?"

Ames was silent for a moment. He looked down at the barrel of the shotgun between his legs and said, "People don't read much anymore."

Then Ames said, "In a village of La Mancha the name of which I have no desire to recall, there lived not so long ago one of those gentlemen who always have a cane in the rack, an ancient buckler, a skinny nag, and a greyhound for the chase."

"Which one of us is Quixote and which one is Sancho Panza?" I asked.

He looked straight ahead and said, "Let's find us more windmills."

We were making good time going north on Tamiami. We were both quiet while I thought about what to do next. Then I spoke. I didn't think about what I was saying. There were consequences, but there was the promise of windmills.

"How are things at the Texas?"

"Fine," he said.

"Think you might want to become my partner?"

"Already am."

"Officially, I mean."

"The pay would be bad, the hours all over the place, the job dangerous sometimes, no benefits?" said Ames.

"And those are the incentives," I said.

"Sounds good to me," said Ames.

"And there's always a chance I'd get in this car one morning and just drive away for good."

"Understood."

"And your job at the Texas?"

"Could still do the cleaning up in exchange for my room. Big Ed'd be amenable."

"Then it's done?"

"Seems," Ames said.

And it was done. I wasn't sure what it meant, but I knew something had happened, something I would have to talk to Ann Hurwitz about.

"Dunkin' Donuts to celebrate?" I asked.

Ames had said enough. He nodded in agreement and we pulled into the parking lot of the Dunkin' Donuts across from Sarasota Memorial Hospital.

Our partnership was confirmed over coffee and chocolate iced doughnuts.

"Someone's been following us," Ames said after wiping his mouth.

"Blue Porsche."

"Yes."

"She parked in the lot?" I said.

"Yes."

"Maybe we should bring her coffee and a muffin?"

"No need," Ames said, looking past me. "She's coming."

There were three chairs at our small table, the only table at which anyone was sitting. The sound on the television set mounted on the wall was off. On the screen, a very pretty blonde with full red lips and perfect teeth was looking out at the world and talking seriously about something.

The woman from the blue Porsche sat between me and Ames.

"Can we get you a coffee and doughnuts or a muffin?" I asked.

"Coffee, black, that's all," she said.

She was Corkle's daughter and the mother of my teenage babbling client, Greg Legerman. She was dark and beautiful, her make-up perfect, not a hair out of place. Her skirt was blue and her long-sleeved cashmere sweater white. A necklace of large Chinese green jade and small jet black beads was all the jewelry she needed.

For an instant, just an instant, I remembered Catherine on the night we went to a concert at Orchestra Hall in Chicago. The symphony played Grieg and Brahms, and I watched my wife smiling and held her hand.

"You all right?" Alana Legerman asked.

"Perfect," I said.

I introduced her to Ames. He nodded in acknowledgment. She didn't offer her hand. Ames rose and headed for the counter to get her coffee. She sat up straight, probably a payoff from yoga classes.

"You didn't give my son back the money he paid you to find out who really killed Horvecki."

"If he wants his money back —"

"He won't take it," she said.

"No, he won't."

"You'll get my son killed."

Ames was back. He placed the coffee in front of Alana Legerman.

"Who would want to hurt him?" I asked.

"Whoever killed Horvecki," she said, looking at the steaming coffee but not picking it up.

"You don't think Ronnie Gerall did it?"

She considered the question. She took a breath, picked up the coffee, and said, "Ronnie has a temper and caustic verbal bite, but he hasn't the fire inside for the kind of brutal thing that was done to Horvecki."

"You know Gerall well?" I asked.

"Well enough."

I pictured the two of them together. She was twenty years older than he was, but she was a beauty, and he was a good-looking kid. Stranger things had happened.

"How did you meet him?"

"That's not relevant," she said, drinking some coffee.

A fat man sat two tables away with a small bag of doughnuts and a large coffee. He was wearing a suit and a very serious look on his face. I watched him attack the bag and come out with an orange-iced special.

I looked at Ames, who sat with his large hands folded on the table. He understood what I wanted. Neither of us spoke. It was her move.

"I'd like you to continue to look for whoever killed Philip Horvecki. You return whatever money my son and my father gave you, and I'll give you double the amount in cash. In addition, you make it clear to everyone you come in contact with that you are working for me. I'll do the same."

She touched the corner of her mouth with a little finger to remove a fleck that wasn't there.

"So, whoever killed Horvecki won't have any reason to harm your father and your son?" I asked. "If the killer wants my investigation to stop, he'll go after you."

"Yes," she said, "If that's what it comes to. Whoever it is is already trying to kill you."

I didn't see how changing clients would make a difference to someone who might want to kill me because I was looking into Philip Horvecki's murder, and I wasn't sure how accepting her offer might make her father and son a lot safer than they were already.

"How about this?" I said. "I keep the money you, your father, and your son give me, and the killer has to do a lot of thinking before going after your family. What's Greg's father like?"

"As some of Greg's friends might say, Greg's father is, like, dead. Heart attack. The world did not grieve at his passing."

"Nine hundred and thirty dollars," I said.

"A nice round number," she said, reaching into her oversized Louis Vuitton purse. "Will a check do?"

"Nicely," I said. "Make it out to cash."

She had a checkbook in front of her and a lean silver pen in her hand. When she finished writing the check, she tore it out of the book and handed it to me.

"Then there's nothing more to say," she said, getting up.

"You could thank my partner for the coffee."

"I'm sorry," she said. "Thank you."

This time she held out her hand, and

Ames took it.

"Report to me when you have anything and try not to upset my father and Greg. Oh, and one last thing. When I said 'everyone you come in contact with' — don't tell them you are working for me."

She gathered up her purse and moved quickly toward the door. The fat man in the suit paused in his chewing to admire Alana Legerman as she went into the sunlit morning.

"Pretty lady," Ames said.

"Very pretty," I agreed.

"What's next?"

"We do just what she doesn't want us to do. We talk to Greg and Corkle."

Greg was still in school. I left a voice message asking him to call as soon as he could.

D. Elliot Corkle answered the phone. I asked if I could come over.

"Something happen to Gregory?"

"No."

"Come on over."

"Be there in half an hour."

He hung up. On the way to his house we stopped at a Bank of America and cashed the check. I gave half the cash to Ames. Alana Legerman hadn't followed us — we would have known. It's hard to hide a neon blue Porsche being driven by a beautiful woman.

The Saturn still made some voodoo sounds. Ames said he would engage his magical skills and take care of the Saturn's remaining problems the next day.

My cell phone rang.

"You weren't going to call me, were you?" Sally asked.

What was it I heard? Disappointment? Simple weariness? A headache in progress?

"I don't know."

"Dinner Saturday. Just you and me. No kids. Walt's. Six-thirty."

"You want me to pick you up at home?"

"You have a car?"

"Bought it today."

"Acquiring property."

"It can be abandoned or given away," I said. "It's not worth much."

"Or you can drive it into the sunset," she said.

"Yes."

Ames had put on his glasses and was reading a small blue book to let me know he was in no hurry for me to end the call.

"Pick me up at six-thirty," she said.

"Six-thirty," I repeated.

She hung up.

Ames took off his glasses and put the book

back in his pocket. I drove. We were on our way to talk to an odd and possibly demented man with many millions of dollars.

Corkle answered the door. He was wearing a green polo shirt and navy pants with a welcoming smile.

"Can we come in?" I asked.

Corkle stepped back and wrung his hands just the way he did in his infomercials when he was about to offer "a sweet deal." He may not have needed the money, but he couldn't resist two customers.

"This is my partner, Ames McKinney."

It was the first time I had said that. I felt a little like Oliver Hardy introducing himself in one of their movies — "I'm Mr. Hardy and this is my friend Mr. Laurel. Say hello Stanley." — but Ames was no Stan Laurel.

Corkle stopped wringing his hands and reached out to shake. He looked delighted as Ames took his extended hand.

"Come in," said Corkle. "The library. You remember the way Mr. Fon . . . Fonesca."

"Yes," I said.

"Beer? Lemonade?"

"Lemonade?" Ames asked as I started toward the area with the yellow leather furniture.

"Yes, thanks," I said.

"Three glasses," said Corkle.

Ames and I sat on the uncomfortable leather sofa and waited. Corkle appeared in a few seconds with a tray on which rested a pitcher of iced lemonade and three glasses.

"Best lemonade in the world. Made with whole lemons from the tree right outside, seed and rind turned to a smooth pulp. More nutritious than the juice alone and it can be made in my D. Elliot Corkle Pulp-O-Matic in five seconds. Of course, you have to add sugar. I'll give you a Pulp-O-Matic when you leave."

All three of us drank. He was right. The lemonade was the best I had ever tasted.

"Blue Berrigan. Name mean anything to you?"

"No," he said. "D. Elliot Corkle has never heard of him."

"He was an entertainer," Ames said. "Sang kids' songs, had his own television show."

"Didn't know the man," Corkle said, holding up his glass of lemonade to the sun to watch the tiny pieces of pulp swirl like the snowy flecks in a Christmas bubble.

"You knew Philip Horvecki," I said. "You said . . ."

I paused to pull my index cards out of the day planner I kept in my pocket. I flipped through the cards and found the one I wanted.

"You said, 'Horvecki is not a nice human being.'"

He sat back, folded his hands in his lap and looked up at the ceiling for about ten seconds before saying, "D. Elliot Corkle is considering lying to you. I could do it. I can sell almost anything, especially a lie."

"But you won't," I said.

"I won't. I knew Philip Horvecki. He had a three-acre lot at the fringe of downtown. He wanted me to buy it from him. I wanted to buy it, but not from him. D. Elliot Corkle did a background check. He was a weasel. I told him so. He didn't like it."

"You didn't happen to kill him?" I asked.

"No."

We all had more lemonade.

"Did you ever threaten to kill him?" I asked.

"No. Am I a suspect in Horvecki's murder?"

"Ask the police that one," I said.

"Then why are you still looking for someone else besides Gerall for the murder? Gerall is a smart-ass and a . . . a . . ."

"Weasel?" asked Ames.

"Weasel," Corkle confirmed. "He bamboozled my grandson and my daughter.

Neither has the good judgment of a John Deere tractor, which, by the way, is one of the finest pieces of machinery ever invented.

"You know what happened to Augustine?" he asked. He was looking directly at me, lips tight.

"I think he went back to acting," I said.

"He's a terrible actor. I used him on some of my infomercials because he looked tough and had muscles and D. Elliot Corkle wanted someone who could try to open The Mighty Miniature Prisoner of Zenda Safe, which can go with you wherever you go and is housed inside a candy or cigar box you could leave in plain sight."

"I remember that," said Ames.

"I'll give you one when you leave," said Corkle. "The Mighty Miniature Prisoner of Zenda Safe could not be opened unless you had a blow torch, but it had two defects. Want to guess what they were?"

"You advertised the safe on television," I said. "People know what the safe looked like."

"Several million people," Corkle said, proudly pouring us all more lemonade. "Yes, it was hard for D. Elliot Corkle to come up with someplace the little safe could be hidden in the average house. And then, how was I to let them know where the safe

218

should now be hidden? What's the other problem with it?"

"The safe might be hard to open, but it can be carried away and opened somewhere else later," said Ames.

"On the button," said Corkle, closing one eye and pointing a finger at Ames. "Still sold enough to make a small profit on them."

"I've got some questions," I said.

"Shoot," said Corkle.

"Do you know who killed Horvecki?"

"I believe in our justice system, in our police," he said emphatically. "It's the sacred duty of any citizen to help the police in any way that citizen can. People should not commit murder. Evidence should never be withheld."

"Are you withholding evidence?" I asked.

"There are secrets inside the office of D. Elliot Corkle. Next question."

"Secrets? Evidence?" I asked.

"Next question," he said.

"No, that'll do it," I said. "Sorry about the intrusion. Thanks for your hospitality."

At the front door, Corkle said, "Wait."

We stood there until he returned with two boxes for me and two for Ames.

"You each get a Pulp-O-Matic and a Mighty Miniature Prisoner of Zenda Safe."

"Heavy," said Ames, holding a gift box in

each arm. "You could beat a man's head in with either one of these."

"Wait," Corkle said hurrying off, ducking into the closet and popping right back out with two more packages, both small. "The Perfect Pocket Pager."

He stuck one in one of my pockets and did the same for Ames. We left the house and started down the path. It wasn't until we hit the street that we heard the door close.

"Secrets," Ames said. "Believe him?"

"Strongly suggests that he knows who did it or has a pretty good idea," I said.

"Think he has something?"

"Maybe we can find out," I said.

I had some trouble getting the trunk of the Saturn open, but when I did we placed our gifts inside, got in the car, and drove away from the Bay and from Corkle.

"Where to now?" asked Ames.

"Ronnie Gerall."

11

Ronnie Gerall agreed to see us when I sent him a message saying that I had something important to tell him. Ames stayed in the waiting area of juvenile detention with his book, and I took off my Cubs cap and followed the guard down a brightly lit corridor that smelled of Lysol and bleach.

Ronnie Gerall was waiting for me when the door to the visitors' room was opened. Ronnie was getting special treatment because he was accused of murder — and murder of a prominent, if not much loved, citizen.

Ronnie, his hair freshly combed, looked good in orange and a sullen pout. He did not offer to shake my hand, and I wasn't about to be rejected.

"I have a new client," I said as I sat.

I got an impatient look at this news.

"A client who's willing to pay for a new lawyer," I said.

"Why would I want to replace the guy from the public defender's office? He's inexperienced, stupid, and has no confidence. I was thinking of representing myself. Who's my benefactor?"

"A woman who thinks you're innocent."

He stiffened and I knew he would come up with the right name if I pushed him.

"I thought you were going to find out who killed Horvecki and set me free to enjoy the sunlight, baseball, and pizzas."

"It's always good to have well-paid backup," I said.

"What do you want to tell me?" he asked.

"Do you know Blue Berrigan?"

"Blue Berrigan? The dolt who used to have the stupid kid show on television?"

"Yes."

"I don't know him," Gerall said.

"Someone murdered him yesterday."

"I'm sorry, but I have problems of my own."

"I'm pretty sure he was killed because he knew who killed Philip Horvecki."

This got Gerall's interest.

"Then nail him," Gerall said. "You know what it's like in here? You have any idea of what kind of people are in here, people I have to be nice to when I want to punch their few remaining teeth out?"

"I'm still trying to find Horvecki's killer. But I need you to answer one question."

"What?"

"Does Corkle or Greg know about you and Corkle's daughter?"

"Know what?"

His fists were clenched and he started to rise from his chair. I sat still and looked at him. I was getting to know his moves. I met his eyes. The menace slipped away.

"No, they don't know," he said sitting. "But when this is over, they'll be told."

"Why?"

"Because Alana and I are going to get married," he said.

It didn't have to be said, and I didn't say it, but the observation hung in the dusty room. Either Corkle or Greg might prefer to have Ronnie in prison than living as Corkle's son-in-law and Greg's stepfather.

"I know what you're thinking. She's old enough to be my mother, but you've seen her," Ronnie went on as if he were announcing the new issue of a Salmon P. Chase postage stamp. "She loves me."

"I'm happy for you both," I said.

There was nothing else to say. Ronnie folded his arms and watched me head for the door.

Ames and I split a medium moussaka pizza — eggplant, cheese, sausage, and extra onion — at Honey Crust on Seventeenth Street. We were celebrating our partnership.

"Too many suspects," he said, wiping his mouth with a napkin.

He was right.

"Who's your pick?" I asked.

"Don't know, but Corkle's looking ripe for it."

"His grandson, daughter, Pepper the Preacher, Williams the Cop, and Ronnie Gerall. Just because he's in jail it doesn't mean he's innocent."

"And maybe Gregory's friend Winston," said Ames.

"And half the students at Pine View."

The next line should have been one reflecting incredulity that someone might murder over retaining a high school educational program. But both Ames and I knew that people had been murdered over a lot less. A few days earlier a Bradenton police officer had interrupted a ninety-dollar drug sale, and the buyer killed him. Two homeless men in Sarasota had fought, and one had died from a jagged Starbucks Frappuccino bottle to the throat. The fight had been over who had more teeth. Homeless Man Number One had more teeth, but Number Two said his were in better shape. Number Two pushed Number One into the concrete arch of a medical office building on Bahia Vista. Number One lost most of his remaining teeth and his life, blood and Frappuccino dribbling down his chest.

"What do we do now?" Ames asked.

"I'm going home to bed."

"It's three in the afternoon."

"A good time to close my door, pull down the shade, take off my shoes and pants, and go to sleep."

But such was not to be.

My cell phone sang "Help!"

The number of people who had my cell phone number, at least the ones I wanted to have it, was four: Ames, Flo, Adele, and Sally.

"Yes," I said.

"Lew," said Sally. "Darrell walked out of the hospital less than an hour ago."

"Is that good or bad?"

"Bad," she said. "He put on his clothes and walked out before he was discharged. He's supposed to be at home resting."

"You try his mother? Their apartment?"

"I called her. He isn't at the apartment

225

and he didn't call her."

"We'll find him," I said.

"Call me when you do, all right?"

"I'll call you," I said.

Sally hung up. So did I.

"Darrell?" asked Ames as he stood up with a box holding the last three slices of the pizza.

I nodded and put a twenty-dollar bill on the table. I was on my feet now and heading for the door. Nothing had to be said. Both Ames and I would have given twenty-to-one odds that we knew where Darrell was.

And we were right.

When I opened the door to my new home, Darrell Caton was sitting in the chair behind my desk. Victor Woo sat across from him. They had been talking. I tried to imagine what the two of them would have to say to each other. Then I saw the small photograph in front of Darrell. I knew what it was. I had seen it before, on a table in the booth of a bar in Urbana, Illinois. Victor had shown me the photograph of his smiling wife and two small, smiling children.

"Mind reader, Lewis Fonesca," said Darrell. "Knew where to find me and knew I was hungry. What kind of pizza you bring me?"

"Moussaka with extra onion," I said.

Ames placed the box on the desk. Darrell opened it and examined the pizza.

"What the f . . . hell is musical pizza? Beans?"

"Let's get you back to the hospital," said Ames.

"Hell no," said Darrell, handing a slice of lukewarm pizza to Victor. "They've got diseases and all kinds of shit in there. Worst place to be when you're sick. I read about it."

"Let's get you back," Ames said again.

"Your mother's worrying about you. Sally is worried about you," I said.

"Think about it, Lewis Fonesca," said Darrell. "Four people may be worrying about me. Four. You. Big Mac here. My mother and Ms. Porovsky. Him?" he added looking at Victor. "I don't know what he's thinking."

"What about Flo and Adele?" I said.

"They know I escaped from Alcatraz?"

"No."

"Then they can't be worried, can they? Pizza's good. What's that yellow thing?"

"Eggplant," I said.

"Woo," Darrell said. "I'll wrestle you for the last piece."

Victor shook his head no. Darrell picked

up the last slice of pizza. He tried to hide a wince as he brought it to his mouth. Darrell was fifteen. No father. His mother had kicked a crack habit two years earlier and was holding down a steady job at a dollar store.

"You're going back to the hospital," Ames said.

"Don't make me run," said Darrell chewing as he spoke. "You won't catch me and running could kill me. Besides, if you do get me back in the hospital, I'll just get up and leave again."

"Why?" Victor asked.

We all looked at him.

"Why?" asked Darrell. "Because I'd rather die than be hooked up to machines waiting for Dr. Frankenstein and a bunch of little Frankensteins to come in and look at me."

"Fifteen," said Victor.

"Fifteen little Frankensteins?" asked Darrell.

"You are fifteen. You wouldn't rather die."

Victor looked at me. There were times after Catherine died that I wouldn't have minded dying, but I never considered suicide as an option. There were times, I knew, that after he had killed Catherine, Victor had considered death as an option.

"Mr. Gloom and Mr. Doom," said Darrell. "You didn't answer your damn phone. I broke out because I have to tell you something, Lew Fonesca."

"Tell it," I said.

"You should have brought more pizza."

"That's what you have to tell me?"

"Hell no. I had a visitor during the night in the hospital. I was asleep and drugged up. Room was dark. Machine was beep-beep-beeping, you know. Then I heard him."

"Who?"

"A man, I think, or maybe a woman. He was across the room in the dark. He thought I was asleep. At least I think he thought I was asleep. He said something like, 'I'm sorry. My fault. Silky sad uncertain curtains.' Shit like that. Creepy. Then he said he had to go but he'd be back. I could do without his coming back. So, I got up and . . ."

"Anything you could tell from his voice?" I asked. "Young? Old?"

"Like I said, couldn't tell," said Darrell. "No, wait. He had one of those English accents, like that actor."

"Edgar Allen Poe," said Ames.

"Edgar Allen Poe, the guy who wrote those scary movies?" asked Darrell.

" 'The silken sad uncertain rustling of each purple curtain wrought its ghost upon the floor,' " said Ames.

"Yeah, creepy shit like that."

"It's from a poem by Poe, 'The Raven,' " said Ames.

"I guess. You know him? This Poe guy?"

"He's been dead for a hundred and fifty years," I said.

I knew one person involved in all this that had what might pass for an English accent.

"I don't believe in ghosts," said Darrell. "You should have bought more pizza. Next time just make it sausage."

"Let's get you back to the hospital."

"Let's order a pizza to go," said Darrell. "Do that and I go back to the hospital."

"Ames and Victor will get you the pizza and take you back to the hospital."

Darrell looked decidedly unwell when they went through the door. I called Information and let them connect me with the number I wanted. The woman who answered had a pleasant voice and a British accent. She told me that Winston Churchill Graeme wasn't home from school yet, but soon would be. She asked if I wanted to leave a message. I said no.

When I hung up I walked over to the wall where the Stig Dalstrom paintings were and looked for truth in black jungles and mountains and the twisted limbs of trees. I focused on the lone spot of yellow in one of the paintings. It was a butterfly.

I folded the empty pizza box and carried it out with me. At the bottom of the steps I dropped the box into one of the three garbage cans and called Sally. With no preamble, I said, "We found Darrell."

"Where?"

"My place. Ames and Victor are taking him back to the hospital."

"I'll call his mother."

"Are you at work?"

"Yes."

"What can you tell me about Winston Churchill Graeme?"

Twenty minutes later I was parked about half a block down and across the street from the Graeme home on Siesta Key. The house was in an ungated community called Willow Way. The house was a lot smaller than others in the community, but it wasn't a mining shack.

Winn Graeme hadn't called back to set up a time to talk. I wondered why.

I didn't think Winn Graeme was home yet but, just to be sure, I called the house. I was wrong again. He answered the phone.

"This is Lew Fonesca," I said.

"Yes?"

"I'm parked on your street, half a block West."

"Why?"

"I'd like you to come out and talk."

"You can come in."

"I don't think you want your mother to hear what we have to talk about."

"I don't . . ."

"Your visit to the hospital last night."

It was one of those silences, and then, "I'll be right out."

There was no one on the street. A white compact car was parked in the driveway of the house from which Winn Graeme emerged. The house was at the top of a short incline with stone steps leading down to the narrow sidewalk. Trees and bushes swayed in the cool wind from off the Gulf.

Winn saw my car, adjusted his glasses, and headed toward me. He walked along the sidewalk, back straight, carrying a blue gym bag. He walked like a jock and looked like a jock.

He opened the passenger side door and leaned over to look at me before he decided to get in. The door squeaked. He placed the gym bag on the floor in front of him.

"I have soccer practice in half an hour," he said, turning his head toward me. "Someone is picking me up."

"We shouldn't be long," I said. "You have a car?"

"Yes," he said. "It's in the garage. Why?"

"Early this morning," I said. "Say about two o'clock. Where were you?"

"Why?"

"Darrell Caton," I said. "The hospital."

Winn Graeme took off his glasses, cleaned them with his shirt and looked through the front window into a distance that offered no answers. Then he nodded, but I wasn't sure whether he was answering my question or one he had asked himself.

"Is he going to be all right?"

"I don't know."

"We're fragile creatures," he said.

"You told him you were sorry. Sorry for what?"

"For not stopping what happened."

"Greg shot Darrell, right?"

No answer from Winn, so I went on.

"He was aiming at me, but Darrell got in the way."

Still no response.

"Okay, not Greg. You shot Darrell."

Now he looked at me, and I at him. I saw a boy. I wondered what kind of man he was looking at.

"To scare you into stopping your investigation," Winn said.

"First he hires me and then he tries to stop me," I said.

He said nothing, just nodded, and then, after heaving a breath as if he were about to run a hundred-yard dash, he spoke.

"He found out something after he hired you, something that made him want you to stop. Firing you didn't work. You found someone else to pay you. So he tried to frighten you into stopping. He hoped you would weigh your safety and possibly your life against the few dollars you were getting. He only made it worse."

"He shot at me in the car with Augustine, and then he shot Darrell."

"Who's Augustine?"

"Cyclops."

Winn looked out his window. A woman was walking a small white dog. She was wearing a business suit and carrying an empty poop bag. Winn seemed to find the woman and dog fascinating.

"Both times he shot at me he sent someone else to the hospital," I said.

"Your life is charmed."

"No, Greg's a terrible shot."

The god of irony was at it again.

"Blue Berrigan," I said. No response, so I repeated, "Blue Berrigan."

"The clown," he said softly.

234

"He wasn't a clown."

"Greg didn't do that."

"Horvecki?"

"Greg didn't do that. We weren't unhappy about it, but he didn't do that."

"Did you?"

"No," he said.

A yellow and black Mini Cooper turned the corner and came to a stop in front of the Graeme house.

"I've got to go," he said. "I told you all this because I'm sorry that I didn't do anything to stop Greg. He's my friend. Whatever I've said here I'll deny ever saying."

"Why?" I said though I knew the answer.

"Why what?"

He had the door open now.

"Why is he your friend?"

"We need each other," he said as he got out of the car. "Greg didn't kill anybody."

He closed the door, crossed the street and raised his hand in greeting to the boy who leaned out of the window of the Mini Cooper.

The boy in the car was Greg Legerman.

Greg looked back at me and ducked back through the window. Winn Graeme crawled in on the passenger side, and they drove off.

I could have confronted Greg Legerman, but sometimes it's better to let the person you're after worry for a while. I had learned that as an investigator with the state attorney's office in Chicago. Patience was usually better than confrontation, especially with a nervous suspect, and they didn't come any more nervous or suspicious than Greg Legerman. I wasn't afraid of Greg's not talking. I was afraid that he wouldn't stop.

I did follow the little car down Midnight Pass and off the Key, but I kept going straight when they turned left on Tamiami Trail.

My cell phone rang. I considered throwing it out the window, but I answered it.

"Lewis, I have a death in the family," said Ann Hurwitz.

"I'm sorry."

"My cousin Leona was ninety-seven years old," she said. "She's been in a nursing home for a decade."

"I'm sorry," I said.

"Lewis, you are one of the few people I know whose expression of sorrow over the death of a very old woman you don't know I would believe. I must cancel our appointment tomorrow so I can attend the funeral in Memphis."

"All right."

"But I have an opening today," Ann Hurwitz said.

"When?"

"Now."

"I'm on the way."

"You did your homework?"

My index cards were in the notebook in my back pocket.

"Yes."

"Good. Decaf with cream and Equal. Today I feel like a chocolate biscotti."

"With almonds?"

"Always with almonds," she said and clicked off.

Fifteen minutes later I picked up a pair of coffees and three chocolate biscotti from Sarasota News and Books and crossed Main street. I was about to go through the door to Ann's office on Gulfstream when he appeared, mumbling to himself.

He was black, about forty, wearing a shirt and pants too large and baggy for his lean frame. His bare feet flopped in his untied shoes. He looked down as he walked, pausing every few feet to scratch his head and engage himself in conversation.

I knew him. Everyone in this section of town near the Bay knew him, but few knew his story. I'd sat down with him once on the park bench he lived under. The bench was across the street from Ann's office. It had a good view of the small boats moored on the bay and the ever-changing and almost always controversial works of art erected along the bay. He had been evicted from his bench in one of the recurrent efforts to clean up the city for tourists. I didn't know where he lived now, but it wasn't far. Even the homeless have someplace they think of as home.

"Big tooth," he said to himself as he came toward me.

"Big tooth," I repeated.

The bag in my hand was hot and the biscotti must have been getting moist.

He pointed across the street toward the bay. There was a giant white tooth which was slowing the passing traffic.

He scratched his inner left thigh and said, "Dentist should buy it. Definitely."

One of the charms of the man was that he never asked for money or anything else. He minded his own business and relied on luck, the discards of the upscale restaurants in the neighborhood and the kindness and guilt of others.

I reached into the bag and came up with a coffee and a biscotti. He took them with a nod of thanks.

"You, too?" he asked, tilting his head toward the nearby bench — not his former residence, but the one right outside Ann's office.

"Can't," I said. "Appointment."

"Old lady who talks to ghosts and crazy people?"

"Not ghosts," I said.

"I'm not a crazy person," he said.

"No," I agreed.

"You a crazy person?"

"I don't know."

"You should maybe find out," he said, moving toward the bench, his back to me now.

"I'm working on it," I said and stepped through the door.

Ann's very small reception area was empty except for three chairs, a neat pile of copies of psychology magazines, and a small Bose non–boom box playing generic classical music. The music was there to cover the voices of any clients who might be moved to occasional rage or panic, usually directed at a spouse, child, sibling, boss or themselves. The music wasn't necessary for me. My parents never raised their voices. I have never raised mine in anger, remorse, or despair. All the passion in our family came from my sister, and she more than compensated for it with Italian neighborhood show-manship.

Ann was, as always, seated in her armchair under the high narrow horizontal windows. I handed her the bag. She smelled it and carefully removed coffee and biscotti and placed them on the desk near her right hand.

"No coffee for you?" she asked, handing me a biscotti.

"No," I said. "Caffeine turns me into a raging maniac."

I took off my Cubs cap and placed it on my lap.

"Levity," she said, removing the lid of her coffee and engaging in the biscotti-dipping ritual.

"I guess."

"Small steps. Always small steps. Progress," she said. "Biscotti are one of the tiny treasures of life. When one of my clients tells me he or she is contemplating suicide I remind them that, once dead, they will never again enjoy coffee and biscotti."

"Does it work?"

"Only one has ever committed suicide, but I can't claim that the biscotti approach has ever been the reason for this high level of success. Did your mother make biscotti?"

"No, she ate it. My father made *pignoli.*

My uncle made biscotti."

"Pignoli?"

"A kind of cookie with pine nuts."

"My mother made mandel bread," Ann said. "That's like Jewish biscotti, made with cement, at least the way my mother made it."

I looked at the clock on the wall over her head. Five minutes had passed.

"You want to know when we are going to start," she said. "Well, we already started."

"I asked Ames to be my partner."

"Putting down roots," she said, finishing her biscotti. She had eaten it in record time.

I handed her mine.

"You sure?" she asked. "I didn't have time for lunch."

"I'm sure about you having my biscotti. I'm not sure about asking Ames to be my partner."

"Why?"

"He'll expect me to stay around."

"Yes."

"Besides, I make just enough to live on."

"Yes, but you asked him and he said yes.

"He said yes."

"Sally's leaving, moving North. Better job."

Ann said nothing, just worked on her biscotti, brushing away stray crumbs from her

241

white dress with dancing green leaves.

"Did you ask her to stay?" she said finally.

"No."

"Do you want her to stay?"

"Yes."

"Is there anything you could say or do that would make her stay?"

"I think so. Maybe."

"But you won't say it."

"I can't. You want to hear the first lines I've collected?"

"Not this session," she said.

The phone rang. She never turned off the phone during our sessions and I guess she didn't turn it off during anyone else's sessions either. She had too much curiosity to turn off her connection to anyone who wanted to confess or try to sell her something.

"Yes, I'll take it," she told the caller after listening for a few seconds.

She hung up.

"I'm going to give you a conundrum, an ethical dilemma, a moral puzzle," she said. "With that call, I just paid to become beneficiary of a life insurance policy for a ninety-one-year-old man. He gets paid with my cash offer immediately. I double or triple my investment when he dies, providing he dies before I do and, given my age, while the odds are in my favor, I stand some chance of losing. I have six such policies. What do you think?"

"Do you meet these people?" I asked.

"Absolutely not," she said, sitting back and folding her hands.

"Life insurance is gambling on beating or forestalling death," I said.

"Precisely, Lewis. Still?"

"I don't know. It doesn't feel right."

"No, it doesn't, but why not? Does it challenge God or the gods who might decide to strike you down instead of the person from whose death you would profit?"

Her eyes were dancing. We were getting somewhere or going somewhere. She leaned forward.

"I lied, Lewis," she said. "I didn't buy life insurance for a dying man. I told my stockbroker to go ahead and buy pork belly futures. I'm betting on people who might profit from the slaughter of pigs."

"That's comforting."

"Your opinion of me faltered for a moment," she said.

"Yes."

"But it's all right if I profit from the death of pigs."

"Yes," I said.

"We bet against death every day," she said.

"But it is taboo to bet for death. We don't want to make those gods angry even if they exist only in our minds."

"Someone may be trying to kill me," I said.

"This has happened before."

"Yes."

"You invite it?"

"I don't know."

"You gamble with your life."

"I suppose," I said.

"And the irony is that you keep winning."

"I don't want to die anymore," I said.

"I know. But you haven't decided what to do about staying alive."

"I don't want anyone else I know to die."

"But they all will," she said, looking over her shoulder at the clock on the wall.

"Some of them have."

"Catherine," she said.

"Yes."

"The world is not perpetually sad in spite of the fact that the ones we love will all die," Ann said.

"Yes it is," I said.

"Time to stop. Next time, I hear your first lines."

She clapped her hands and rose. Her fingers were thin and the backs of her hands freckled with age. The wedding ring she wore looked too large, as if it would fall off.

I got up and put my Cubs cap back on my head. We faced each other for a moment. She seemed to be trying to convey some question with the tilt of her head and a few seconds of silence. I felt the answer but had no words for it. I nodded to show that I had at least a glint of understanding. I got twenty dollars out of my wallet and handed it to her.

When I stepped out into the sun, the homeless man was still on the bench squinting out at the setting sun. He had finished his coffee and biscotti, and his arms were spread out, draped over the bench. He was at home. He scratched his belly. I sat beside him and looked at the boats bobbing in the water. He didn't acknowledge my presence.

"You have a favorite first line from a book?"

"Uh-huh."

"What is it?"

" 'Kelsey Yarborough hated grits with salt but he ate them anyway because his mother told him it was good for him.' "

"What's the book?" I said, writing the line on one of my cards. I had a neat little packet of them now.

"Kelsey Plays the Blues."

"Who wrote it?"

"Kelsey Yarborough."

I looked at him, but he was too busy looking toward the sun. I thought I knew the answer to the unstated question, but I said nothing.

He helped me out by saying, "Me. I'm Kelsey Yarborough." He pointed a thumb at his chest.

"You wrote a book?"

"Hell no," he said. "I wrote the first line of a book. "The rest of the book's in my head and it's never gonna come out. I wrote the music for the first notes of a song. That ain't never gonna come out either. You know why?"

"No."

"Because," he said, tilting his head up so he could catch the dwindling warmth of the setting sun. "Got no creative juice. Got no interest. Now I got a question for you, but I don't want no answer. My time's too precious to spend getting involved."

"The question?"

"Who is in that car comin' this way down the block. Been circling ever since you went into the doctor's office."

I looked down the street. There was a dark Buick of unknown age moving slowly in our direction. When it got close enough, I could see that its windows were tinted and dark.

The passenger side window facing us came down slightly and the car stopped about fifteen feet in front of us.

"Get down," I said, going to the pavement prone and scurrying under the bench.

Kelsey didn't move other than to look down at me. The two shots came in rapid succession. Both seemed to whiz precariously close to Kelsey.

Then the car sped away with a screech. I turned my head to catch the license plate number. I think it was one of the save-the-manatee plates, or tags, as they call them in Florida. It began with the letters C and X. The rest was obscured by dirt.

I slid out from under the bench, picked up my hat, dusted it, and then wiped away the worst of the garbage that covered the front of my shirt and jeans.

"That was for you," he said. "Only reason anyone wanting to be shooting me is because I'm a black man and a homeless eyesore. More likely the message was for you."

"It was," I said, putting on my cap.

I left him sitting on the bench and moved down the street to my Saturn. There was a folded sheet of notebook paper, the kind with ragged edges and punched holes. I retrieved the note. It read:

What Part of Stop Don't You Understand?
Would you understand a death march
band?
Listen to the distant Orleans clarinet.
Turn away. There's still time yet.

It was written in a cursive script you don't often see anymore.

I had learned something in my session with Ann. I tried to figure it out as I drove, but I was distracted by the background voice on a talk radio station. The host, who had a New York accent, wanted callers to tell him what they thought about bombing Iran and sending troops if Iran continued to defy the United States and continued their race to build a nuclear weapon.

The car from which someone had shot at me was not the one Greg Legerman had driven to pick up Winn Graeme. The shots that had been fired at me a few minutes earlier had not come from a pellet gun, but from something with real bullets. Either Greg had another car and a more impressive gun, or this was a new shooter.

About seven or eight minutes later I was parked outside the Texas Bar and Grill on Second Street. I was calm with a this-isn't-real calm. My hands didn't tremble. I didn't weep.

When I stepped through the door of the Texas, Big Ed was behind the bar. He nodded at me and adjusted his handlebar mustache. Guns of the old West hung on the walls, and the smell of beer and grilled half-pound burgers and onions perfumed the air. Around eight round wooden tables people, almost all men, were having a heavy snack before heading home for healthy dinners.

"Ames here?" I asked Big Ed.

"Back in his room," Big Ed said, nodding over his left shoulder.

Ed was a New Englander who loved old Westerns and would have worshiped Lilly Langtree were she to return in ghostly form.

"You know Wild Bill Hickok wasn't holding aces and eights when he died? Bartender made it up. No one knows what he had. Grown men still feel a little panic when they look down at the dead man's hand in a game of poker."

"I didn't know that," I said.

"You want a beer, a Big Ed Burger?"

"Beer and a Big Ed with cheese."

Behind the bar there was a horizontal mirror with an elaborately carved wooden frame, painted gold.

"The same for Ames," I said.

I looked at myself in the mirror and saw a

short, balding Italian with a sad face wearing a Cubs baseball cap.

"He told me," Big Ed said, adjusting the curl in his waxed handlebar mustache with both hands. "About partnering up with you."

"You all right with that?" I asked.

"Ames has partnered up with you since he met you. I'd like him to put in some hours here, too, in exchange for his room, providing you don't have too much work for him to do."

"I don't expect to overwhelm him with work."

"Good," said Big Ed after calling back to the tiny kitchen for two half-pound burgers.

He poured two mugs of beer from the tap and clunked them down in front of him.

"Work on your beer. I'll go back and tell Ames that you're here."

When Ames came out, tall, hair shampooed and white, he was dressed in his usual freshly washed jeans and a loose-fitting long-sleeved white flannel shirt with the sleeves rolled up.

We moved to a table next to two guys speaking in Spanish and sounding like they were having an argument half the time and telling each other jokes the other half.

"You play poker?" I asked Ames.

"I do."

"How good are you at it?"

"Middling good," he said. "But then most I've played think they're middling good."

"I'm less than middling bad," I said. "Remember Corkle saying he had something on Ronnie Gerall?"

"I do."

"We're going to try to find it."

We listened to the guys speaking Spanish and drank our beers until Big Ed motioned and Ames moved around the tables to pick up our burgers.

"You good enough in a seven-card stud game to help someone else win?" I asked.

"Depends on who's watching and playing."

We ate as we talked. More people, including the two Spanish speakers at the next table, left and a few others came in. Big Ed handled them all, nodding just right at each new customer as if he had known them all his life.

"Players are multimillionaires . . ."

"Corkle," said Ames.

"Yes, and four others. They have a game every other week at Corkle's house. Stakes are fifty and a hundred. You need four thousand to sit down."

"I've got two thousand," he said.

"I've got another two," I said. "We'll borrow a few thousand more from Flo in case we run out."

"Not like you to be beholding."

"Little by little, day by day, I'm trying to change," I said.

"How's it going?"

"Not too good," I said, taking a bite of burger.

The grilled burger was handmade by Big Ed from extra-lean meat and cooked to greasy perfection by the kitchen cook. I was hungry. The slightly burnt beef reminded me of a taste from the past that I couldn't quite place.

"How you gonna get in this game?"

"Kidnap one of the players," I said.

Ames gave me a slight nod and worked at chewing the large bite of burger in his mouth.

"Only way?" he said.

"Only one I can think of," I said. "You in?"

"We're partners," he said. "When we doing this?"

"Tonight," I said. "It's game night. Wednesday."

"What'll I be doing while you're playing poker?"

"Searching through Corkle's office."

"Corkle carries a handgun," Ames said.

"I know. I'll be careful," I said, pushing the now-empty plate away.

"I trust you," he said.

"I know."

"What time?"

"Midnight," I said.

"You planning to win?"

"No," I said. "Just to fold a lot, hang in as long as possible and not lose everything."

"If they catch us?" Ames asked. "They'd have to own up to gambling for big stakes."

"Yes, and it'll be in the newspapers and on television," I went on. "The fines won't mean anything to them, but the fact that they'll have to close down their game for good will mean something. And Corkle might have to leave the house and go down-town."

The bar in the Texas was a small one. Not much space behind it and only six high, wooden swivel stools. At that moment a man and a woman were arguing at the bar and getting louder — loud enough for us to hear the drunken slur.

The couple were probably in their fifties and looked like they had spent their days behind desks taking and giving orders.

She slapped the man hard, a slap that stopped conversation and echoed around the room. The man was exhausting his vituperative vocabulary now, and quickly worked his way up toward a punch. Before he could throw it Big Ed reached over his arm and grabbed his wrist. That gave the woman an opening to attack again. This time she punched. The man slipped from the stool and fell flat on his back, his head thumping on the hardwood floor.

"You want to help Big Ed?" I asked.

"No," said Ames. "He's happy. Genteel barroom brawl."

"See what the boys in the back room will have," I said, watching the woman dropping to her knees on the floor and touching the fallen man's cheek.

"Warren," she whimpered, "I'm so, so, *so,* so sorry."

The bar noise level in the room went back to prebrawl level. It was then that I noticed Ed Viviase, alone at a table near the window. He must have come in while the man and woman were doing battle.

When he saw that he had our attention, he got up and sat between me and Ames.

"See the fight?" I asked.

"Yeah. Over in one minute of the first round. You're easy to find, Fonesca. You only go to five places regularly. I found you at the third one on my list."

"A beer?" asked Big Ed.

"On the clock," said Viviase.

We sat at a table, Viviase, Ames, and me. The detective watched as the woman helped the fallen man to his feet and then out the door, an arm draped over her shoulder.

"Love," Viviase said with enough sarcasm so we wouldn't think he was genuinely moved. "Always a bad call for a cop, couple fighting. They don't want a man or woman of the law stepping between them. Sometimes a cop will get hurt more than the battlers. I once got a steak pounding mallet on the side of the head — you know the kind with the nubs?"

"Yes," I said.

Viviase shook his head, remembering.

"She was a chef," he said. "I was lucky she didn't have something even more lethal in her hand, like whatever it was that killed Blue Berrigan. The chef and her husband were divorced a few months after I met and arrested them. Neither of them did time. I had headaches for more than a year."

"Tough," I said.

"There are tougher things," Viviase said. "Like finding out your daughter went behind your back to involve a process server in a murder case."

"I'm sorry," I said.

"Of course you are. People who commit crimes are always sorry when they get caught."

"She didn't hire me," I said.

"I know. The hell with it. I'll have a beer. A beer ain't drinking."

It was Edmond O'Brien's line from *The Man Who Shot Liberty Valance,* forever to be honored by alcoholics.

Ames rose to get the beer.

"I'll get the tape back to you," Viviase said.

"No hurry," I said. "You ground her?"

"For what? Disappointing me?"

"Guess not."

"You really think Gerall didn't kill Horvecki?"

"Yes. And he couldn't have killed Blue Berrigan. He was in jail."

"Who says he killed Berrigan?" asked Viviase as Ames came back with three beers.

"The angel of common sense," I said.

"Only thing holds the two murders together is you," Viviase said, drinking the beer directly from the bottle. "And I'm reasonably confident that you didn't kill either one of them, unless you've gone Jekyll and Hyde on me."

"The Gerall boy's a bad apple, but he didn't kill anybody," said Ames.

"Ames and I are partners now," I explained.

"Partners in what?" asked Viviase, shaking his head. "Operating an illegal office of private investigation."

"We find people," I said.

"You find people who commit murder," Viviase said.

"Sometimes," I admitted.

"Ames have a process server's license?"

"Not yet," he said.

"Not never," answered Viviase, after nearly finishing his bottle of beer. "He's a convicted felon."

"We'll work on that," I said. "He's my partner either way."

"You and Ames here bothered a Venice policeman, a detective."

"We talked to Detective Williams," I said.

"Mr. McKinney here fired a weapon at him after you practically accused him of murder."

A bustle of businessmen and -women came through the door, laughing and making in-jokes that weren't funny, but when you want to laugh any flotsam of intended wit will do.

"What does he want?"

"Nothing now, but for you to stay away from him."

I knew why. If Ames and I were arrested,

the story of his aunt and mother being raped would hit the media again.

Viviase finished his beer while Ames and I kept working on ours. He rolled the empty bottle between his hands. No genie emerged. Viviase got up.

"You find anything, let me know," he said. "Don't do anything stupid."

He left.

Then Ames and I decided to do something stupid.

■ ■ ■ ■ ■

II
PLAYING FOR KEEPS

■ ■ ■ ■ ■

12

I was holding two pair, jacks and fours, in a five-card stud game. That was the only game being played in the card room of Corkle's house. The old doctor with the slight tremor was the only one left in the hand with me. The pot stood at four hundred dollars and change. The doctor had a pair of sevens showing. He could have had three of them or, since one of his cards showing was a king, he could have had a higher two pair.

On my left was Corkle, clad in a green Detroit Lions sweatshirt. Next to him was a bulky man who had been introduced as Kaufmann. "You know who he is," Corkle had said in his initial introduction when I had sat at the table three hours earlier. I didn't know who Kaufmann was, but about an hour into the game Corkle asked him something about a union meeting. On his left, across from me, was a kid, college age. Corkle introduced him as Keith Thirlane.

Keith Thirlane looked like an athlete, a very nervous athlete trying to look calm. He was tall, blond, and wearing black slacks and a black polo. The last player at the table was "Period Waysock from out of town." Period was about sixty, bald, and slowdown fat. He did everything from betting to going to the snack table with the deliberation of a large dinosaur.

I pushed in another hundred dollars and looked at the steel clock on the wall. It was almost one in the morning.

Ames and I had pooled our money. I had cashed the check from Alana Legerman. We came up with the requisite four thousand, with another thousand borrowed from Flo Zink. We had a slight cushion. Then I had called Laurence Arthur Wainwright, who was one of the poker players Corkle had mentioned and the only one whose name I recognized. Wainwright was a state representative, a lawyer who owned pieces of banks, mortgage houses, property, and businesses worth who knows how much. Wainwright made the local news a lot, partly because he did a lot of donations to charities and looked good in a tuxedo at society dinners. Wainwright, also known as LAW or Law by the *Herald-Tribune,* was in constant trouble for his business practices, which were often barely legal.

On the phone, I told Wainwright that I had some documents he had been looking for. There are almost always documents a person like Wainwright is looking for.

"What documents?" he had asked.

Ames had gone through past newspaper articles mentioning Wainwright and come up with a list of four prime names. The best bet seemed to be Adam Bulagarest, a former Wainwright business associate who had moved out of Florida before the law could catch up with him.

"Does the name Bulagarest ring a bell?" I asked.

"Is this extortion?"

"I hope so," I said.

"How did you get these documents?"

"They're originals taken from papers in possession of Mr. Bulagarest. You can have them for a nominal fee. We will provide you with a signed and notarized guarantee that there are no copies."

There was no chance Wainwright could check on my tale with Bulagarest. In researching the poker players, Dixie had discovered Bulagarest was serving time in a Thai jail for child molestation.

"How do I get these documents?" Wainwright asked with a tone of clear skepticism.

"Come tonight to the Ramada Inn at Disney World. Register as F. W. Murnau. We'll meet you at the bar at midnight."

"To Orlando tonight? What's the hurry?"

"My associates and I are not comfortable in Florida. Bring one hundred thousand dollars in cash. If you don't come, we have another buyer."

"I don't . . ." Wainwright said, but I hung up.

People like Wainwright always had piles of cash handy in case the real law was about to knock at their door.

I waited an hour and then called Corkle to ask when there might be an opening at his poker table.

"You have four thousand dollars?"

"Yes."

"You're in luck. One of our regulars can't make it."

Two hours into the game, I was ahead about three hundred dollars. After three hours I was ahead by almost eleven hundred dollars. It wasn't that I was a particularly good player. They, including Corkle, were all incredibly bad, but I was learning that in a five-handed game, the odds of one of the bad players getting lucky was fairly high. Besides, I had to remember that I wasn't there to win, just to keep the players busy.

From time to time, when they were out of a hand, the others at the table either ambled to the snack table in the corner for a plate of nuts and a beer or to the toilet just off the room toward the front door.

I didn't meet the first raise on the next hand and moved toward the small restroom. It was a minute or two after one. Law Wainwright was sitting in a hotel room at Disney World with one hundred thousand dollars or a pistol with a silencer in his lap. I didn't care which.

I looked back. The players were bantering, betting, acting like their favorite television poker pros. I moved past the restroom, turned a corner and went to the hall beyond to the front. I opened it quietly. Ames, flashlight in hand, stepped in. I closed the door and pointed to a door across the hallway. He nodded to show that he understood and showed me the Perfect Pocket Pager, one of the gifts Corkle had given us. I had an identical one in my pocket. Both Ames's and my pager were set on vibrate. Each pager had originally been offered not for $29.95 or even $19.95, but for $9.95 with free shipping if you ordered now, but the "now" had been a dozen years ago and, until we had tested them, we didn't know that they would work.

On the way back to the poker table, I reached in and flushed the toilet. The same hand was still being played, but only Corkle, who never sat out a hand, was still in it against Waysock from out of town. The pot, a small mountain of crisp green, looked big.

Corkle won the hand with a pair of fours. Both men had been bluffing.

I was worried about Ames. He wasn't carrying a gun. I didn't want a shoot-out and Ames was not the kind of man to give up without a fight. Ames and I were partners now. I was, I guess, senior partner. I know he felt responsible for me and to me. I felt the same.

Ames was going through Corkle's office in search of the evidence Corkle had mentioned — evidence that might tell us who had killed Blue Berrigan and Philip Horvecki. Or maybe it wouldn't. Maybe it was just another invention proceeding from Corkle's heat-oppressed brain.

I was having trouble concentrating on the game.

"Two hundred more," Keith the Kid said.

He hadn't been doing badly. At least not in the game. He was a little over even. He winced in periodic pain or regret and gulped down diet ginger ale.

We were down to three players in the

hand. I saw the bet and, for one of the few times during the game, Corkle folded. When the next cards were dealt to Keith and me by Kaufmann, Corkle got up and headed for the restroom. I watched him walk past it. I pressed the durable and easy-to-clean replaceable white glow-in-the-dark button on the pager in my pocket.

"Your bet, Lewie," said Kaufmann.

"What's the bet?" I asked.

"Three hundred," said Kaufmann. "Keep your eyes on the prize."

Period Waysock from Out of Town had waddled to the snack table.

I was holding two fours down and a third four showing on the table with one card to go, a set of three in a five-card-nothing wild game. The Kid could have had three sevens, eights, or jacks or just a pair of each. He wasn't betting like a player with a set. I reluctantly folded, got up from the table and hurried after Corkle.

I caught up with Corkle in the foyer where he was pacing and talking on a cordless phone in front of the front door.

"No, D. Elliot Corkle is not sorry that he woke you. There are more important things than sleep. I did not make my money by sleeping. I made it by staying awake. You can sleep later."

He looked around at the three closed doors and the elevator and kept pacing as he listened.

"Not everyone who goes to jail gets raped," he said. "D. Elliot Corkle will put up the bail in the morning. Watch him all the time. Do not let him run away . . . All right. Let me know."

Corkle pushed a button on his phone and I ducked into the bathroom and closed the door. I heard him walk past, come out, pushed the button on the pager twice and watched while Ames stepped out of Corkle's office. He headed for the front door holding up an eight-by-eleven brown envelope for me to see. Then he went through the front door and closed it as I turned to return to the game.

Keith the Kid was standing across the foyer looking at me. He didn't say anything, but he did give me a look of slight perplexity.

"Stretching my legs," I said. "Bad knee."

"What'd you have?" he asked. "That last hand."

"Queen high," I said.

"No," he said. "Not the way you bet."

"I figured from the way you were betting that you had a set. The odds were against me."

"You gave me the hand," he said. "I don't want anyone feeling sorry for me."

"I don't," I said. "I didn't."

He touched his cheek nervously.

"I thought I could make back some of the money I lost here last time," he said. "My father was a regular in this stupid game. He's not well enough to play again. Heart. I took his place. I don't want to lose, but I don't want any gifts either. Besides the ones Corkle gives out in boxes as we leave."

"Kaufmann won't play a hand unless he's holding an initial pair," I said. "Period bluffs half the time, no pattern. Corkle never folds unless he's beaten on the table."

"And me?"

"You shouldn't be playing poker."

"You?"

"I don't like to gamble," I said.

"Then . . ."

"Hey, you two," Corkle called. "Clock is moving and a quorum and your money are needed."

I moved past Keith and took my place at the table. Keith came behind me and sat.

"Question," Period Waysock From Out of Town said. "You wearing that Cubs cap for luck or because you're going bald."

"Yes, in that order," I said.

269

"Let's play some poker," Corkle said, and we did.

At two in the morning, the last hand was played, the cash was pocketed and the lies about winning and losing were told. I estimated that Ames and I had come out about five hundred dollars ahead.

On the way out, Corkle handed each of us a small box about the length of a pen.

"See Forever Pocket Telescope with built-in sky map," he said. "Specially designed lenses. You can clearly see the mountains of the moon or the party your neighbors are having a mile away, providing trees or buildings aren't in the way."

We thanked him. I was the last one at the door. Corkle stopped me with a hand on my arm and said in a low voice, "D. Elliot Corkle knows what you did here."

I didn't answer.

"You did some losing on purpose," he said. "You're a good player. You're setting us up for next time."

I didn't tell him that I was sure I had come out ahead and not behind.

"Well," he went on. "I don't think that opportunity will be afforded to you. You're a decent enough guy, but not a good fit here."

I agreed with him.

"One more thing," he said. "My daughter has bailed out Ronnie Gerall."

He looked for a reaction from me. I gave him none.

"She stands to lose a quarter of a million if he skips," said Corkle. "I'll be grateful with a cash bonus of four thousand dollars if he doesn't skip."

He didn't tell me why Alana Legerman would bail Ronnie out, but I could see from his face that we were both thinking the same thing.

I took my See Forever Pocket Telescope with sky map and went out the door.

Ames, leaning over so he couldn't be seen from the door, was in the backseat of the Saturn. He didn't sit up until we hit Tamiami Trail.

"What'd you find?" I asked, looking at him in the rearview mirror.

"Our chief suspect has a lot of explaining to do," he said.

Victor wasn't around when we got to my place.

Ames waited for me to sit behind my desk, and then produced the envelope he had taken from Corkle's office. He opened it and placed the first two sheets next to each other in front of me.

They were birth certificates. The one on my left was Ronald Gerall's. It said that he was born in Palo Alto, California, on December 18, 1990. The birth certificate on the right gave his date of birth as December 18, 1978. If the certificate on the right was correct, Ronnie Gerall was 29 years old.

"I'm betting that one," Ames said pointing at the certificate on my right, "is the right one and the other one's the fake."

"We'll find out," I said. "You know what this means?"

"Gerall started high school here when he was twenty-five or twenty-six years old," said Ames.

He reached back into the envelope and came out with two more pieces of paper. He handed them to me and I discovered that our Ronnie had graduated from Templeton High School in Redwood City, California, and California State University in Hayward, California.

"Best for last," Ames said, pulling one more sheet of paper out of the envelope.

It was a marriage certificate, issued a year ago in the State of California to Ronald Owen Gerall and Rachel Beck Horvecki. Ronnie was married to Horvecki's missing daughter.

We had more questions now. Why had

Ronnie Gerall posed as a high school student? Where was his wife? What was Corkle planning to do with the documents that were now on my desk?

It was three in the morning. We said good night and Ames said he would be back "an hour or two past daybreak." I told him nine in the morning would be fine.

I handed the papers back to Ames and said, "You keep them. If Corkle finds that they're gone, he might think I'm a logical suspect."

Ames nodded and put the documents back in the envelope.

When Ames left I went to my room and closed the door. The night-light, a small lamp with an iron base and a glass bowl over the bulb, was on. I had been leaving it on more and more when night came. I put on my black Venice Beach workout shorts and went back through my office to the cramped bathroom. I showered, shaved, shampooed my minor outcropping of hair; I did not sing. Catherine used to say I had a good voice. Singing in the shower had been almost mandatory — old standards from the 1940s had been my favorites and Catherine's. "Don't Sit Under The Apple Tree," "To Each His Own," "Johnny Got a Zero," "Wing and a Prayer." I had not sung or considered it after Catherine died. When I turned off the shower, I heard someone moving around in the office.

I got out, dried my body quickly, put on my Venice shorts and stepped into the office while drying my hair.

Victor Woo was sitting on his sleeping bag on the floor in the corner. He had placed the blanket so that he could look up at the Stig Dalstrom paintings on the wall. He glanced over at me. He looked exhausted.

"I called my wife," he said.

I draped the towel over my shoulder.

"What did you say?"

"I didn't. I couldn't. But she knew it was me. She said I should come home, that she's been getting my checks, that the children miss me. She didn't say that she missed me."

"Go home Victor," I said.

"Can't."

"I forgive you. Catherine forgives you. I don't think Cook County forgives you, but that's between you and the Cook County state attorney's office, and I don't plan to give them any information."

It was pretty much what I had been saying to him for more than two months. I didn't expect it to work this time.

"Forgive yourself," I tried. "Hungry?"

"No."

"You can do me a favor," I said. "In the morning, go to Starbucks or Borders, plug your computer into the Internet, and find some information for me."

"Yes."

"You might have to do some illegal things to get what I want. I want whatever you can find about a Ronald Gerall, probably born somewhere in California."

It was busywork. Dixie would get me whatever I needed in the morning.

"Yes," he said.

"You want me to turn the light out?"

"Yes."

"Good night."

I went into my room, placed the towel on the back of my chair, put on my extra-large gray T-shirt with the faded full-color image of Ernie Banks on the front.

I turned the night light to its lowest setting and got on the bed. I stayed on top of the covers, lay on my back, and clutched the extra pillow.

The room was bigger than my last one in the office building behind the Dairy Queen. I looked up at the angled ceiling.

I like small spaces when I sleep. This room wasn't large, but it was bigger than I liked. I would have slept in a closet were there one large enough to sleep in. I cannot sleep outdoors. I can't look up at the vastness of the sky without beginning to feel lost, like I'm about to be swept into the universe. This room was tolerable, but it would take some getting used to.

I lay without moving, looking upward, growing too tired to move, going over whether Ronnie Gerall had killed his father-in-law and why, and wondering if he had killed his wife and Blue Berrigan.

Thoughts of Sally Porovsky came and went like insistent faces of forgotten movie actors whose names just managed to stay out of reach.

Sometimes when I fall asleep, an idea comes, and I feel energized.

Usually, if I don't write down the idea, I'll lose it with the dawn. I did get an idea, then, or rather, a question. Why were all the Corkles paying me to save Ronnie?

His family would be better protected by having Ronnie locked away until he was too old to appreciate a handy dandy Corkle Electrostatic CD, LP, and DVD cleaner. I didn't write down my idea, but this time I remembered it. When I sat up in the morning, I heard my dark curtains open, saw bright morning light, and looked up at Greg Legerman and Winston Churchill Graeme.

"He's out," said Greg, handing me a

276

steaming Starbucks coffee.

"Who?"

"Ronnie. Who did you think I was talking about, Charlie Manson?"

"What time is it?"

"Almost nine," said Greg.

"I know Ronnie's out," I said. "Who let you in?"

"The Chinese guy," said Greg.

"He's Japanese," Winn Graeme said.

"He's Chinese," I said.

Greg took the only chair in the room and pulled it over to my bedside.

"You want your money back?" I said. "Fine."

"No, you need it. You live in near squalor."

"Greg," Winn warned.

Greg Legerman's response to the warning was to reach up and punch the other boy in the arm. Winn took it and looked at me.

"How long have you known old Ronnie?" I asked.

Greg thought about it, but Winn answered.

"He transferred to Pine View after his sophomore year. Came from Texas, San Antonio."

"He have a girlfriend?"

"Lots. He had a fake ID," said Greg. "Went out to bars, picked up women. Said he wasn't into high school girls. Why?"

"He ever mention Rachel Horvecki?"

"Horvecki's daughter? No," said Greg. "I don't remember. Why?"

"Have any idea where he might be now?"

I got up and went to the closet for a clean pair of jeans and a blue short-sleeved Polo pullover.

"No," said Winn.

"Any idea where your mother is?"

"My mother?"

"Your mother."

"No. Home. Shopping. Buying. I don't know. I don't keep track of her. Why do you want to know where my mother is?"

"Just a few questions I need to ask her."

"My mother?"

"Your mother."

"I said no. Have you found out who killed Horvecki yet?"

"No, but I will."

Greg had clasped his hands together and was tapping his clenched fist against his chin.

"You need more money?"

"More time," I said. "Now, it would be nice if you left."

"Sorry," said Winn.

He adjusted his glasses and reached over to urge his friend out of the chair.

"I've got more questions," said Greg.

"I can't give you answers now," I said. "Ronnie's out on bail."

Greg reluctantly rose from the chair, nodded a few times as he looked at me, then turned and, after a light punch to Winn's arm, went through the door. Winn Graeme hesitated, looked at me and whispered, "Nickel Plate Club."

Then he was gone. I stood listening while they opened the outer door and moved into the day.

I put on my Cubs cap and stepped into my outer room. Victor was sitting on the floor on his sleeping bag, a cardboard cup of coffee in his hand, looking up at one of the Stig Dalstroms on the wall.

A cup of coffee sat on my desk alongside a paper bag which contained a Chick-Fil-A breakfast chicken sandwich. I sat and began working on my breakfast. I put the coffee in my hand next to the one on my desk.

"I looked," he said.

"At . . ."

"Internet. Ronald Owen Gerall."

The door opened, and Ames came in bearing a Styrofoam cup of coffee. He nodded at Victor and handed the coffee to me. I put it alongside the others.

"I just had a visit from Winn and Greg," I said working on one of the coffees. "They think we haven't made any progress. Progress is overrated. Victor has some information for us about Ronnie."

"He is married," said Victor. "To Rachel Horvecki."

"That a fact?" Ames said, looking at me for an explanation for why we were listening to something we already knew.

"Ronald Owen Gerall spent a year in a California Youth Facility when he was sixteen. Assault."

That was new information.

"There's a little more," said Victor, showing more signs of life than I had ever seen in him before. "Because he was underage when he came to Sarasota and he claimed to have no living relatives, he needed someone to vouch for him, help him find a place to live, and accept responsibility."

"Who?"

"Sally Porovsky."

While Ames, riding shotgun, went off with Victor to try to find Ronnie Gerall, I went to Sally's office at Children and Family Services to do the same thing. I could have called to find out if she was in or off to see a client, but I didn't want to hear her say that she was too busy to see me. Besides, I don't like telephones. I don't like the silences when someone expects me to speak and I have nothing to say or nothing I want to say. I use them when I must, which seemed to be a lot more of the time.

I parked the Saturn in the lot off of Fruitville and Tuttle where Children and Families had its office. Then I picked up my ringing phone and opened it. It was Dixie.

"Your Ronnie Gerall problem just got a little more complicated."

"How?" I asked.

"Ronnie Gerall is dead."

"When?"

"Six years ago in San Antonio," Dixie said. "Which means . . ."

"Ronnie Gerall is not Ronnie Gerall. He stole a dead boy's identity."

"Looks that way," she said. "But there's more. I tried a search of the back issues of the San Antonio newspaper for a period a year before your Ronnie got here. I tried a match of the photograph of him in the Pine View yearbook."

"And?"

"Bingo, Bango, Bongo. Newspaper told me his name is Dwight Ronald Torcelli. He fled an indictment for felony assault. Then I did a search for Dwight Ronald Torcelli. He's twenty-six years old. His birthday's tomorrow. He'll be twenty-seven. Maybe you should buy him a cake or give him some Harry & David chocolate cherries."

"Is that a hint?"

"Hell yes. I love those things. Want me to keep looking?"

"Try Rachel Horvecki or Rachel Gerall," I said.

"They may have a license and a minister's approval, but they are definitely not married."

"I wonder if she knows that."

"Good luck investigating, Columbo."

We hung up, and I looked at the entrance to Building C of a complex of bored three-story office buildings that couldn't decide whether to go with the dirt-stained brick on the bottom half or the streaked once-white wooden slats on top. Building C was on the parking lot between A and D. There was a neatly-printed sign plunged into the dirt and grass in front of the space where I parked. The sign said there was an office suite available and that it was ideal for a professional business.

The offices were almost all occupied by dentists, urologists, and investment counselors who promised free lunches at Longhorn for those who wanted to attend an equally free workshop on what to do with their money. A four-man cardiology practice had recently moved out and into a building they had financed on Tuttle, about a mile away.

Cardiologists, cataract surgeons, specialists in all diseases that plagued the old and perplexed the young are abundant in Sarasota, almost as abundant as banks.

John Gutcheon was seated at the downstairs reception desk making a clicking sound with his tongue as he wrote on a yellow pad.

John was in his mid-thirties, blond, thin, and very openly gay. His sharp tongue protected him from those who might dare to attack his life choice, although he had told me once, quite clearly, that it was not a choice and it was not an echo. His homosexuality was a reality he had recognized when he was a child. There were those who accepted him and those who did not. And he had come to terms with that after many a disappointment.

"Still wearing that thing," he said, looking up at me and shaking his head. "Lewis, when will you learn the difference between an outrageous fashion statement and bad taste."

"I like the Cubs," I said.

"And I like sea bass but I don't wear it on my head. There are other ways of expressing your bad taste," he said.

"My wife gave me this cap," I said.

"And my cousin Robert wanted to give me an introduction to a predatory friend at a gay bar," he said. "I made the mistake of accepting that introduction. You could at least clean that abomination on your head."

"I'll do that," I said.

"Lewis, 'tis better to be cleanly bald than tastelessly chapeaued."

"I'll remember that."

"No, you won't, but I feel as compelled as a priestly exorcist to remind you."

"Sally in?" I asked.

"All in," he said folding his hands on the desk.

"How is your writing coming?"

"You remembered," he said with mock joy. "Well, thank you for asking. My writing career is at a halt while several online and one honest-to-God publisher decide whether it's worth continuing."

"Ronnie Gerall," I said.

He looked up. I had struck home.

"He . . . I can't discuss clients," he said, measuring his words careful. "Lawsuits. Things like that. You know."

"You've talked to me about lots of clients."

"Have I? Shouldn't have. She's in. I assume you didn't come to see me."

"You have a favorite first line of a novel?" I asked.

He pulled open a drawer of his desk and came up with a thin paperback with ragged pages. He opened the book and read: " 'Where's Papa going with that ax? said Fern to her mother as they were setting the table for breakfast.' "

"Stephen King?" I guessed.

He held up the book to show me its cover. *Charlotte's Web,* by E. B. White. Then he said, "Where's Lewis going with that ax?"

"No ax," I said.

"Liar," said Gutcheon.

"No," I said.

"Always a pleasure to talk to you," he said as I headed for the elevator.

The elevator rocked to the hum of a weary motor. I wasn't fully certain what I was doing here or what I expected when I talked to Sally. I had a lead. I was following it. At least that's what I told myself.

The elevator door opened slowly to a Wall Street stage, only the people in front of me in two lines of cubicles were dealing in human misery, not stocks and bonds and millions of dollars. It was a busy day for the caseworkers at Children and Families. There was no shortage of abuse, anger, and neglect.

A few of the dozen cubicles were empty, but most were occupied by a caseworker and at least one client. Almost all the clients were black. Sometimes the client was a tired parent or two. Some were sullen or indifferent, others were frightened. Some were children. The mornings were generally for taking in clients at the office. The afternoons and evenings were for home visits throughout the county. Sometimes the day was interrupted by a court appearance. Sometimes it was interrupted by something personal — personal to the life of the harried caseworker, something like Lew Fonesca.

Sally's back was to me. In the chair next to her desk sat an erect black man in a dark suit and red tie. In the man's lap was a neatly folded lightweight coat. He was about fifty and lean, with graying temples. He looked at me through rimless glasses. He reminded me of a sociology professor I had at the University of Illinois, a professor who, when he looked at me, seemed to be in wonder that such a mirthless silent specimen should have made it to his small classroom.

I stood silently while Sally went over a form in front of her. When she spoke, she had to raise her voice above the hubbub of voices around her.

"He's in school now?" she asked.

I stood back, knowing that she would eventually turn and see me, or her client would gaze at me again and catch her eye.

"Yes, he is. At least he is supposed to be."

His voice was deep, even.

"Thurgood is a good student?" Sally said, looking up from the form.

"When he goes to school, and if you should meet him, he will not answer to the name 'Thurgood.' His middle name is Marshall. Thurgood Marshall Montieth."

"He is," said Sally, "twelve years old."

"Soon to be thirteen," said Montieth. "And, if I may, I will encapsulate the data you have in front of you in the hope of speeding the process so I can get back to work. My name is Marcus Montieth. I'm forty-seven years of age. I am a salesman and floor manager at Joseph Bank clothing store in the Sarasota Mall. My wife is dead. Thurgood is my only child. He is a truant, a problem. He has run away four times. I do not beat him. I do not slap him. I do not deprive him of food. I do not try to instill in him a fear of God because I do not believe in a god or gods. My health is good, though there is a history of heart attack in my family."

"Thurgood is an only child?" asked Sally.

"And for that I would thank God were I to believe in one. May I ask you two questions?"

"Yes," said Sally.

"What can be done for my son, and why is that man hovering over our conversation?"

Sally turned enough in her desk chair to look over her right shoulder at me.

"Lewis, could you . . ." she began.

Something in the way I looked told her this was not one of my usual visits. Usually, I called before I came. Usually, I waited downstairs and listened to John Gutcheon while I waited for her to be free. Usually, there was no sense of urgency in my appearance. Usually, I did not hover near her cubicle.

"I'll be with you in a few minutes," she said.

I thought it unlikely she would ever be with me. I had let Sally Porovsky move into my life — no, to be fair, I had moved into hers — and let the ghost of Catherine begin to fade a little, but just a little.

"Mr. Montieth, when would it be possible for you to come back with Thurgood?"

"Please remember to call him Marshall. During the day he is supposedly in school.

In the evenings I work. He comes home to my sister Mae's apartment after school. I do get Wednesdays off."

"Wednesday after school?"

"Yes," he said. "Time?"

"Four-thirty," said Sally, reaching over to write in her desktop calendar.

"We will be here," he said rising.

He was tall, six-four or six-five, and when he passed me I expected a look of disapproval at my intrusion. He smiled in understanding, assuming *What? A fellow parent with a troubled child? A homeless creature in a baseball cap, some scratches on his face?*

"I've got a client coming in ten minutes, Lewis," she said.

I stepped forward but I didn't sit. She looked up at me.

"What is it?"

"Ronnie Gerall," I said. "When he supposedly transferred from San Antonio to Pine View, you vouched for him, signed papers of guardianship, found him a family to live with."

"Yes," she said. "Lewis, please sit."

Her full, round face was smooth, just a little pink, and definitely pretty. She was tired. Sally was tired much of the time.

I sat.

"What's your question?" she asked with a

smile that made it clear that she did not expect me to ask if she would run away with me to Genoa.

"Two questions to start," I said. "How did Ronnie Gerall get in touch with you? How old was he when he entered Pine View School for the Gifted?"

Sally blew out a puff of air as she leaned back in her chair and looked up at the white drop ceiling.

"A letter and records came from Ronnie's caseworker in San Antonio addressed to me. The caseworker said Ronnie's parents had recently been killed in a small plane crash and that Ronnie had no other relatives, though his father had once had a brother in Sarasota. There was a possibility that other relatives might be found. The records showed that Ronnie was sixteen when he arrived here.

"I called the number I'd been given," she said. "A woman answered, gave her name, said she was Ronnie's caseworker and had heard of me through an attorney who had moved to San Antonio a few weeks earlier. She didn't have his name, but could get it if I needed it."

"You were conned," I said.

"I know."

"Ronnie Gerall was twenty-five when he

came here," I said.

"Almost twenty-six," she said.

"His real name is Dwight Torcelli. When did you find out?"

"Two years later," she said. "Just before I met you. How did you find out?"

"Dixie."

Sally shook her head. She looked more tired than I had ever seen her.

"I was suspicious," she said. "Dwight Torcelli is a very good-looking, charming, smart, fast-talking young man. With my experience, you might think I wouldn't fall for things like this, but he took me in and made it clear that he was interested in me as someone other than a caseworker."

"And?" I said, knowing, almost welcoming yet another blow.

"I let him get close, not so close that we . . . but close. By that time I knew he wasn't a teenager. I should have turned him in, but he was persuasive, claimed he had never finished high school, that he wanted to go to college and . . ."

"Yes?" I said.

"By that time he was in his senior year. We saw each other once in a while, but we never . . ."

"I believe you."

"Don't," she said closing her eyes. "There

were two times, both in the last year. I . . .
I'm forty-three years old, two young children, a job that never stops, sad stories
around me all day and here was a young
man who reminded me of a very white-
toothed young James Dean."

"That's why you're moving?" I said.
"Because Torcelli is here?"

"That and the other things we talked
about."

We were silent for a while, looking at each
other.

"You think he killed Horvecki?"

"I don't know," she said. "Why would he?"

"He's married to Rachel Horvecki. She
inherits her father's money."

Sally looked over the top of her cubicle at
the ceiling.

"If Ronnie left Sarasota, would you stay?"
I asked.

"Probably not. I broke the rules, Lew,"
she said, turning in her chair and putting a
hand on my arm. "I'm sorry."

The phone rang. Sally picked it up and
said, "All right."

When she hung up, she said, "My next
appointment's here."

I stood.

"You know where I might find him?"

She pulled over the notepad on her desk,

paused to look at the framed photograph of her two kids, and jotted something down. Then she tore it from the pad and handed it to me.

"I'm really very good at what I do here," she said.

"I know."

"I'm sorry. Lew . . ."

"Yes."

"Get the son of a bitch."

I nodded, said nothing and left the cubicle. It was the first time I had heard her utter any epithet more harsh than "damn." I didn't want to run into Sally's next client or clients getting off the elevator. I didn't want to imagine what it would be like for Sally after our conversation. I took the stairs.

John Gutcheon looked up at me with sympathy. He knew.

"I'm sorry," he said.

Everybody seemed to be sorry, including me. I wondered how Gutcheon had found out about Dwight Torcelli and Sally, but I guessed that he had seen it in Dwight's triumph and Sally's guilt. He saw a lot going by as he sat behind that reception desk. Sometimes one learns more by sitting and watching than running and listening.

13

I called Ames.

"We've been parked outside Gerall's apartment," said Ames. "Nothing yet."

"That's not where he is," I said.

I told him where I was going and asked him to get there soon, and armed.

"You sound like someone hit you with an andiron."

"Yes," I said. "I know. I've got some things you should know. I'll tell you when I see you."

"Saturn needs more work," Ames said. "Best do it in the morning."

"Right," I said, and hung up.

Saturn, Mars, Jupiter, and the Earth all needed more work. The Universe needed more work. I tried to concentrate on a new metallic banging under the dashboard. It sounded like an angry elf had had enough of this rust of metal and motion. Up Tamiami Trail into Bradenton and a turn at

Forty-seventh. I parked at the address Sally had written for me. Gerall's car was there. So was a perfectly polished, sporty-looking new Mazda with all the bells and whistles one could buy, enjoy, and show off. I probably wasn't too late. He could have run away on foot. Unlikely. He could have taken a cab. Possible. Someone could have picked him up and taken him to another refuge. I sat and waited for Ames to arrive.

The apartment building was small, two stories, brick, in need of a serious blasting to reveal whatever color was under the dirty earth and etched-in dripping patterns from the building's old drains. The weight of leaves, brush, twigs, and tree branches gave the illusion of a sagging middle to the roof. A sign, as abused as the building, said that choice studio apartments were available in the Ponce De Leon Arms. The dried-up tiny fountain near the take-it-or-leave-it sign let tenants know they had not come to the right place if they were planning to live forever. What the building and the sign did say, without words, was, "If you're low on the pole and looking for what you can get by on, this is as good a place as any."

Victor pulled his car in behind mine and remained behind the wheel, while Ames got out wearing his weathered yellow duster.

"I'll go in first. You stand outside his door," I said.

Ames nodded in understanding. We crunched over a layer of dead and dying yellow, orange, and black leaves dropped by two massive native oak trees. The entryway door of the building was open. The small foyer, tiled in cracked, ancient squares, had nothing to offer but a bank of twelve mailboxes, one of which hung open, and a collection of flyers and giveaway newspapers promising two slices of flavorless pizza for the price of one. The apartment marked GERALL was number seven.

We went through the inner door, also open, and down the narrow, carpeted corridor to apartment seven. Someone inside was talking. I could have strained to pick up some of the conversation. The voices belonged to a man and a woman.

I knocked.

The people inside the apartment stopped talking and went silent.

"Who is it?" came Ronnie's voice.

"Police," Ames said.

The room went silent. The pause was long.

"Police," Ames repeated. "Open it or step out of the way."

The lock was unbolted as Ames stepped back against the corridor wall where he couldn't be seen unless Dwight Torcelli or whoever was inside stepped out to look. The door opened slightly more than a crack.

"Fonesca?"

"Who is it?" a woman's voice from inside the room asked.

"Not the police," Torcelli said.

"May I come in, Dwight?" I asked.

"How did you find . . . ?"

He stopped after quickly and silently going through the very short list of those who would know about this second apartment and his real name.

"Sally," he said.

"May I come in?" I asked again.

He stepped back to let me enter and closed the door behind me. Alana Legerman stood in the center of the room next to the bed on which a large brown cloth suitcase stood open. It looked full and ready to be closed.

"Sally who?" asked Alana.

"My caseworker," he said.

His denim pants were tan, pressed, creased, and tight fitting. His shirt was a Polo pullover, green and white stripes, and not tight fitting.

"We're in a hurry here, Mr. Fonesca," Alana said.

"I'll bet you are. Bail jumping, especially

on a murder charge, can make someone move in a hurry. You're going to lose a lot of money."

"I can afford it," she said. "You plan to tell anyone?"

"Yes, the police."

She motioned to Torcelli to close the suitcase. He did and pulled the cracked leather straps tight.

"You still work for me, Mr. Fonesca," she said.

"I resign. Job-related stress."

"I have a secret you may wish to know before you make a decision," she said.

"You're really his mother," I said, nodding at Torcelli.

"No," she said, pausing to show that she didn't appreciate my attempt at humor at her expense. "You stole something from my father."

"What?" asked Torcelli.

"I don't know," she said. "He just told me Fonesca and the old man he hangs around with broke into the house and stole something."

"The old man is my partner," I said. "His name is Ames McKinney. And a copy of what we stole is here."

I took the folded pieces of paper from my pocket and handed them to her.

"We have to go," Torcelli said while she looked at what I had handed her.

"I find people for a living," I said. "I'm good at it. It may be the only thing I'm good at. I could find you no matter where you go, and so could the police."

"Not true," he said, folding his arms and standing erect with his arms folded. "Alana, those things in your hand are fakes. He's . . ."

She held up a hand to indicate that she wanted him quiet while she looked over the papers. After no more than two minutes she handed me the documents and spoke.

"Two questions, and I expect the truth: First, are you really twenty-seven years old? Second, are you married?"

The answer was a long time coming, and he looked at me with something less than friendship before answering.

"Yes, and no," he said. "I am twenty-seven years old. At least I will be tomorrow."

"Happy Birthday," she said, folding her arms across her chest."

"I can explain why I . . ."

"Are you married?"

"No," he said. "I was. She died."

"You married Philip Horvecki's daughter," I said. "Is she dead?"

"No."

Alana Legerman was freeze-framed in a look of disappointment which turned to anger and then to acceptance with a shake of the head.

"Alana," he said. "You know I love you."

"You love me? Who are you?"

"His name is Dwight Torcelli," I said.

"Mr. Fonesca, do you have any objection to my leaving?" she asked.

"No."

"I won't be missing anything else I should know?"

"No."

"Good. Don't let him get away. Good-bye."

"If you let me . . . ," he began, but he didn't finish because she was out the door and gone.

I wondered what she would make of Ames in the hallway with a shotgun. There was no scream. I heard no voices through the thin door.

"I didn't kill Horvecki or anyone," he said. "I swear. Believe me."

"What I believe doesn't matter."

"You're taking me back to jail."

"But not to juvenile. You're an adult. We'll let the district attorney's office figure it all out."

"No," he said. "When you give them those

documents about me, I probably won't even be able to get a public defender who believes I didn't kill Horvecki."

I wanted to ask him about Sally, but I didn't. He would either lie or tell the truth, and both would hurt.

"Let's go," I said.

"No," he repeated.

"Suit yourself. Run, hide. Maybe Alana Legerman won't turn you in. Maybe she really won't care about losing the bond money. Maybe."

I stepped away from the door. He picked up his suitcase and moved toward me.

"Step away," he said.

I stepped away, but something I couldn't control came over me. I moved in and punched him in the nose as hard as I could. I felt bone break and electric frozen pain in my knuckle.

There was no satisfaction in throwing the punch. It just felt like something I had to do.

He let out a groan and dropped the suitcase. Blood gushed from his nose. Rage was in his eyes and his fists were clenched. He was almost twenty years younger than I. I was in good shape from my almost daily workouts at the downtown YMCA, but I was probably not a match for him. The one thing I was sure of was that I could take whatever he threw and keep on coming. I didn't know how much he was willing to take.

"You lunatic," he screamed, doing nothing to stop the blood.

He looked like a much different person from the one who had opened the door. This was not a young James Dean sans mustache. This was Mr. Hyde played without his hair draped haphazardly down his forehead. His now inflamed nose suggested drunkenness. His eyes were wide and wild.

"You broke in here and tried to kill me," he said.

I knew where this was going. I took a step toward him. A gun, a small gun, appeared in his right hand. He wiped blood from his nose with the back of his left hand.

"You told me that someone hired you to kill me," he said. "Maybe Corkle."

"Might work," I said. "But probably not."

He was flexing his grip on the gun which was now aimed at my stomach.

"Why aren't you scared?" he almost screamed.

"Nothing you'd understand," I said. "Lift the gun a little if your plan is to hit my heart."

"You are a lunatic," he said.

His gun hand moved down so that it was now aimed at the floor. That was when Ames came in, shotgun at the ready and aimed at Torcelli who took a step back.

"You okay?" Ames asked me. "You've got blood on you."

"His," I said.

"I'm the one hurt," Torcelli said, pointing to himself to be sure we knew who and where the injured party was.

"Put your little gun down," said Ames, "and we'll get that bleeding stopped."

Torcelli placed the gun on the bed.

Ames asked, "What happened?"

"He punched me. No warning. Just punched me in the nose," said Torcelli.

Ames looked at me and before saying, "That a fact?"

"Yes," said Torcelli. "It's a fact. I'm running out of blood."

"Let's go save your life," said Ames. "Where's the bathroom?"

"There," said Torcelli, bloody shirt pulled up to his nose.

Ames touched my shoulder as he followed Torcelli through a door. Then I heard running water. Then my legs began to shake. There was a chair against the wall next to the door. I managed to sit. My hands were trembling now. Was it because Torcelli had almost shot me? No, that didn't feel right. It was because I had felt something uncontrollable and powerful when I hit him. The operative word being "felt." *Feeling,* strong emotion had come back, if only for a few seconds. I almost didn't recognize it. I know I didn't like it. I didn't like it at all.

When they came back in the room, Torcelli was holding a towel to his nose. His voice was muffled, but I could understand him.

"You could have driven bone into my brain," he said.

"You'll be fine," said Ames, standing behind him.

"Yeah," said Torcelli, sitting on the bed.

"Why did you do it?" I asked.

He took the towel from his face and looked at it to see if his nose had stopped bleeding. It hadn't.

"I didn't kill anyone," he said.

"No, everything else."

"It's a long story."

"Make it short," said Ames.

"What am I going to look like?" Torcelli asked. "I have to look good. It's what I've got."

"Story," Ames said.

Towel to nose, he turned to look at Ames over his shoulder then back at me.

"I met Horvecki's daughter in San Antonio. I was working in a Sharper Image store in a mall. She came in. She was visiting a fellow high school friend from Pine View. We started to talk. I said we should talk more. So we made a date for that night. And the next. And the next. I learned that her father was rich. Her father was a jerk. No way he would just accept me."

"You had already discussed marriage?" I asked.

"We applied for the license the second week I knew her."

"Love?"

"On her part. I've done some acting. I was convincing. I got the idea of using information she had given me to persuade Horvecki to give me a job and pay me at a level that would suit his son-in-law."

"That didn't work, did it?" I asked.

"He said that he had another idea. I'd have to register as a high school student at Pine View. He would handle the paperwork. All I had to do was gather examples of how the school was screwing up. He said he wanted to bring down Pine View and the Bright Futures program. I'm sure he also wanted to see how low I would sink to be sure Rachel and I would inherit his money. He had hired a detective to look into my past. He insisted that I change my name, even told me how to do it and how to get a convincing set of documents that established me as Ronald Gerall, a transfer student in very good standing. He said he'd provide us with enough money to keep us comfortable while I accomplished what he demanded."

"You brought these documents to Sally," I said.

"I did."

"What about running from a grand jury in Texas?" I asked.

"A mistake."

"A mistake Horvecki used to keep you in line."

"One of them. Maybe I should see a doctor about this nose. The blood is still coming."

Ames produced a dry towel from behind his back and handed it to Torcelli, who dropped the bloody one on the floor and pressed the fresh one to his nose.

"Thanks."

"Welcome."

"Sally authenticated these documents," I said.

"With a little friendly persuasion," Ronnie said.

I should have been able to muster enough

anger to at least consider another punch to Ronnie's expanded red-and-purple nose, but I found nothing to call on. Hitting him again would not take care of what I was now feeling.

"Last question," I said. "If you get it right, you win the prize."

"Okay," he said.

"What really happened the night Horvecki died?"

"I called him, told him I wanted to see him, that he was screwing me around, that he was just trying to stall until he could get rid of me, poison Rachel against me. I told him I was coming over. He said, 'Not now. I've got a friend visiting.' "

"Did he sound like he meant it?"

"He smirked," Ronnie said.

"Over the phone?" I asked.

"Yes. Philip Horvecki was good at that."

"Go on."

"When I got there, the front door was open. I went in. Someone was going out the window. Horvecki was on the floor. I could see he was dead. Rachel was in the bedroom doorway. Horvecki was on the floor. I told Rachel to get out of the house, get down to Main Street."

"Why?" Ames asked.

"I panicked," he said. "I had to almost

push her out. She went, and I ran after her, looking for whoever had gone through the window."

"You didn't see anyone?" I asked.

"I did," he said. "There was someone in a pickup truck across the street. I had seen him when I went into the house. I thought he was waiting for someone in one of the other houses. I told you all this."

"We like hearing it," said Ames.

"I went back in the house. I was sure Horvecki was dead, but I went over to him to be sure. I've seen people beaten, but nothing like this. His face was a mess. A bone in his left arm was pushed through the skin. I started to get up to call 911. The door opened. Two cops were pointing guns in my face. Find Rachel. Find the guy in the pickup truck. Rachel and the guy in the truck both saw the killer go through the window. That's the story. It's true."

"You believe him?" I asked Ames.

"Some."

"It's the truth. Oh, shit. Is this a piece of bone?"

He pinched a small piece of something between his thumb and nearby finger and held it up.

"Can't tell," said Ames. "Maybe."

"I'm going to need a plastic surgeon,"

Ronnie said.

"Probably, but you can afford one now," I said. "If Horvecki really left his money to his daughter."

"That do it for here?" asked Ames.

I nodded. Ames helped Torcelli to his feet.

"I'm still out on bail."

"I don't think the police are going to want you out on the streets of Sarasota, or Rio, or Brussels," I said. "We've got a place you can stay for a while."

"You're taking me in," he said.

"No, not yet," I said. "We're taking you somewhere safe."

"You'll be safe," Ames said.

"Safe from what?"

"From whoever it is who's going to try to kill you. My guess is that if he or she catches you, you'll decide to commit suicide," I said.

"Why would I kill myself?"

"Guilt over killing your father-in-law," I said.

"Remorse," said Ames.

"Case closed," I added.

"The killer will try to make it look like I killed myself?"

"That's what I would do," I said. "Tell us about Blue Berrigan."

"The clown?" he asked, examining the second blood-drenched towel. "I told you before. I don't know anything about who killed him. I didn't. Why would I?" He paused to look at us. "You're going to find the killer and keep me out of jail?"

"At least for a day or two, if we can," I said. "Ames, I forgot the introduction. This is Dwight Torcelli."

"Can't say I'm pleased to meet you," Ames said.

"Okay. I'm sure Alana will get me a real lawyer. I can talk her into it. She'll calm down. Now, will you please take care of my nose."

I wasn't as sure as he was about Alana Legerman coming up with money for a lawyer.

14

He wasn't wearing his uniform when he came through my door that night. The door had been locked, but Essau Williams was a cop. There are many ways to get through a locked door, short of breaking it down. Besides, most people carefully lock their doors at night but leave their windows open with only a thin screen to protect them.

I was lying in bed, my eyes closed, my reading lamp still burning on the chair next to my bed. I had fallen asleep with a book on my chest. The book was a list of boys' names and their meaning. Lewis means "fame and war." I hadn't looked up Essau.

He grabbed me by my blue Chicago cubs sweatshirt with the sleeves cut off and lifted me from the bed. We were face-to-face. There was no anger in his face. There was nothing but frigid appraisal. Before he had come in, and before I fell asleep, I was considering a last stop in the restroom. Now

I had to pee. I had to pee very badly. I did not tell him.

"I did not kill Horvecki," he said.

"Okay," I said.

"The Gerall kid did it. Don't come to my house again."

I didn't answer. I had nothing to say.

"You understand?"

"Yes," I said.

"Say what you've got to say," Essau said.

He hadn't addressed that to me but to someone I now made out in the darkness near the door. Jack Pepper, Reverend of the Self-Proclaimed Ministers of God, stepped forward.

"Do you know who killed Philip Horvecki?" asked Pepper, every bit as calm as Essau Williams who stepped back from me but continued wearing a look of menace. He had it down. He was playing bad cop to Pepper's good Reverend. Or maybe he wasn't playing.

"Was it Ronald Gerall?"

"I don't think it was Gerall."

"If you discover who the person was who killed the bastard of hell, you will call one of us," said Pepper stepping forward. "But it might be best if no one finds out who did it. You understand?"

"Yes."

"But if you find the avenging angel —," Pepper began.

"I call you so you can do what?" I asked.

"Protect him," said Pepper. "The killing was not murder. Whoever did it, it was an execution. You find him. You tell us. You go about your business. You understand?"

I nodded, but the nod was too small and went unseen in the darkness.

"Understood?" asked Essau Williams.

"Yes," I said.

"Good," said Pepper.

"No," I said. "I understand, but I won't do it."

Essau Williams got a one-handed grip on my already crumpled shirt.

"You could have lied to us," said Pepper. "You're an honest man. But honesty is not always its own reward."

"I have a question," I said.

"Yes?" asked Pepper.

"How did you two team up?"

"In search of retribution from the system of men," said Pepper, "we've encountered each other through the years in our several attempts at trying to seek justice for our families and punishment for Philip Hor-vecki."

"Find him, tell us," said Essau.

"We decided that neither of us would

exact physical retribution," Pepper continued ignoring Essau Williams. "But if someone were to do so, we would put the full
extent of our gratitude toward him and pray
for the mercy of Jesus upon him."

"*You* would pray for the mercy of Jesus,"
Essau Williams amended.

"What will you do?" asked Pepper, now
only a few feet from me.

"Get a lock for my door," I said.

Silence. I prepared to be hit, as well as
anyone can prepare. The instant the blow
came I would go with it, fall back. Then
again, Essau Williams might simply decide
to strangle me.

"You're not afraid," Pepper said.

"No."

"You know you are in the hands of Jesus,"
said Pepper.

"No."

"Then . . . ?" Pepper asked.

"I have another question," I said.

"What?" asked Pepper.

"Do you have a favorite first line from a
book?"

" 'Behold, I send my messenger before thy
face, which shall prepare thy way before
thee. Prepare ye the way of the Lord, make
his paths straight.' The Gospel according to
St. Mark."

"You left out a little," I said.

"What the fuck is this?" Williams said. "Are you both crazy?"

"I was going to ask the same thing," I said.

"We have a damn good reason if we are, Philip Horvecki. What's your damn good reason?"

"There's someone in the dark," I said.

"What is that supposed to mean?" Williams said.

"Me," came the voice from the door.

Victor Woo had entered while they were doing their best to intimidate me.

Williams and Pepper turned toward the door. Victor flipped on the light switch. He was barefoot, wearing clean jeans and an orange University of Illinois sweatshirt with the sleeves rolled up. In his right hand was the old aluminum softball bat I'd found in the closet when I moved in here.

I could see now that Williams was also wearing jeans. His long-sleeve T-shirt was solid blue. Pepper, pale, his straw hair slightly tousled, wore brown slacks and a white shirt and tie. I wore my underpants with the penguins and my Cubs sweatshirt with the cut-off sleeves. No one wore a smile.

"Victor batted leadoff for two Tigers farm teams," I said.

I might analyze that instant lie sometime later with Ann Hurwitz. Anyway, it didn't seem to have any effect on my visitors.

"We've said what we have to say," Pepper said calmly.

"You can put the bat down, Jet Li," said Essau Williams.

Victor moved away from the door so they could pass. Pepper went out first. Williams paused at the door and said, " 'Once upon a time, there were three bears, a papa bear, a momma bear, and a baby bear.' A favorite first line. My mother used to tell me that one when I was a baby. That was long after Philip Horvecki raped her and my aunt, and long before he came back eight years ago and turned her and my aunt into cowering old women and ended my family's history."

He closed the door behind him. Victor followed them out to be sure they left and then returned, bat still in hand.

"Tea?" he asked.

"Sure," I said. "You?"

"I don't like tea," he said. "But I have Oreo cookies and milk."

"That'll work for me."

We woke Dwight Torcelli, who was sleeping on a blanket in the room next to mine. Victor had been in that room, too, lying on his bedroll in front of the door to keep Torcelli from deciding to wander. There was a strip of white tape across his swollen nose. The skin under both of his eyes had turned purple. I almost apologized, but I wouldn't have meant it.

"What?" he asked sitting up, blinking, not sure of where he was, and then slowly understanding.

"You had visitors," I said. "You missed them. Victor and I are going to have Oreo cookies and milk. Want to join us?"

"I guess," he said, looking at me and then at Victor, who still bore his softball bat.

I was reasonably sure now who was responsible for the death of both Philip Horvecki and Blue Berrigan. When I got up in the morning, I'd share my thoughts with Ames.

I checked the clock when we went back into the room where my desk sat. It was almost three in the morning.

We had cookies and milk.

I was up by six. I showered, shaved, shampooed what little hair I have remaining with a giant container of no-name shampoo-conditioner purchased at a dollar store, and examined the scratches on my face. It didn't look as bad as I thought it would. I certainly looked better than Jeff Augustine.

317

I was dressed in my jeans and a fresh green short-sleeve knit shirt with a collar. It didn't go well with my blue and red Cubs cap, but I had no plans for meeting royalty. If I did run into any, I could tuck my cap away. Lewis Fonesca was prepared for anything except intruders, unbidden emotions, disarming surprises, life's horrors, and the pain and death of others.

When Ames and Darrell Caton walked in together just before eight, I was eating an Oreo cookie with the full understanding that I would have to brush my teeth again.

"Met him downstairs," Ames explained.

"Takes me a while to get up the stairs since I got shot with an Uzi," said Darrell.

"It was a pellet gun," Ames said.

"Shot is shot," said Darrell. "I can't go around telling people I was in the hospital for three days because I was shot in the back with a BB."

"Guess not," said Ames.

It was obvious Ames and Darrell liked each other, though I couldn't quite figure out what the essence of that friendship might be.

"Cookies?" I asked.

Both Darrell and Ames took one.

"He safe?" asked Ames, pointing at the door of the second bedroom.

"Victor's in there with him," I said.

"With who?" asked Darrell.

"Visitor," I said.

"You're my big brother, big sister, uncle, Santa, whatever," said Darrell. "You're supposed to tell me things. Share confidences, you know?"

"You're getting a bit old to have a big brother," said Ames. "And what are you doing roaming the streets when you're supposed to be in bed."

"Okay," said Darrell, "we'll call it even. Then we're . . ."

"Friends," said Ames.

"Friends," I agreed.

"Sometimes I think my mother would rather have me hang with safer friends, like drug dealers and gangbangers."

I offered him another cookie. He took it. Ames decided one was enough.

"Let's get some breakfast," Ames said. "We can bring something back for Victor and our guest."

"You two are playing with me," Darrell said. "That's it, right?"

"No," I said. "Let's go downstairs slowly and walk over to the Waffle Shop and I'll tell you the story about two night visitors."

"No," said Darrell, "I know that one. Amal and camels. I know that shit."

"This one," I said, "is about different night visitors. I think you'll both like it."

"Okay," said Darrell. "Let's get waffles."

It was Saturday morning, bright, sunny, cloudless, Floridian-winter cool. No one shot at us as we walked down the stairs, Ames in front, Darrell second, me in the rear. Darrell moved slowly, wincing, trying to cover it. We were only two blocks from the Waffle Shop but I suggested we drive. Darrell said no.

When we entered the Waffle Shop it was crowded, but a family of four was just getting up from a table at the front window. We waited, then sat, and I pretended to look at the menu, which both Ames and I had long ago memorized.

Greg Legerman and Winn Graeme came in about two minutes later, looked around, saw us, and headed for our table.

Greg and Winn stood next to our table. Greg's arms were folded over his chest, his look a demand before he spoke.

"Where is he?" he asked.

"Greg, Winn, this is Darrell Caton," I said by way of introduction. "He was shot and almost killed on the steps of my office a few days ago."

For a beat they both looked at Darrell who

held out his hand. First Greg, and then Winn, took the extended hand.

"They look kind of shook," said Darrell first to me and then to Ames. "One of them shoot me?"

"Possible," said Ames.

"This won't work," said Greg. "You are working for everyone in my family and you owe me the information first. We're worried about Ronnie."

"We?" I asked.

Greg and Winn had to pull in close to the table as one of Gwen's daughters came by with an armful of platters, calling, "Out of the way."

"We," Greg repeated. "Me, Winn, my mother, my grandfather. We."

"Find a seat," the now-platterless waitress said just above the patter of the other customers.

She said it with a smile, a warm voice, and a hand on Winn's shoulder, but it was a command.

"Sit," Ames said.

They sat, losing the supposed advantage of our looking up at them.

"I'll be right back for your order," the daughter said. "Coffee?"

"Yes," said Greg.

"Orange juice," said Winn.

"How'd you know Ames and I were here?" I asked.

"Went to your place," Greg said. "Your car, the Chinese guy's car, and the old cowboy's scooter were there. The Chinese guy wouldn't let us in, said you were out for breakfast, so we . . ."

"His name is Victor," said Ames. "Victor Woo. Mr. Woo till he tells you to call him otherwise."

Ames was calm, but I knew by the number of words he had used that he was not pleased by our new breakfast companions. The only one who had spoken less was Winn Graeme, who sat reasonably erect and adjusted his glasses.

"We didn't mean any disrespect," said Greg. "I'm a flaming all-inclusive open-the-borders liberal. Right, Winn?"

He gave Winn a shoulder pop with his fist. Winn nodded to confirm Greg's political assessment.

"My mother bailed Ronnie out," Greg said. "We all hired you. We want to know what's going on."

"His name isn't Ronnie," I said.

"What?" asked Greg.

"His name is Dwight Torcelli," I said. "He's twenty-six years old and he's married to Philip Horvecki's daughter."

Greg looked stunned. Winn sat silently. It was time again to adjust his glasses.

"Your mother wants to know where he is?" asked Ames.

Greg looked at Ames as if Ames had not been paying attention.

"My mother . . ."

He was interrupted by Gwen's daughter bringing breakfast for Darrell, Ames, and me, orange juice for Winn and coffee for whoever wanted it. Darrell, Ames, and I were all having the waffle special with eggs and three slices of bacon.

"Go ahead," said Greg. "We don't mind if you eat."

He said the last part of this after the three of us had already begun to eat.

"Okay," came a shout above the voices and clattering plates and cups. "Listen up."

Two tables from us, a trucker in a blue baseball cap and a denim vest over his T-shirt was standing and waiting for attention. His beard was just beyond stubble and he looked more than serious.

"My friend here says Elvis never ate here, that Gwen's mother just put up that poster and the sign."

"That's right," said the friend, now standing.

He was shorter than the other guy but in

better shape, biceps like cement.

"February 21, 1956, Elvis played the Florida Theater in Sarasota," said Winn aloud. "He had breakfast here on the morning of February 22 and headed immediately for an appearance that night in Waycross, Georgia."

The breakfast crowd applauded.

"The kid don't know *shit,*" the muscled trucker said, with a special emphasis on the word "shit."

The restaurant went silent.

Gwen's other daughter, the one with two babies and another on the way, was behind the counter where I usually had breakfast.

"You calling my family liars?" she said.

"My grandfather was here when Elvis came in," said Winn.

"Bullshit," said the trucker.

"His grandfather's still alive and almost ninety-five," added Greg. "Reverend Graeme of the First Episcopalian Church of Christ the Redeemer would, I'm sure, be happy to come by and settle this."

People began to applaud and laugh. The defeated trucker mumbled a few obscenities and sat down as the first trucker raised a hand in historic triumph.

"Your grandfather really in here when Elvis came in?" asked Darrell.

"Don't see how he could have been," said Greg. "He was in Korea."

"Yes," said Winn.

"And," added Greg, favoring his friend with another punch in the arm, "he's dead and he wasn't Reverend Graeme. He was Russell Graeme, co-owner of Graeme-Sydney Chrysler Motors in Sydney, Australia."

Greg was grinning.

Darrell mumbled something to himself and went on eating. I was sitting next to him and heard, though no one else did.

"Rich white kids," Darrell had said.

"That the truth about Ronnie?" asked Winn.

"Truth," I said.

"Why do you want to find him?" asked Ames.

"To talk to him about getting a new lawyer," Greg said leaning forward. "My grandfather said he'll pay to get the best available defense team in the nation. The plan was for us to set it up with Ronnie and you keep looking for whoever killed Horvecki. But he's not Ronnie. I don't understand."

"What about Berrigan?" asked Ames.

"Berrigan?" asked Greg.

Gwen's daughter, the one who had waited

on us, touched Winn's shoulder and quietly said, "Your breakfasts are all on the house."

Then she moved away to the waving hand of a customer who wanted more coffee or his check.

"Blue Berrigan," I said.

"What kind of name is that?" asked Greg.

"Dead man's," said Ames.

Winn Graeme's eyes were closed for an instant. Then he removed his glasses, opened his eyes and put the glasses back on.

"The singer?" he asked.

I nodded.

"Where? When did he . . . ?" asked Greg.

"Day ago," said Ames. "Beaten in his car."

Darrell was giving his full attention to the conversation now.

"Who is Blue Bennignan?" Darrell asked.

"Berrigan," Winn corrected. "I used to watch his show when I was a kid. My mother took me to see him when he was at the Opera House in Sydney when I was six."

"You going to cry?" Greg asked his friend in disbelief before looking around the table to see if anyone else found this particularly bizarre. No one seemed to.

"I know a guy in a gang in Palmetto called Black Brainbanger," said Darrell. "And there's a whore up on the Trail goes by Red

326

Alice because . . ."

"Her hair's red?" said Ames.

"You know her?" asked Darrell.

Ames took it and Darrell laughed.

"Got you, old cowboy," Darrell said.

Ames gave a small shake of his head. No one joined the laughter.

Darrell looked and me and said, "I'm just breaking it down and bringing it down Fonesca. Lightening it up, you know what I'm saying?"

Unordered breakfasts for both Greg and Winn arrived, the same thing all of us had.

"Anything Ronnie needs?" asked Greg.

"His name is Dwight Torcelli," Winn said.

"The best criminal defense attorney in the United States would help," I said.

We ate for a while, and I thought in silence.

Then Darrell whispered to me, "You don't need more money? I do. Rich white boys probably have their pockets full of twenties. You take it, give it to me. I keep a little and give the rest to my mother."

I shook my head, but it didn't stop him. He whispered to me as he finished his breakfast.

"I took a bullet in the back for you, Fonesca," he said.

"Pellet," I said. "Maybe you were the one

being shot at."

"People from my part of town don't use pellets and BBs after they're five years old. They don't shoot people with toys. Someone after me'd have a serious weapon."

"Because you're so bad?" I asked.

"No," he said. "I'm just saying."

"You didn't tell people you got shot with a pellet gun."

"Hell no."

After we were finished with breakfast, Greg and Winn stood, and Greg said, "You'll let me know?"

"I'll let you know," I said, though at this point I wasn't sure about what it was I would be letting him know about.

"Sorry," said Winn, though at this point I wasn't completely sure what it was he was sorry about.

When they left, Ames finished a second cup of coffee and said, "Smart boys."

I wasn't sure how he meant it, and I wasn't going to ask him to explain.

We picked up carryout breakfasts for Victor and Torcelli. The same truckers we had seen earlier were in line behind us at the cash register.

The one with muscles and, I could now see, fading tattoos on his arms, said to

Ames, "Your grandkids cost me forty bucks."

I touched Ames's arm in the hope that he wouldn't respond, but he said, "Cost yourself forty dollars."

"Not the way I see it," said the trucker.

"Let it go, Ben," said the trucker who had won the bet.

"You let it go, Teek. Easy for you. You won. Way I see it, old bones here owes me."

It was our turn to pay now. I handed over cash for the carry-out to Gwen's daughter at the register. She pushed it back to me.

"Ames owes you shit," said Darrell. "Right, Fonesca?"

"Right," I said.

"Mess with Ames, he'll shoot your ass," Darrell said. "Mess with Fonesca he'll break your nose. Ames shot and killed a man and Fonesca just broke a fool's nose."

"That a fact?" said Ben the trucker with the biceps.

"Fact," Darrell said.

The trucker reached for Darrell. Ames put his arm in the way.

"You want to take this outside," said Ames. "I'll accommodate."

I led our happy band out the door.

"Parking lot," said Ben.

"I'm having no part," said Teek.

When we got to the parking lot next to the restaurant, Ames opened his jacket so Ben could see an old, but very large, well cleaned, and shining pistol tucked into his belt.

"Bullshit," said Ben, now glaring. He took a step toward Ames, who calmly removed the weapon from his belt and fired into the ground at the trucker's feet.

"Another step and you'll be on your way to the emergency room," said Ames.

"He means it," I said.

Ben backed away three steps and raised a fist, but didn't say anything.

Teek took Ben's arm and started to pull him away.

"Crazy old fucker," said Ben, looking over his shoulder as he wisely allowed himself to be escorted from the lot.

I didn't ask either trucker if they had a favorite first line from a book.

"You did him, Ames," said Darrell holding up his right hand for a high five, which Ames didn't deliver.

"Best we go now," Ames said.

"Best," I agreed.

15

"I'm not an unreasonable man," Horvecki said, professionally looking at the camera and away from the SNN interviewer.

He was looking directly at me as I sat in my room with Ames, Darrell, Victor, and Ronnie watching the DVD Greg Legerman had given me.

Horvecki had the raspy voice of a smoker and a haunted look. He was slightly frail and definitely on the verge of being old. He had a well-trimmed, close-cropped head of dyed black hair and the slightly blotched skin of a man who had spent too many hours outside without benefit of sunblock.

"I pay taxes — a hell of a lot of taxes to this country, this state, and this county," he said, looking back at the interviewer, a pretty young brunette who couldn't have been more than twenty-two and who was definitely uncomfortable as she tried to control the interview. "So do thousands of other people who don't have children in school, don't have grandchildren in school. We pay to give a third-rate education to kids who aren't even ours, and no one gives us a choice. Well, I'm fighting for that choice."

"But this is a matter of funding a much-needed program for gifted students," the young woman tried.

"So all students aren't created equal?" he said. "Some get a better education. No one asked me what I thought about that. Did they ask you? Your parents? Did you go to Pine View?"

"No," the girl said protectively, "I went to Riverview."

"Education should be paid for by parents and anyone who wants to give money," Horvecki said. "I don't want to give money for the children of the people who should be paying."

"And Bright Futures?" she asked.

"Same thing," he said. "A big, phony boondoggle. Take lottery money and tax money and give it to smart kids instead of distributing it evenly among all the kids who want to go to college."

"That's what you believe, that the money that — ?"

"I don't think there should be any Bright Futures program or any Pine View School funded by my BLEEP money."

"So?" she asked.

He turned again to face the camera and said, "Vote no on the funding referendum."

Cut to a silver-haired man behind a desk with sheets of paper in his hand.

"Philip Horvecki," he said. "Man on a mission with a gift for making political enemies and a record of convincing voters in the past fifteen years to vote for his self-named Self Interest Initiative Voters Alliance."

The television screen went gray with thin white fizzling lines.

Darrell reached over, ejected the disk and turned off the television.

"See," said Torcelli. "That man was a monster."

"Your father-in-law," said Ames. "Your wife's father."

"Yes," Torcelli said, touching the bandage on his nose to be sure it was still there.

"So you went to see him because of your commitment to Bright Futures," I said.

"Yes," he said.

"Nothing to do with your wanting to be his true son and heir?" said Ames.

"A little, maybe, but does that negate what I was trying to do?"

"A little, maybe," Ames said.

"I'm a con man, a fraud, an opportunist, a —"

"Asshole," said Darrell.

"All right," Torcelli conceded, "but if you came from the background I had —"

"Wrong road to go down with me," said Darrell. "I'll take you home for the night, and we'll tour my neighborhood. We'll play Mr. Rogers. And check out Fonesca's tale. His —"

"Where is your wife?" I interrupted.

Torcelli shook his head to show that none of us understood the weight of his life or the toll it had taken.

"She's not well," he said.

"Sorry to hear that. Where is she?" I asked again.

He looked past us out the window at the slightly fluttering leaves of the tree outside.

"Want to have Viviase ask the same question?" I said. "He might add a few questions about your friendship with his daughter."

"She's a kid," he said.

"Your wife or Viviase's daughter?"

"My wife is staying at the Ocean Terrace Resort Hotel on Siesta Key," he said. "Waiting for her father's lawyer to tell us what she's inherited."

"You told us you didn't know where she

was," I said.

"You said you wanted us to find her to give you an alibi," Ames said.

"I did. I did, but I wanted to protect her. I was confused and you were . . ." He put his head in his hands.

"She's registered under the name Olin. I'll call her and tell her to talk to you."

"Don't call," said Ames.

"You got anything to eat in the refrigerator?" asked Darrell.

"You just had breakfast," said Ames.

"I'm still growing and I need food to keep me going. I was shot and almost dead. Remember that?"

"You plan on letting us forget it some time?" asked Ames.

"Hell no," said Darrell.

"Go look in the refrigerator," I said. And he went off to do just that.

"You believe me about what happened?" said Torcelli. "You believe I'm innocent?"

"Greg Legerman thinks you're innocent," I said, "but then, he doesn't know about you and his mother."

"Don't tell him," Torcelli pleaded.

"You were using Alana Legerman as backup in case your wife didn't get Horvecki's money?" I said.

"I wouldn't put it like that," he said,

touching his bandaged nose again.

"Course not," said Ames.

Darrell came back into the room with a bowl of Publix sugar-frosted wheat and milk.

"What'd I miss?" he asked.

"Nothing," said Torcelli sullenly.

Victor got up and left the room, brushing past Darrell who crunched away at the cereal.

"The State of Florida is going to try to kill me when they find out I'm an adult, but my wife will get me a great lawyer and you'll keep looking for whoever killed Horvecki, right?"

"Your wife know you're not really married?" Ames asked.

"We'll get married again," he said.

I thought of him with Sally, overworked Sally, caring Sally, Sally with a deep laugh and a soft smile when she looked at her children. I tried to conjure up the other side of Sally I'd glimpsed a few times, the Sally who had no compassion for the parents who took drugs or were religious lunatics or just plain lunatics. She was calm and determined with such people. She was relentless and willing to fight the courts and the law to see to it that they couldn't destroy their children. She lost more often than she won, but she kept fighting. I thought about these two Sallys, and I tried not to imagine her with the man who sat across from me, the man whose nose I had broken, the man who wanted Ames and me to save his life.

Victor came back into the room. He had another bowl of cereal and milk. Less than an hour after breakfast Darrell and Victor were hungry. So was I.

Someone was knocking outside the door in the other room.

"I'll get it," said Ames, moving out and closing the door behind him.

Then we heard a voice, a familiar voice. I got up and went out to meet our visitor.

"He's here, isn't he?" said Ettiene Viviase.

"He's here," I said.

It wasn't rage in his eyes exactly, but personal determination. The source, I was sure, was his daughter's involvement with the man he still thought of as Ronnie Ger-all.

"Haul him out," he said.

"What's happened?" I asked.

"Just came from my third visit to his apartment," he said. "This time I found something new, found it under a bookcase. I turned it over to the lab about ten minutes ago."

"What?" I asked.

"The weapon that was used to kill Blue Berrigan."

Ames went in to get Torcelli who came out black-eyed and slightly bewildered. The confident and angry young man of a few days ago had been replaced by this pained creature with a swollen and bandaged nose and black and blue eyes.

"What happened?" Viviase asked.

"I hit him," I said.

"You?"

"Yes."

"There's hope for you, Fonesca," he said. Then he looked at Torcelli and said, "Back to a cell. We've got lots to talk about."

"Fonesca, tell . . ." Torcelli began, but he was no longer sure about who he might call for help.

"I didn't kill anyone," Torcelli insisted as Viviase put handcuffs on him behind his back. "Fonesca, we're both Italians, Catholics. I swear to Jesus. I swear on the life of the Pope. I didn't kill Philip Horvecki."

"He's Italian?" said Viviase.

I didn't bother to tell Torcelli that I wasn't a Catholic and that some of my best enemies were Italian.

Victor and Darrell came out of my room, bowls in hand, still eating their cereal.

"You make an interesting quartet," Viviase said. "One more thing. What did your two middle-of-the-night visitors want?"

I didn't answer, so he added, "We had a man watching last night. Thinks he recognized Essau Williams, a Venice police officer. Who was the other man?"

"It was personal," I said.

"The other man," Viviase insisted.

"Jack Pepper, a radio evangelist from Cortez," I said.

"Mind telling me what they wanted, or did they just drop by to give you legal and spiritual counseling and a cup of tea?"

"They wanted me to find a way to get Dwight Torcelli free of the murder charge."

"Dwight Torcelli?"

"Ronnie's real name, but we can still call him Ronald. It's his middle name. He's twenty-seven years old today."

"You can prove that?"

"Listen . . ." Torcelli started to say, but Viviase was in no mood to listen to him.

"You can prove it," I said, and told him how to do it.

"No point in my telling you not to do anything dumb," he said. "You're going to do it anyway."

When Viviase and his prisoner were gone and Darrell and Victor had finished their

339

second breakfast, we all got into Victor's car, Ames in front, Darrell and I in the rear.

"How come you're not telling me to go home?" Darrell asked.

"Because," I said, "you'd remind me that I'm responsible for you all day. You'd tell me that being with me when I'm working is the most important thing in your life."

"I'm into girls now," he said. "Don't overestimate your charisma." He hit each syllable in the word.

"I'm impressed."

"You're learning," Darrell said as Victor drove to Siesta Key.

"I'm entering a new phase," I said.

And I was pretty sure I was.

The Ocean Terrace Resort Hotel was on Siesta Beach. It had a swimming pool, but it was no resort. It was a one-story dirty green stucco line of thirty-five rooms and a slightly moldy-smelling carpet in the hallway. The Ocean Terrace lived on the spillover from the bigger, fancier, more up-to-date and upscale motels that called themselves resorts and sold postcards proclaiming that they were the place for Northerners, Canadians, Frenchmen, Germans, Norwegians, and Japanese to spend a week, or the whole winter. The Ocean Terrace of-

340

fered nothing but its own existence.

The desk clerk, a woman with an unruly pile of papers in front of her and a head of equally unruly dyed red hair looked up at us as we entered the lobby. She was maybe in her fifties, clear-skinned, buxom, and looking as if she had suffered a few setbacks in the last ten minutes.

"What have we here, the road company of the Village People? A baseball player, a cowboy, a Chinese guy, and a black kid," she said.

We didn't answer her.

"Sorry. That was uncalled for," she said. "We have no vacancies and you appear to have no luggage. Would you like a bottle of water?"

"Sure," said Darrell.

"Rachel Olin," I said.

The woman bent down out of sight and then came up with a bottle of water which she handed to Darrell, who said, "Thanks."

"A guest," I said. "Rachel Olin."

"Checked out about an hour ago," the woman said.

"She pay with a credit card?" I asked.

"Cash. Who are you?"

"Her husband is looking for her," Ames said.

"He's pining for her," said Darrell.

She looked at Victor but he had nothing to add.

"Left with a man," she said.

"She call him anything?" Ames asked.

"No, I don't think so."

"What did he look like?" I asked.

"Who are you?" she asked.

I produced my process server license card and handed it to her.

"You look different in that baseball cap," she said, handing the card back. "These gentlemen are your backup?"

"Ames is my partner," I said. "I look after Darrell on Saturdays."

"And I killed his wife," Victor said.

She turned her attention to Victor, who was definitely not smiling.

"The guy she went with was a little older than you maybe," she said. "Good shape. Nice looking."

"Anything else?"

"Yes," she said. "He had a patch over his left eye."

"Thought he left town," Ames said from the front seat as Victor drove through Siesta Key Village, avoiding collision with shopping bag–laden tourists.

"So did I," I said.

"Who?" asked Darrell.

"His name is Jeff Augustine," I said.

342

"He kidnapped her?" asked Darrell.

"I don't know. Maybe. Doesn't look that way," I said.

"He's not the upchuck who shot me, is he?"

"Someone shot him, too," Ames said.

"Fonesca, what is going on?" Darrell asked, turning in his seat to face me as fully as he could.

"I'm not sure," I said.

"Can't do no better than that?" he asked.

"Can't do *any* better than that," I said. "I'm not sure, but I'm getting some ideas."

"Good ones?"

"I don't know."

"Where are we going?"

"To the home of D. Elliot Corkle," said Ames.

"Why?"

"So he can give you a handy dandy super automatic CD sorter which normally sells for nineteen ninety-five," I said.

"I don't need a CD sorter," Darrell said.

We were crossing the bridge off the Key.

"Don't worry," said Ames, "he's got lots of things he likes to give away."

Ames told Victor how to get to Corkle's. When we hit the mainland, Victor turned north on Tamiami Trail.

"Victor," I said. "Would you do me a favor?"

"Yes."

"Stop telling people you killed my wife."

"But I did."

"You may want to hear it, but other people don't."

"You don't want me to say it, I won't."

"I don't want you to say it to anyone but me when you feel you have to."

"I'll remember," he said.

There were no cars parked in front of Corkle's or in his driveway, but that didn't mean no one was home. If he had told me the truth, Corkle didn't leave his house. Doctors, barbers, dentists, I'm sure, came to him. I wouldn't have been surprised if he had an operating room somewhere behind the walls.

The last time I was in Corkle's home, Ames stole the Ronnie documents, and I won a few dollars playing poker. This was not a place I wanted to be.

"Ames, find a way in the back," I said. "See if you can find her."

Ames looked straight ahead. Victor looked at the steering wheel and Darrell said, "No way. You said he'll give us something?"

"We'll come up with something," said Ames.

Ames stayed seated while I went up the path to the front door. A tiny lizard skittered in front of me. I pulled my foot back to keep from stepping on it. A flock of screaming gulls spun over the Gulf of Mexico about forty yards down the street to my right.

I took off my cap, put it in my back pocket and rang the bell. It didn't take long, maybe forty seconds. Corkle opened the door.

"Ah, the thief in the baseball cap. Come in."

He stepped back and looked over my shoulder at Victor's parked car. Corkle was wearing blue slacks and an orange shirt with the words CORKLE'S RADIO TO OUTER SPACE. Under the lightning black letters was a picture of a plastic radio the size of a cigar box.

"You like the shirt?" he asked, leading me toward the office Ames had broken into. "On the way out, remind me and I'll give you and your friends in the car one each."

"Could you really hear outer space?" I asked as he opened the door to his office and let me pass.

"I'll give you one. You try it. Let me know. Truth is, you can tune in outer space on any radio. You just won't hear much of anything. But the CROS is perfect for AM and FM and has an alarm clock that plays 'So in Love With You Am I.' Have a seat."

I sat, not across from him at his desk but at a table in the corner near a window.

Corkle picked up a glass sphere about the size of a softball. He shook it gently and held it up so I could see the snow under the glass gently falling on . . .

"Rosebud," he said. "This is an exact replica of the one in *Citizen Kane.*"

He handed it to me.

"See the sled?"

"Yes," I said handing it back. "You sold them for nine ninety-five?"

"No, I didn't sell them. I had this one made to remind me not to go looking for other people's Rosebuds. Are you looking for someone's Rosebud, Lewis Fonesca?"

"My own maybe," I said.

He made a sound I took as a sign of sympathy or understanding. Then he put the glass ball gently atop a dark wood holder on the table and began rummaging through the drawers of his desk.

"I don't stay in this house because of any phobia," he said. "I just don't find things out there very interesting anymore. You know what I mean."

"Yes."

"I wasn't asking a question," he said, bouncing from the chair and looking at his shelves for something else to play with. "I know the answer."

"What's the answer?" I asked.

"Catherine," he said. "Am I right or am I right?"

"You're right," I said. "Now I've got a question."

"Want a drink? You drink Diet Coke, right? Or how about lemonade?"

"Not now, thanks. The Kitchen Master Block Set."

"A good seller, not great, but good. Sold seventy-four thousand in 1981."

"There was a meat pounder in the set," I said.

"Meat tenderizer," he corrected.

"A big wooden mallet with ridges on the head."

"Yes. You want one?"

"My sister has one."

"Nice to know it's still in service," he said. "Sturdy. Made in the Philippines."

"I think one of them was used to murder Blue Berrigan," I said. "I saw the postmortem photographs. They left a dent in his skull like a fingerprint."

"Could be a different manufacturer's," he said.

Corkle found what he was looking for in the deep file drawer in the desk. It was a jar full of what looked like pennies. He rolled the jar in his hands. The coins made the sound of falling rain as it turned.

"You give away a lot of Kitchen Master Block Sets here in Sarasota?"

"I give my Corkle Enterprises helpful house, car, and kitchen aids to anyone who comes in this house. I give them for Christmas, Hanukkah, Kwanzaa, and birthdays."

The rolling coins in the jar grew louder as he moved toward me.

"You're a generous man," I said.

"I like to think so."

"You haven't asked me about Ronnie Gerall."

"I assume that you'll tell me if you have anything to say that will help him."

"His name isn't Ronnie Gerall, but you already know that."

"Do I?"

He was behind me now. I didn't turn my head, just listened to the coins.

If I were ever to really believe in God, a primary reason would be the existence of irony in my life. There had to be some irony in the possibility of my getting killed with a jar full of pennies.

There is a mischief in me, even with the coins of death over my head. Death wish? Maybe. Ann Hurwitz thought so. Now she thinks I may be getting over it. If so, why did I then say, "Jeff Augustine."

The coin rattling turned to the sound of a thunderstorm in the Amazon and then suddenly stopped.

"He didn't leave town," I said.

Corkle moved back to the wall, deposited the jar, and sat behind his desk.

"He convinced you he was going, didn't he?"

"Yes," I said.

"Good actor. C-plus real-life tough guy."

"Where is he?"

"I don't know," Corkle said, "but I do know where your cowboy friend is."

"Where?"

"Searching the rooms upstairs for Rachel Horvecki."

He pushed a button under the desk and a section of the bookcase popped open to reveal a bank of eight full color television screens. They were all numbered. On number three Ames was talking to a young woman sitting on a bed.

"Why did you take her?"

"Protect her," he said. "My daughter and

grandson believe in Ronnie's . . . What's his real name?"

"Dwight Ronald Torcelli. He's still Ronnie."

"I don't want her threatened to the point where he feels he can't proclaim his innocence."

"You think he'd do the noble thing?"

"No," said Corkle, swiveling his leather chair so that it faced the window and presented me with the back of his head. He had a little monk's bald pate you couldn't see unless he was seated like this and leaning back.

"Don't ask me why my daughter and grandson believe in him."

"Their belief may be eroding."

"I wouldn't try to talk them out of it," he said. "On the other hand, I wouldn't say a word against . . ."

"Dwight Torcelli," I said. "You let us steal those documents about Ronnie Gerall while we played poker the other night," I said. "You dropped a hint about them and left them on your desk. You had a pretty good idea we would come the night I bought into your poker game."

"Why would I do that?"

"To give us reasons to believe that he was guilty without handing us evidence."

"You think I'm that devious?"

"You're that devious," I said.

He swiveled back to face me and looked up at the television monitors.

"Persuasive," he said.

I looked at the monitors. Ames and the young woman were coming out of the bedroom. He led the way to some narrow steep stairs just off the kitchen. The young woman followed him.

"Augustine?" I asked.

"You think he killed Horvecki and Berrigan?"

"The thought had entered my mind."

"Anything else?"

"Are you paying me to clear Torcelli or to find something against him?"

"Given his relationship with your friend Sally Pierogi . . ."

"Porovsky."

"Porovsky," he amended. "Given that, I think you might have an interest in proving Torcelli is not a nice person. There, they've left the house."

I looked up at a screen in the lower left-hand monitor to see Ames and the young woman hurrying across the back lawn.

"You're good at all this," I said.

"Couldn't have sold forty-eight thousand copies of the Guitar Master 12-Lesson Plan and almost twenty thousand guitars to go with it if I weren't good at sizing up the potential customers."

"What are you trying to sell me?" I asked.

"I'm buying," he said.

"What?"

"The truth," he said. "Not the big truth. Just a small one about who killed Horvecki. If it clears the dago weasel, so be it. You don't believe me?"

"No. Police will be coming to talk to you about what they found in Torcelli's apartment."

"The meat tenderizer?"

"The meat tenderizer."

"They're waiting for you in your car," he said.

He got up and so did I.

"You get your choice of items in the closet," he said.

"Some other time," I said, going to the office door.

"D. Elliot Corkle has irritated you," he said following me. "The dago remark? I was just pulling your chain." He reached up and pulled once on an invisible chain.

"I know," I said.

He grinned and pointed a finger at me to show I had hit the mark.

"Answer four questions and we're friends

again," I said.

"Ask."

We crossed the foyer to the front door.

"You know a policeman named Essau Williams and an Evangelist named Jack Pepper?"

"D. Elliot Corkle knows who they are," he said. "Wait a moment."

He hurried to the closet off the front hall, opened it and disappeared for no more than a few seconds before coming out with a white cardboard box and handing it to me. Second question?"

"Have you given money to either one of them?" I asked as we went out onto the red-brick path.

"Nothing to Williams but I did volunteer to put up a suitable headstone of his choice for his mother when they die. Five thousand dollars to Pepper to help support his ministry."

"In exchange for?"

"Nothing, but I did indicate to both of them that I appreciated their efforts to bring Philip Horvecki to justice."

"Blue Berrigan?" I asked.

"Unfortunate. No, tragic. No, shocking. A terrible coincidence. If you see my daughter . . ."

"Yes?"

"Nothing," he said. "She'll come back here. She always does when her funds get down to the level of the gross national product of Poland. Another question."

"Does Jeff Augustine play golf?"

"Why? Do you want him to join you on the links at the Ben Hogan Gulf Club? I don't know if he plays golf. I do know that if he does it will be a bit difficult for him now with but one eye."

He closed the door and I carried my prize to the car, where Rachel was sitting in the front passenger seat. I got in beside Ames and Darrell.

"Where are you taking me?" Rachel Gerall said.

"Wherever you want to go," I said.

"To see Ronnie," she said, her voice in twang from the center of the State of Florida.

She was frail and pale, red of hair and green of eyes. She should have been Irish. She had a pinched face and thin lips. She could have been cast as a tubercular resident of an Irish mining town a century ago. Either that or a hardcore drug user.

"Who are you people?" she said, half turning to look at me.

"People trying to help the police find whoever killed your father," I said.

"I don't trust you," she said, giving me the evil eye.

"Trust him," Darrell said. "He ain't lying."

"Ronnie's in jail," I said.

"Big boy jail," said Ames.

"And his name ain't Ronnie," Darrell added.

"That's no never mind to me," she said. "I want to see him."

"Do you know what happened to the one-eyed man who took you from the motel?" I asked.

"No."

"Would you like a drink?"

"Of what?"

"Whatever you want to drink," I said.

"I'd like an iced tea with lemon," she said.

"We'll stop," said Ames.

Victor drove to the Hob Nob on the corner of Seventeenth and Washington. The Hob Nob isn't trying to look like a fifties diner. It is a fifties diner. It hasn't changed in half a century. It's open air with a low roof, picnic tables, a counter with high stools and bustling waitresses who call you "honey." Smoking is permitted. You could be sitting next to two local landscape truckers, a couple who've just escaped from a drug bust, or a retired stockbroker from

Chicago and his wife. There's not much privacy at the Hob Nob, but the food is good and the service is fast.

Darrell lived within walking distance of the Hob Nob, passed it almost every day, ate at it almost never. He ordered a burger and a Coke.

"I know what you want," Rachel said after I ordered her an iced tea with lemon.

Ames, Victor, Darrell, and I all wanted different things, none of which we could imagine Rachel providing.

"You want me to tell you that Ronnie killed my father."

"Did he?" Ames asked.

"No, he did not," she said, raising her head in indignation. "It was that other man."

"What other man?" asked Ames.

"The one who went out the window. I heard the noise, my father shouting. I was in my room. I opened the door and saw this man climbing out the window and Ronnie, all bloody, kneeling next to my father."

"What can you tell us about the man who went through the window?" I asked. "White, black, tall, short, young, old?"

"He was white and he had an orange aura," she said with confidence.

"Orange aura?" asked Darrell.

She turned to Darrell and said, "Orange is anger. Yours is green, nervous."

Connecting thoughts did not seem to be a strong element of Rachel's being.

"You watchin' too much TV," said Darrell. "A wife can't be forced to testify against her husband, but if she wants to nail his ass, it's party time. If you want to help him, you'd be best off sticking with the guy through the window and forgetting auras. Tell her, Fonesca."

"He's right," I said.

Her iced tea had arrived. She slowly removed the straw from its wrapper, dropped the wrapper in the black plastic ashtray on the table, and inserted the straw into her drink.

Rachel was a little slow in everything she did — thinking, talking, moving. My first thought was drugs, but my second thought was that heredity had not been kind. Or maybe it had. There was an almost somnambulatory calmness to the young woman. Daddy had bullied his way through life. His daughter was sleepwalking through it.

She sipped her drink loudly with sunken cheeks.

"Could your husband have killed your father, maybe with the other man's help?" I asked.

"You're trying to trick me, like the one-eyed man," she said coming up for air.

"The one-eyed man tried to trick you into saying Ronnie killed your father?"

"He did," she said emphatically. "But I told him no such thing. He was on television."

"The one-eyed man?"

"Yes. I watch television," she said. "Good, clean entertainment if you are discerning. *Rockford Files* on the old TV channel."

"He was on the *Rockford Files*?" Ames asked.

"What's the *Rockford Files*?" asked Darrell.

The marriage of Torcelli and Rachel had been made in heaven or in hell. He exhaled a slick veneer of deception and she floated on a vapor of ethereal innocence.

"Did he kill your father?" Ames asked.

"The one-eyed man?" she asked, bubbling the last of her iced tea through the straw.

"Your husband," I said.

She thought, looked down at her drink, and said, "May I have another one?"

I ordered her another iced tea. Rachel wasn't brilliant, but she wasn't a fool. If she was playing with us, we were losing.

"Ronnie," I repeated. "Did he kill your father?"

She sucked on her lower lip for a few seconds as she considered her answer and said, "I wouldn't have blamed him if he did. My father was not a good man. He never hurt me, but he wasn't a good man. No, he was definitely a bad man. Ronnie saved me from him. When I finish my second iced tea, I'd like to see him."

"You're very rich now," I tried.

"Lawyer said. Policeman said. Man with one eye said," she said. "Ronnie married me for the money."

"He did?" I asked.

"He did," she said as she worked on her drink. "He never denied it. He said when my father died we would be rich and he would be a good husband. Ronnie's a looker and though I am somewhat plain and wistful, he treats me nicely and I tell him he is smart and beautiful which he delights in hearing provided I don't overdo it, and he pleases me in bed or on the floor. He likes sex."

"More than I need to know," said Darrell with a mouthful of hamburger.

"Did Ronnie kill your father?" I tried once more.

"No. I saw the other man do it."

"You actually saw him do it?" asked Ames.

"Yes. He was all bloody. He was there

earlier. Had words with my father, who called him a 'shit-bastard-cocksucker.' "

"And you didn't recognize the killer?" I asked.

"I had a little dog and his name was . . . ?" she said with a smile.

"Blue," said Ames.

"Yes," she said.

"Old song," said Ames.

"New suspect," I said.

"Please take me to Ronnie now, after I pee," Rachel said.

Victor got the washroom key and walked with her to the rear of the Hob Nob, where he waited outside the door.

"Lady's on a cloud," said Darrell finishing off his burger. "What time's the next cloud? I might want to hitch a ride."

"Believe her?" Ames asked.

"You?" I answered.

"She didn't see Berrigan kill her father, just heard it," said Ames.

"Or maybe didn't hear it. Or maybe just wants to get her husband off the hook and the murder of her father blamed on a dead man."

"She's just acting?" asked Ames.

"If she is, she's really good."

"Ain't nobody that good," said Darrell.

"Yes," I said. "There is."

360

16

"He's too smart for that, the little bastard," Detective Ettiene Viviase said.

He was seated behind his desk at police headquarters on Main Street. Ames and I were across from him, in wooden chairs that needed a complete overhaul and serious superglue to forestall their inevitable collapse.

Victor and Darrell were at Cold Stone ice cream store, across the street and half a block away.

Viviase was talking about Dwight Torcelli.

His door was open. Voices carried and echoed from the hallway beyond, where the arrested and abused sat after they got past the first line of questioning and into the presence of a detective.

"The weapon we found in Torcelli's apartment is a now-bloody wooden meat pounder."

"Tenderizer," I said.

Viviase was working on a plastic cup of

coffee of unknown vintage.

"The girl makes little in the way of sense."

"Some things she said make sense," I said.

"What?"

"Berrigan."

"Says her father knew Berrigan, used him as a greeter at a weekend sale at his Toyota dealership in Bradenton."

"He owned a Toyota dealership?" I said.

"Now she owns it and if luck or you turn up something to keep Torcelli from going to jail, the Horvecki estate will be his too. And weirdest goddamn thing is that they both really seem to like each other. She said she'd remarry him."

I said nothing. I didn't want to open the door to Alana Legerman and possibly to Sally and possibly to who knows how many others.

"Treats her like a nine-year-old," said Viviase, finishing his coffee and looking into the cup to see if he had missed something.

"She says Berrigan killed her father," I said.

"Convenient," Viviase said, looking into his empty cup for some answers.

He dropped the cup into the garbage can behind his desk.

"Williams and Pepper," I said.

"You make them sound like a law firm, a

men's clothing store, or a mail-order Christmas catalog."

Someone screamed down the hall, not close, but loud enough. I couldn't tell if it was a cackle, a laugh, or an expression of pain.

"Williams and Pepper both have solid alibis for the times of death of both the Horvecki and Berrigan murders."

"They weren't each other's alibis, were they?"

"I'm in a good mood, Fonesca. Truly. I don't look it, but I'm in a good mood. My daughter, I've discovered, has not been fooling around with our heartthrob prisoner."

"That's good."

"No," he said. "She's been fooling around with a high school senior. She assures me and her mother that 'fooling around' is all that she's been doing, whereas if she were fooling around with Ronnie the words would take on a whole new meaning. So, I'm in a good mood. I'm waiting for a DNA report on Horvecki and the blood on the meat pounder."

"You checking Berrigan's DNA too?"

"We are."

"I think the blood on the tenderizer is Berrigan's, not Horvecki's."

"Why would our boy want to kill Berri-gan?"

"Maybe he wouldn't, but somebody else might and then hide the murder weapon where it was sure to be found in Torcelli's apartment.

"Life is complicated," I said.

"Life is uncooperative."

"Yes."

"Can I talk to him?"

"He doesn't want to see you. He's only talking to his wife and his lawyer — the lawyer courtesy of your very own D. Elliot Corkle and his daughter, the same daughter who put up the charming Ronnie's bail."

The first words Ames uttered since we entered Viviase's office were, "We'd best go."

"Fine," said Viviase, turning to me. "Let me know if you and your sidekick find more of Ronnie's or Torcelli's wives or girlfriends kicking around."

His eyes didn't meet mine but I sensed something and that something was the name of Sally Porovsky.

Rachel didn't want a ride. She asked the receptionist at the jail to call her a cab so she could be taken to the nearest hotel, which happened to be the Ritz-Carlton on Tamiami Trail just outside of downtown.

The Ritz-Carlton was about a three minute ride from the jail. She told Ames, who was waiting for her, that her husband had reminded her she was rich and could now stay anywhere she liked and didn't even need to pick up the clothes she had left at her father's house.

"How did she seem to you?" I asked.

"Something on her mind wherever her mind was," Ames said as he, Victor, Darrell, and I walked over to the pizza shop next to the Hollywood 20 Movie Theaters on Main Street.

"So," said Darrell, "who killed those two guys and who shot at me and you, Fonesca?"

"I'm not sure," I said.

"But you think?" said Darrell.

"Yeah," I said.

Victor said nothing. Victor was extending his silence. He was waiting for something, something for me to say or do, or something he had to decide to do, or something that came down from heaven or up from hell.

"Movie?" asked Darrell as we all shared a large sausage pizza.

"Next week," I said.

"When's the last time you went to a movie, Fonesca?" Darrell asked.

It had been June 6, 2003. Catherine and I

went to see *Seabiscuit* at the Hillside Theater. We both liked it. We usually liked the
same movies. Since then the only movies I
had seen were on videotape or television,
almost all made before 1955, almost all in
black and white.

"I don't remember," I said.

"We're right next door to the fucking
place," Darrell said. "They've got *Saw 8* or
9 or something. And you Ames McKinney,
what was the last time you went to a movie
in a real, honest-to-god theater?"

"Can't say I remember," Ames said.
"Maybe forty, fifty years ago."

"I need some help here," said Darrell.
"Victor, you, when? Or don't they have
movies in China?"

"I've never been to China," said Victor. "I
went to this movie the night before last."

"That settles the issue," said Darrell. "The
Chinese guy who's not from China and me
are going to see *Saw.*"

"No," said Victor. "I won't see movies in
which women or children are killed."

"Fonesca, I'm pleading with you," said
Darrell.

"All right," I said. "I'll go."

"I guess I will, too," said Ames.

"Depends," Victor said.

We spent two hours in darkness watching

beautiful women with too much makeup saying they were witches and trying to kill bearded guys who looked like Vikings by sending monkey-faced creatures riding on short but fast rhinos with short fire-spitting spears in their hands. Darrell drank a seemingly gallon-sized Coke and a giant popcorn.

When we got out, it was dark.

"Help that near-crazy lady," Darrell said as we let him off outside the apartment building on Martin Luther King in which he lived with his mother.

I didn't answer. Neither did Ames. We drove off with Victor.

"Someone beat Horvecki to death," Ames said. "Someone killed Blue Berrigan almost in front of our eyes. Why? Who?"

"And someone shot Darrell in the back and put a pellet through the window of Jeffrey Augustine's car," I said. "Who? Why?"

Victor parked in the narrow driveway next to the house. We all got out.

"You've got some ideas," said Ames.

"An idea," I said.

"Partners, right?"

"Right," I said.

"Ideas?"

I told him. He rolled his scooter out from under the stairs and drove back to his room at the back of the Texas Bar and Grill.

Victor took a shower and then settled into his sleeping bag in the corner of the office. I got into my black Venice beach shorts and my *X Files* black T-shirt and spent about an hour in bed, just looking up at the ceiling. I considered calling Sally. I didn't. Sleep snuck up on me, as it usually does just when I'm convinced insomnia will have me waiting for the sun to rise.

No wandering preachers or wayward policemen woke me. No new great ideas came to me in dreams. I remembered no dreams. I woke up three minutes after six in the morning. My *X Files* shirt was soaked with sweat, though the room felt cold. I got up, dressed in clean jeans and a plain blue T-shirt, and picked up the Memphis Reds gym bag I had purchased for two dollars at The Women's Exchange.

In the outer office, Victor was tossing on his sleeping bag. Half of him was on the bag. The other half was on the floor. I made it out the door without waking him and went down the stairs to retrieve my bicycle from the shed under the stairs.

The morning was cool, maybe in the seventies. The sky was clear and traffic on 301 was lighter than usual. The YMCA was on Main Street in the Mall next to the

Hollywood 20 Movie Theaters.

I saw a few people I knew as I did my curls with fifteen-pound weights. It felt better after I got them done and began my second set. Then I did crunches, bends, and heart-breakers until my shoulders began to ache.

After I finished my workout, I showered, put on my clothes, and stepped out onto Main Street where someone took a shot at me.

I stood on the sidewalk for a few seconds, not quite registering what had happened. A trio of teens passed me laughing, noticing nothing. An elderly woman with a walker slowly crossed the street, looking forward and moving slowly. Nothing seemed unusual until the second shot fell short, pinging off the hood of a shiny new red Honda Accord a few feet away from where I was standing. I could see the small dent in the car show-ing silver metal under the red paint. With the second shot I held up my gym bag and bent at the knees. Something thudded into the bag I held in front of my face. I ducked for cover alongside the Honda, hoping the shots were coming from the other side of the street and not from either side of me.

I sat on the sidewalk, my back to the car, my Cubs cap about to fall in my lap. A couple in their fifties came down the sidewalk. They tried not to look at me.

"Down," I said. "Get down."

I motioned with my hand. They ignored me, probably considering me an early-morning drunk. They walked on. No more shots.

After a few minutes I hadn't been killed, so I stood up carefully and looked around. There were places to hide, doorways to consider, rooftops, corners to duck around. I looked at the front of my gym bag. A pellet was lodged in the fabric. I pulled it out, pocketed it, and went to get my bicycle from where it was chained around a lamppost. There was a Dillard's bag dangling from the handlebars. I looked inside and found a folded handwritten note.

Should you survive, think no ill of me.
Folly is as folly always does.
Folly is and never was completely free.
Stop or hear again the bullet's buzz
and it will be as if Fonesca never was.

"High school kid," said Ames, looking down at the poem that lay flat on my desk. "Maybe a girl."

"Real men don't write poetry?" I asked.

"They might write it, but they don't show it to anybody."

"Why write a poem?" I said. "Why not just a note saying, 'Stop trying to help Ronnie Gerall or I'll shoot at you again and next time I won't miss.' "

"Guns are easy to get," Ames said. "Why shoot at you with a pellet gun, especially after having been less than gentle, beating two men to death?"

"Maybe," said Victor who stood looking out the window at nothing.

Ames and I both looked at him.

"Maybe," Victor continued, "the person shooting at you is not the killer of Horvecki and Berrigan."

With my Bank of America pen, we made a list of everyone we could think of who would know I was trying to find a suspect other than the former Ronnie Gerall. The list was long.

"Where do we start?" Ames asked.

I told him and he said, "Dangerous out there for you."

"Whoever is shooting at me," I said, "is a rotten shot. Plus, he won't shoot at me again till he knows I haven't dropped the case."

"She," said Ames.

"Right," I said. "He or she."

"Let's do it," said Ames and we went out the door and down to my car.

Victor sat in the back, Ames next to me. I turned the key and the Saturn powered on with something approaching a purr.

"Worked on it early this morning, before church," Ames said.

"Sounds great," I said.

"It'll do," he said.

I didn't ask Ames what church he belonged to, though I knew he would tell me. I didn't ask Ames if he had a weapon under his well-worn tan suede jacket, though I knew there was one there.

We got to the church in Cortez just before noon. Services were over, but the Reverend Jack Pepper was delivering a pensive message on station WTLW.

"Vengeance is mine, sayeth the Lord," came Pepper's voice over the radio as we sat listening to the man in the small studio in the building just beyond the tall metal mesh gate. "But we are the vessels of the Lord, the instruments of the Lord. What if the Lord calls upon us to seek his vengeance?"

He paused for a few seconds to let his listeners consider what he had just said. I imagined a 1930s farm couple, Dad in his overalls, Mom wiping her hands on her apron, son on the floor looking up at an old Atwater Kent radio as if it might suddenly turn into a television set. I wondered how many people actually listened to Jack Pepper.

"Ponder this further," Pepper said. "How will we know when it is the Lord commanding us? We have free will for the Lord has given it to us along with many of the blessings of life including the bounty of the seas right in our own waters — fish, shrimp, crab, scallops, lobster. When are we really hearing the Lord? I'll answer this after these messages from the good Christian business in our own neighborhood."

I got out of the car after telling Victor to get behind the wheel and Ames to stand by the gate and be ready. I wanted to talk to Jack Pepper alone.

As Ames and I walked to the gate, I could hear Victor behind us, listening to Jack Pepper urging his good listeners to buy their bait and tackle at Smitty's Bait and Tackle.

I pushed the button next to the gate. Pepper, complete in suit and tie, came out, told the dog to go sit "over there," and let me in.

"You find something that will help Gerall?" he asked opening the gate to let me in.

"Maybe," I said. "I've got a few questions."

"I've got to get back on the air," he said,

motioning for me to follow him. I did.

There was no one but Pepper and me in the reception room, and through the glass window I saw no one in the studio. Pepper opened the studio door, hurried in and sat just as the commercial ended. The speaker connected to the studio crackled with age, but it worked. Pepper put on his earphones, hit a switch and said, "You are waiting for an answer to the question I posed before the break, and I'll give it to you. You'll know that it is the voice of the Lord because your heart is cleansed and you follow the Ten Commandments and the teachings of Jesus. The wayward will hear the voice of the Devil; the good will hear the voice of the Lord."

He said he would take calls if anyone wished to ask questions or give testimony. He gave the number and repeated it.

The phone rang.

"A call," Pepper said hopefully. He picked up the phone in the studio and said, "Jesus and I are listening to you."

At 1 p.m. Jack Pepper signed off, saying, "WTLW will return to the air tomorrow morning at ten. Join us if you can and trust in the Lord."

Back in the reception area, Jack Pepper said, "We've got Dr Pepper, Mr. Pibb, canned iced tea, and all kinds of Coke in the refrigerator."

I declined. He moved behind the receptionist and manager's desk and came up with a can of Coke, which he opened, drank from, and said, "Parched."

"Which of you was at Horvecki's house the night he was murdered?"

He swished some Coke around in his mouth wondering if he should lie.

"Rachel Horvecki and Ronnie Gerrall both say they saw a pickup truck in front of Horvecki's house that night," I went on. "There was a man in it. You or Williams?"

"And if I say neither?"

"Then you'd be lying and Ronnie would be one step closer to death row."

"I think the Lord sent you," he said softly. "It was me. We'd been watching Horvecki's house whenever we could, waiting for him to commit a new abomination. A man cannot help being the creature the Lord created, but he can do battle with his nature."

"You saw and did what?"

He took another drink, let out an "aah," and said, "A few minutes after midnight I hear voices inside the house, voices filled with hate. And then a thudding sound. Ronnie comes down the street just about then and goes in the house. Man in a watch cap climbs out the window at the side of the house and goes running down the street. Ronnie comes outside like a flash, looks around, and goes back inside."

"How loud were the noises and voices inside the house before Ronnie showed up?" I asked.

"Loud enough," he said. "Police came just about then, went in, and you know the rest."

"How long between the time Ronnie came out to look around and the time the police arrived?"

"Less than a minute," he said. "No noise. Police there almost instantly, which could mean —"

"Whoever called 911 did it before Ronnie got there," I said.

"The murderer called 911?" asked Pepper.

"Where was Williams that night?" I asked.

"I'm not my brother's keeper," he said.

"Did either Ronnie or Rachel see you in front of the house?"

"Probably," he said. "I wasn't hiding. I wanted Horvecki to know I was there watching. The police will want a statement from me, won't they?"

"They will," I said.

"There is a restraining order against Essau and me. I prayed it wouldn't be necessary for me to come forward," he said. "I prayed that the real killer would step forth or be exposed before I had to speak out, but it looks as if the Lord has chosen me to speak the truth. It will be in the newspapers won't it?"

"Yes. I'm sorry."

He clasped his hands, closed his eyes, and dropped his head in prayer.

I left the building.

The dog got up, looked at me, and growled deeply. I wouldn't make it to the gate if she didn't want me to, and she didn't look as if she wanted me to. I looked at the door. Pepper did not come out.

"Steady on, girl," Ames called.

The big dog took slow, stalking steps in my direction. Pepper still did not appear. The dog rocked back, ready to pounce, when Ames's voice boomed with authority.

"I said steady on."

The dog looked at him as he took another step toward me. Ames came out with a small gun, which slipped out of his sleeve and into his hand.

I hadn't moved, but the dog had. She was a few steps from me, now, and growling again. Ames fired into the air and the dog scampered off to a far corner. Then Pepper appeared in the doorway of the building.

He looked at me and Ames and then at the dog.

"You shot her," he said.

"No," I said. "She's just frightened."

"So are we all," said Pepper. "So are we all."

17

A lean white heron stood on one leg atop the rusting pickup truck on Zo Hirsch's lawn. The bird looked at me, and I looked back. He considered putting his foot back down but changed his mind as I walked up the cracked concrete path to the front door.

"You," Hirsch said opening the door and looking up at me.

"Me," I admitted.

"You've got the papers, right? More courts and lawyers after me? Okay, bring it on."

I handed him the envelope with the summons enclosed.

"They can't get blood out of a banana and I'm a banana."

"Your wife?" I asked.

"And the third-rate shortstop," he said. "I made an offer they couldn't refuse, and they refused it. I'm down to selling off some of my collection. Interested in buying a genuine Cleveland Indians sweatshirt once worn by Larry Doby?"

"How much?"

"Two thousand."

"What do you have under a hundred?"

"Baseball autographed by George Altman, a Cub. Led the National League with twelve triples in 1962."

"How much?"

"My pride is gone. I'll take what you offer over fifty dollars."

I took out my wallet, found two twenties and a ten and handed it to him.

"Can we talk?" I asked.

"We are talking."

"Can I come in?"

"What the hell."

He pocketed the money and stood back to let me in. I moved into the living room and sat down. Black baseball players in poses and smiles looked down at me. Zo Hirsch, summons and the cash I had given him in hand, hurried off to the back of the house and returned almost immediately with the baseball. He tossed it to me. Then he sat in the chair across from mine.

"You want something to drink? I'm down to store-brand ersatz cola and root beer from a dollar store. It tastes vaguely like something besides tap water."

"Tempting," I said, "but no, thanks."

"Simply put," he said, "what do you want from me? There isn't much left, but what there is, with the exception of a few treasures, is for sale."

"Horvecki," I said. "You were his only friend."

"Friend," he repeated the word, more to himself than to me. "We talked baseball, had drinks."

"He talk about anything else? What did he care about?"

"Guns," said Zo Hirsch, "and his daughter, Rachel. I only saw her a few times a couple of years ago. Cute kid, too skinny, didn't talk. My ex-wife was not too skinny and she could talk, mostly in Spanish. She called me 'Pequeño.' You now what that means?"

"Little," I said.

"At first she said it with a smile and a touch. Later she said it with a hiss and folded arms. A piece of work."

"Horvecki," I reminded him. "What else?"

"He liked the ladies. They didn't like him. He paid for companionship. Come to think of it, so did I."

Zo Hirsch sat back in the chair and drummed his fingers on the arms.

"Pine View and Bright Futures," I said.

"Oh yeah, almost forgot. He hated them

both. His kid got turned down by Pine View. He was determined to bring the school and that Bright Futures program down. He didn't talk about it much, but when he did, that was what he said. He supplemented his daughter's education by teaching her how to ride, shoot, learn his truth about history, which was wacky. Next question."

"Wacky?"

"Phil had a long list of groups he hated. The School Board, the ACLU, the Democratic Party, lawyers, psychiatrists, teamsters, television writers, professional tennis players —"

"Enough," I said. "I get it."

"You gotta give him credit," said Zo Hirsch. "The man knew how to hate."

"Your friend?"

"No," he said. "But the man knew baseball."

"He was ruthless in business," I said.

"He was a giant five-story steamroller in business. He crushed and was proud of it."

"What was in it for you?"

Zo Hirsch squirmed a little in his seat, shook his head and looked toward the recently repaired front window.

"He bought baseball memorabilia from me, paid more than top dollar, never even questioned authenticity. Philip Horvecki was a substantial part of my income."

"He was a —"

"Sucker," said Zo Hirsch, "but he knew it. I think he was buying a friend. I was happy to sell. The guy really did know baseball and he served good lunches."

"Why you? There are plenty of people for sale."

"He liked showing me off," said Zo Hirsch. "It made people uncomfortable. A little black man. He liked making people uncomfortable. One more question. Then I've got to go see my lawyer to find out if there's anything to salvage. I hope he suggests that I hire a hit man and get rid of my ex-wife and the shortstop. You on that bicycle again?"

"No. I've got a car."

"Good. You can give me a ride. On the way, I'll give you my all-time favorite Cubs lineup and you can do the same."

I put the slightly tarnished George Altman autographed ball in the glove compartment and drove Zo Hirsch to an office building on Orange, just north of Ringling.

When Hirsch got out of the car, he hesitated and said, "Phil Horvecki was a shit, but he was my friend, sort of, the poor bastard."

I watched him walk to the big double-thick glass doors and reach up for the handle. He pulled the door open with dignity and strength and disappeared inside.

I wondered how he planned to get back home.

After I called her, Alana Legerman met me at the FourGees Coffee Shop on Beneva and Webber. She was reluctant. I was persuasive. I didn't try to tell her that I was still trying to save Ronnie. I told her I wanted to talk to her about her son.

The lunch crowd had cleared out. I had a choice of the bright, sunny room where there were small tables, but I chose the back room, dark and minimally plush, with music piped in at a level where one could still have a conversation.

She came in after I did, just as the last customers, three women, moved out of the side room and left. She saw me, walked over, and sat, hands in her lap. She wore a light blue dress with short sleeves and a black belt with a big silver buckle. She was doing Grace Kelly ice princess, and she was good at it.

"I'm waiting," she said.

A lean girl, barely out of her teens, came in to take our order.

"Coffee and a scone," I said.

"Prune?"

"Plain."

The waitress turned to Alana, who said, "Tea, mint."

"That's it?" asked the girl.

I said it was, and Alana went back to her patient waiting pose.

"Does Greg own a pellet rifle?"

"My son owns whatever he wants. His grandfather doesn't deny him anything."

"So, he owns a pellet rifle?"

She shrugged.

"Who knows? I've never seen him with one."

"Why does Greg want to save Ronnie Gerall?"

"They're friends. That's how I had the bad fortune to meet Ronnie."

"What kind of friends?" I asked.

This time she cocked her head back in a becoming look of surprise.

"You're suggesting my son and Ronnie had a homosexual relationship?"

"No. That didn't occur to me, but I'll think about it. Did Ronnie rule in their relationship?"

"Probably," she said.

"Have you ever seen Ronnie act violent?"

"No."

"Does Greg have any other friends besides

Winston Graeme?"

"No. I don't think so."

"When did they become friends?"

"About a year ago. No, two years ago. Winn Graeme is very protective of my son. My father and I are both very grateful for it, though I must confess that I don't understand why the boy puts up with Greg."

"Greg keeps punching him in the arm," I said.

"A token of my son's inability to come up with a painless way of expressing his friendship. His therapist assures me that when he gets to Duke he will mature. What is this all about?"

Our coffee and tea came. I picked up the check. We drank in silence for a few seconds, and then I said, "Does Greg write poetry?"

"Poetry? You ask the damnedest questions. Greg writes poetry, short stories, does sketches and paintings that could earn him a scholarship, and he reads at a rate that is not a treat to watch. He doesn't just read. He devours books."

"Do you and your father want Ronnie to go to prison for murder?"

"We'll be satisfied to have him sent away for pretending to be a high school student or, better yet, whatever he did in Texas that he and his wife ran away from."

"Your whole family hired me to find evidence that he didn't kill Horvecki."

"My father and I have changed our minds," she said, finishing her coffee. "The job has changed. If you find evidence that he killed Horvecki or that other man . . ."

"Blue Berrigan."

"Blue Berrigan," she repeated with a shake of her head. "What kind of people have we gotten ourselves involved with? No answer is required."

I gave none.

"Are we finished?" she asked.

"Yes."

"Good. I have another appointment."

She got up, picked up her purse, and said, "Nail the bastard."

"Someone else said the same thing."

"A woman?" she asked.

"Yes."

"Of course," she said and strode away.

When she was gone, I made a call and got through after two rings.

"This is Lew Fonesca."

"I know," said Winn Graeme.

"I'd like to see you."

"When?"

"Now."

"Where?"

"FourGees. It's —"

387

"I know where it is. You have something?"

"Maybe," I said.

"I'll be right there."

I had a refill of coffee and waited, listening to Rufus Wainwright sing "Not Ready To Love."

It took him twenty-five minutes before he came into the backroom. He adjusted his glasses to be sure I was the person he was looking for.

"I'm missing golf practice," he said, sitting down in the same seat Alana Legerman had been in. "I had to tell the coach and tell him my mother called and said she wasn't feeling well."

"He believed you?"

"I don't know. He didn't call me a liar. I don't like lying. What's going on? Why isn't Greg here?"

"You go everywhere together?"

"Pretty much," he said. "We're friends."

The waitress came back to take our order and get a good look at Winn Graeme.

"Are you Winston Graeme?" she asked.

"Yes," he said.

"I saw you play Riverview," she said. "You had twenty-four points. My boyfriend was Terry Beacham, but we're not together anymore."

It was a clear invitation, but not to Winn,

who said, "You have a caffeine-free diet cola?"

"Just Diet Coke."

"I'll have that," he said, looking at me and not at the girl, who got the message and moved away.

She had forgotten to ask if I wanted a refill or something else.

"Why?" I asked.

"Why what?"

"Why are you and Greg friends?"

"He's smart and we get along. Sometimes you can't explain things like friendship."

"I think I can explain it," I said. "How much does Greg's grandfather pay you to take care of his grandson and pretend to be his friend."

Winn put his head down and then brought it up, adjusting his glasses again.

"Mr. Corkle pays me fifteen hundred dollars a month in cash."

"How long has he been doing this?"

"Since Greg's sixteenth birthday party. My father lost his job when I was fifteen. He had a drinking problem. He was sixty-one when he lost the job. Since then he's made some money at home on his eBay trades. Some money, but not a lot, and my mother stands on her feet eight hours a day selling clothes at Beals. I need a scholarship. I need Bright Futures. I need fifteen hundred dollars a month. Wherever Greg goes to college, I'll go to college so the money won't stop."

"What else would you like?"

"I'd like it if Greg didn't find out about his mother and Ronnie and about me taking money from his grandfather."

"You think I'll tell him?"

"I don't know," he said.

"I won't tell him. You own a pellet gun?"

"No, why?"

"Someone's been trying to shoot me with one."

"If I were trying to shoot you would I tell you I had a gun?" he asked.

"Good point. People sometimes admit things they shouldn't."

A man in his late forties or early fifties and a woman who might have been his daughter came in the back room. He was wearing a business suit and tie. She was wearing less than she should have been. The man looked at Winn Graeme and me. Then the two of them sat on a sofa in the shadows under the speaker.

"You know that girl?" I asked.

"Why?"

"She nodded at you."

Winn shook his head before saying, "I

know her. She graduated from Riverview last year. She was a cheerleader. Her name is Hope something."

"Small town," I said, looking at the pair, who were whispering now, the girl shaking her head.

"That's not her father," Winn said.

"How do you know?"

"That's Mr. Milikin, lawyer downtown. Wife, four kids. He's on the board of everything in the county."

I looked at the couple. Mr. Milikin looked as if he were perspiring. His eyes darted toward the archway leading into the other room. He didn't want to see any familiar faces.

"Ronnie's going to be like that if he lives long enough," Winn said.

"Like Milikin?"

"No."

"Horvecki," I said.

"We didn't kill him."

"We?"

"Greg and I. We tried to talk to him a few times. So did others. Didn't do any good."

"You went to his house?"

"Once. He wouldn't let us in, threatened to call the police if we didn't go away. He said he had the right to bear arms and protect himself, his family, and his property.

He said, 'Under my roof, we know how to use a gun!' "

"And?"

"We went away. Is that all?"

I looked at him and he forced himself to look back for an instant before giving his glasses another adjustment.

"That's all," I said.

Winn Graeme stood up, started to turn, and then turned back to me to say, "Don't hurt Greg."

"That a warning?"

"A plea."

He didn't look toward Mr. Milikin and the former cheerleader as he left. The girl glanced at him, but Milikin was so busy pleading his case that he didn't notice. He just kept perspiring.

I had almost enough information now. There was only one more person I had to see. I paid the waitress, who said, "He's a fantastic basketball player. Jumps like a black guy. You know where he's going to college?"

"Yes," I said and went around the tables and through the door.

I was careful. I could have been more careful. Ann Hurwitz would know why I didn't exercise more caution. Pellets might fly. I might catch one in the eye like Augustine. I was reasonably sure of who the shooter would be, but Augustine was the person who could make it a certainty.

The shot didn't come until I opened the door to get into the Saturn, which was wedged between two SUVs at the far end of the lot, a few spaces from the exit on Webber.

The shot didn't come from a pellet gun.

The first bullet shattered the driver side window showering shards on the seat. I turned to look in the direction from which I thought the bullet had been fired.

Something came at me from around one of the SUVs. It hit me, knocked me backward to the ground, and landed on me. I panted for breath. A second shot came but I didn't hear it hit the ground or my car or the pavement.

I lay there for a beat, the weight on my chest and stomach, an arm covering my chest, and looked up to see, inches from my nose, Victor Woo.

"You all right?" he asked.

I tried to answer but couldn't speak. He understood and rolled off to the side. I started to get up but he held a hand out to keep me down. He listened, watched for about half a minute, and then helped me up.

"He's gone," he said.

The shooter wasn't trying to frighten me off anymore. We had gone beyond that, to murder.

"I followed you," Victor said at my side.

"Thanks," I said trying to catch my breath.

"That last shot might have killed you," he said.

"Might have, yes," I acknowledged.

"It would have hit you."

He was trying to make a point, but I wasn't sure what it was. He turned around so I could see where the bullet had entered his right arm through the red Florida State University sweatshirt he was wearing, the arm he had draped over my chest. There was remarkably little blood.

"It ricocheted off the ground before it hit me," he said.

"I'll drive you to the ER."

"No," he said. "I'll stop somewhere, clean it, put on a bandage and some tape. The bullet just scratched my arm. It's not inside me."

Clichés abound from old movies. "It's just a flesh wound." "I've had worse bites from a Louisiana mosquito."

"Suit yourself," I said.

"I want to go home," he said. "I saved your life. It is all I can do. It doesn't make up for killing your wife, but it's all I can do."

"I forgave you for killing Catherine."

"But when you said it before, you didn't mean it," he said. "This time you do. I've been away from home too long."

I reached out to shake his hand. He winced as he briefly held my grip.

"My bedroll is in my car," he added. "I'm leaving from here. If I can ever be of any service . . ."

"I know where to find you," I said, but we both knew I would never call.

"You know who's trying to kill you?"

"Yes," I said.

"Stop them," he said.

And he was gone. I held up my hands. I felt calm, but my hands were both shaking. Can the body be afraid when the mind isn't? I knew the mind could be afraid when the body of a policeman went through the door of an apartment where a crazed father held a gun to his ten-year-old daughter's head, or when a fireman made a dash into a burning building where he heard the cry of a cat. It was a question for Ann.

When I opened the car door, I saw the folded sheet of paper with the words:

I whisper your name in the book of one

more tomorrow
knowing your yesterdays were filled with
*   sorrow.*
Migrating birds soar South then North
*   again.*
North into night flying over your solitary
*   den.*
Luck will not last.
Move fast.
Move past.
Thou hast
No more tomorrows.

I cleaned up as much of the glass on the seat and the floor as I could and got in my car. Once I was seated I saw more shining shards on the passenger seat. I swept them on the floor with my hand and called Ames.

"Real bullets this time," I said.

"You all right?"

"Yes."

"Same shooter?"

"Yes."

"Sure?"

"I'm sure. Where are you?"

"The office."

"I'll pick you up in ten minutes. A weapon would be in order."

"Got one," he said.

When I got to the house, Ames was coming down the steps. The day was cool enough that his lightweight leather jacket wouldn't draw attention and whatever weapon he was carrying would remain hidden.

"Watch out for the glass," I said as he started to get in the car.

"I'll fix that window when we're done," he said swiping away at some of the glass bits I had missed.

He sat, looked at me and said, "Let's do it."

18

"Took you a while," Corkle said, opening the door. "Come in."

He was wearing tan slacks, a dark light-weight sweater and a blue blazer. Well dressed for a man who never left his house.

Ames and I followed him as he led the way to the rear of the house and onto a tiled, screen-covered lanai. The kidney shaped pool was filled with clear blue-green water.

A glass pitcher of something with ice and slices of lemon in it sat on a dark wooden table. There were five glasses.

Behind the table stood Jeffrey Augustine, black eye patch and all.

"It's just lemonade," said Corkle. "Mr. Augustine will pour you both a glass, and we can sit and talk."

Both Ames and I took a glass of lemonade from Augustine. I took off my Cubs cap and put it in my back pocket.

"I feel like one of those rich bad guys in a fifties movie," said Corkle, glass in hand, sitting on a wooden lawn chair that matched the table. "Like what's his name, Fred . . ."

"Clark?" I said, sitting next to him.

Ames stood where he could watch Augustine, who was also standing. Augustine wasn't drinking.

"Yeah, that's the guy," said Corkle. "Bald, heavyset sometimes, a little mustache. That's the guy. Fonesca, D. Elliot Corkle is not the bad guy here, Fonesca."

"You kidnapped Rachel Horvecki," I said.

"Mr. Augustine brought her here to protect her," said Corkle, looking at the lemonade after taking a long drink. "She came willingly, and you two executed a flawless rescue."

"Protect her from what?"

"She's rich now," he said. "Someone might be inclined to take a shot at her or drop a safe on her in the hope and expectation of getting her money."

"Ronnie."

"Ronnie Gerall, otherwise known as Dwight Torcelli," he said. "I've known Rachel since she was a baby. Always been a little bit in outer space. Her father put her there. Good kid. She deserves better than Torcelli. So does my daughter."

"Someone tried to kill me about an hour ago in the parking lot at Beneva and Webber."

"With a pellet gun?" he asked looking at Augustine whose fingers automatically reached for his eye patch.

"With a rifle."

"You know why?" he asked, drinking more lemonade.

"Because I've been talking to people."

"People?"

"People who told me who killed Philip Horvecki and Blue Berrigan."

Corkle held up his lemonade and said, "Pure lemonade with small pieces of lemon evenly distributed throughout. Good, huh?"

"Very good," I said.

"Made with the Corkle Mini-Multi Mixer Dispenser. Put in the water, the ice, lemons, push a button. It works almost silently; you just place the individual glass under the spout, and it fills automatically. Same perfect taste every time. Works with lemons, oranges, berries, any fruit or vegetable. Cleans with one easy rinse. I like orange-banana."

"You know who killed them," I said.

"I'll give you both a Corkle Mini-Multi Mixer Dispenser when you leave," he said. "Parting gift. Much as D. Elliot Corkle enjoys your company, he doesn't think we can be friends. Are you owed more money for your troubles?"

"No," I said.

"If there's nothing else . . ."

"Nothing else."

Augustine had placed his empty glass on the table and folded his arms in front of him.

At the front door, we waited while Corkle got us each a boxed Corkle Mini-Multi Mixer Dispenser. Ames handed his to me. They were lighter than they looked.

When we cleared the door, Ames said, "I'll take that now." He took his Corkle Mini-Multi Mixer Dispenser and added, "He was armed. Augustine."

"I know," I said.

"I think it best if I keep my hands free till we're away. Where to now?" Ames asked.

"To see a baby and get something to eat."

"I'll watch for snipers," he said.

About a block from Corkle's I said, "Victor's gone."

"Where?"

"Home."

"Good."

"He saved my life when the shooting started."

"He was waiting for something like that."

"You knew?"

"I figured," said Ames.

"I should have," I said.

Flo was home alone with Catherine who toddled toward us, arms out for Ames to pick her up, which he did.

"Gifts for you," I said, handing her both Pulp-O-Matics.

"Those are the things I saw on television years ago," she said. "Almost bought one then. My friend Molly Sternheiser had one. Said it was a piece of shit. Tried to get her money back. Never did. Now, for some reason, I've got one and a backup."

Flo had given up her flow of curse words when Adele and Catherine came into her life. Every once in a while, however, a small colorful noun bursts out unbidden.

"Don't try to understand," I said. "Just mix."

She reached up, took my cap from my head and handed it to me. I pocketed it.

The music throughout the house wasn't blaring, but it was as present as always.

"That's Hank Snow," she said. " 'Moving On.' "

Flo was wearing one of her leather skirts and a white blouse. She only had six or seven rings on her fingers. She was dressing down.

"Hungry?" she asked.

"Yes," I said, watching Catherine and Ames, who were almost face to face and both very serious.

The baby reached up and touched his nose with pudgy fingers.

"I'll find something to eat," said Flo.

"Adele?"

"School," she said. "How about chili? Got a lot left over from dinner yesterday."

"Fine," I said.

She went to the kitchen while I sat and listened to Hank Snow and watched Catherine and Ames. After a minute or so he handed the baby to me and went toward the kitchen to help Flo.

Catherine was pink and pretty, like her mother. She sat on my lap and started gently bumping her head against my chest until Flo called, "Come and get it!"

The chili was good, not too spicy. We drank Diet Cokes and talked.

Catherine in her high chair worked on crackers. I watched her. I was here for a few minutes of sanity.

I told Flo that Ames and I were now officially partners.

"That a fact?" she said.

"Fact," Ames confirmed.

"How's the new place working out?"

"Fine," I said.

Ames ate his chili straight. I filled mine with crumbled crackers.

I had been aware for some time that if Ames indicated something beyond friendship in his relationship with Flo, she would be receptive. Flo was somewhere around sixty-five years old. Ames was over seventy. Flo had a built-in family to offer — herself, Adele, and the baby, plus the money her husband Gus had left her.

I didn't think Ames was in the market, but the door was open.

Adele called. She was going to be late. Flo told her we were there. Adele said she was sorry.

Catherine was in Flo's arms and George Jones was singing "He Stopped Loving Her Today" when we left. Ames went out first and looked around to be sure no one was about to shoot at me. There was no real cover around the houses in the area, which was almost without trees and bushes. The trees that did exist were, like the houses, only five or six years old.

"Next stop?" asked Ames, riding shotgun again as I drove.

"I've got dinner with Sally," I said.

"Best be looking for whoever's shooting at you."

"I think I know."

I told him. He nodded.

"So," he said. "I keep an eye on the shooter."

"Yes."

We met at Miss Saigon just across 301 from the Greyhound bus station. The restaurant was in a small, downscale mall with mostly Hispanic businesses: a tienda, a travel agency, a beauty shop, a check-cashing service. One of the shops in the mall was, according to Ettiene Viviase, a legitimate business and a front for a neighborhood mom-and-pop numbers racket.

I arrived first, putting my Cubs cap in my pocket. I didn't want it stolen through the broken window of my car. I wore a clean pair of tan wash-and-wear pants and a white shirt with a button-down collar. The cap didn't really go with the dressed-up version of Lewis Fonesca.

I ordered Vietnamese iced tea. Sally arrived ten minutes later, touched my shoulder as she passed, and sat across from me. Coming separately had been Sally's idea.

"I don't want any front door good-byes," she had said.

"I understand," I had said.

"Sorry I'm late," she said.

"Not very."

"Not very sorry or not very late?" she asked with a smile that could have used more enthusiasm.

She ordered an unsweetened iced tea.

When the waiter returned, I ordered noodles with short ribs. Sally ordered duck soup.

We ate in silence. The restaurant was small and busy, with mostly Vietnamese customers. Vaguely Asian music was playing in the background. Voices were low.

"Did you . . . ?" she began, pausing with chopsticks raised. She stopped, question unanswered but understood.

"He'll go away soon," I said.

"Soon?"

"Maybe the next few days."

"Far?"

"Far," I said.

"How do you plan to persuade him?"

"You'll know in a few days."

I didn't use chopsticks, though I could have. My wife had taught me how to use them. At first I had been a poor student, but I caught on. Now, I couldn't bring myself to use them. It was something I did only with Catherine, a small thing but a fine silkscreen for memories.

"Lewis," she said.

"Yes."

"You drifted off somewhere."

"Sorry," I said. "With Ronnie gone, you won't have to leave."

"It was hard for me to come here tonight," she said, looking down at the bowl in front of her. "Hard for me to face you. I can't imagine seeing you day after day."

"You won't get any accusations from me," I said.

"I know, but you don't need any more pain from man or woman."

"Don't leave," I said.

"That's probably the nicest thing you've ever said to me, but where do we go if I stay?"

"Where do you want to go?"

"You answered a question with a question," she said. "I do that all the time with clients."

"So?"

"You don't even know how I look nude and we've never been to bed together," she said. "Almost four years, Lewis."

I tried to stop it, but the image of Sally and Dwight Torcelli in bed came to me. It would come back to me, too. I was sure.

"We can work on it," I said.

"You, me, Ronnie, and Catherine in bed together," she said. "You don't forget anything, Lew. I'll bet you even know the name of your grade school gym teacher and exactly how he looked."

"She," I said, remembering. "Shirley Ann Stoffey. Her husband was Jerry Stoffey, a staff writer for the *Chicago Tribune*. Mrs. Stoffey had a small purple birthmark above her left wrist. She had a Baltimore accent and a tarnished tin whistle she always wore around her neck."

"You see? You can't forget and you can't bring yourself to lie about your memories. You never forget," Sally said.

I didn't say anything. I should have, but I couldn't. This was the moment for sincere, simple eloquence, but it wasn't in me. Sally was right.

She sighed deeply and said, "I'll tell you what. The job in Vermont is open-ended and I could always come back here. I might even get a raise. The kids would be happy if we stayed. I'll tell you what. In Vermont, a year from today, we meet and see . . . Lewis, I'm leaving, not just you but my own memories."

"You can't run away from memories," I said. "I tried. They follow you."

"I've made my decision," she said.

"I understand."

And I did. Sally usually had coffee after dinner. Not this time. I said I would pay. She let me. She gave me a quick kiss and left me sitting there.

I paid in cash and left a big tip. I don't know how much fifteen or even twenty percent is. I don't know how much nine times seven is. I had counted on Catherine to do that. I had counted on Sally to do it, too.

Sally was right, right about everything.

I got in my Saturn, put on my cap, and drove to the place where I was reasonably sure of finding the evidence I needed to convince the police.

I parked a block away and walked back. At the window, I checked, double-checked, and checked again to be sure no one was inside. The next shot from the person who lived here would likely be up close and with a shotgun. The window wasn't locked. I climbed in.

Less than ten minutes later, pocket flashlight in hand, I had found everything I needed. I left it all in place and left.

Tomorrow, it would be over.

It was about eleven at night when I climbed the long flight of stairs to my rooms. With Victor gone, I would be spending my first night alone here. I was looking forward to it. But first I had to deal with the visitor standing on the landing at the top of the stairs.

"Where have you been?" asked Greg Legerman. "No, wait. I take that back. It's none of my business. What I should say is, How is the effort to save Ronnie going? That is my business."

"It'll be over tomorrow," I said.

I opened the door, reached in to turn on the lights. He followed me inside. I closed the door and he moved to the chair behind my desk. I could have told him I didn't want to talk. It would have been true, but I sat.

"Where's Winn?" I asked.

"Home, I think. We don't spend all our time together. Well, most, but not all. I've decided I'm going to Duke. So is Winn."

I shifted my weight, took out my wallet and counted out cash, which I placed on the desk in front of Greg.

"What's this?" he asked.

"What you paid me minus the time I spent working on your case."

"Why?"

"Let's say your mother and grandfather have paid me more than enough."

"I don't understand," he said, looking at the money.

"You will tomorrow."

" 'Tomorrow and tomorrow and tomorrow creeps at a petty pace,' " he said. "That's Shakespeare, sort of."

"I know. Very poetic."

He looked around the room wondering what to say or do next.

"Do you know the history of your semi-profession in the United States?"

"No."

He got up, leaving the cash on the desk, and started to pace as he spoke.

"The first U.S. marshals were appointed by George Washington to serve subpoenas, summonses, writs, warrants, and other processes issued by the courts. They also arrested and handled all Federal prisoners."

"I'm not a U.S. marshal. I'm a private contractor."

"I know, I know. But you see the history, the connection. Our lives, our history, and the history of the entire country — the entire world — are connected by slender threads of seemingly random events."

"Interesting," I said. "Would you like a can of Coke?"

If he said yes I would have given him the caffeine-free variety. Greg Legerman needed no more stimulation.

"I'm sorry," he said. "I get carried away."

"You have any idea who killed Blue Berrigan?"

"No, but I have to tell you something about him. Berrigan."

"Tell."

"I hired Blue Berrigan to lie to you, to tell you he had evidence that would clear Ronnie."

"He tried."

"He wanted more money from me. Said he'd tell the police I had killed Horvecki."

"And you wouldn't give it?"

"No," he said. "I didn't kill him. I don't know who did, probably whoever killed Horvecki."

"Maybe," I said. "How did you know Berrigan?"

"He used to work for my grandfather on his infomercials and at his mall appearances. I've known him all my life. He always needed money. It was a bad idea."

"Very bad."

"I got him killed," said Greg.

I didn't say anything.

"What happened to the Chinese guy?" Greg asked. "His bedroll's gone."

"Went home. A place far away and exotic."

"China?"

"Oswego, Illinois."

"Cheng Ho, fifteenth century admiral,

diplomat, explorer, son of a Muslim, descendent of Mongol kings, was the first real Chinese explorer extending his country's influence throughout the regions bordering the Indian Ocean."

"Greg," I said, trying to slow him down as he paced, speaking so quickly that I missed some of the words.

"Fifteenth century," he said. "Do you know how the Romans numbered the centuries before the Christian era?"

"Greg," I said again as he paused in his pacing to glance at the dark Dalstrom paintings on my wall.

I thought he was going to shift from the Roman calendar to something about art, but he stayed with his history.

"Eleven months, a three-hundred-and-four-day year. But my question was a trick. Your answers to me have been tricks. The Romans didn't number their years. When a new year came, they called it something like 'The Year of the Counsels of Rome.' They didn't think of decades or centuries. Time meant something different to the Romans."

"Greg, how did you get here?"

"I drove, of course."

"How about staying here tonight?"

"Why?"

"Do I have to tell you?"

He went back to the chair, sat, played with the money, scratched his forehead and said, "No."

"I'll call your mother."

"No," he said. "Not necessary. She isn't sitting up waiting for me."

"Your grandfather?"

"No. I won't be missed. I'm never missed. I am a trial and a tribulation to my family," he said, finishing with a broad grin. "Don't worry. I've brought some of my quiet-down tranquilizers. I'll be fine."

"Bathroom is over there. I'll get my sleeping bag out of the closet."

"I need a pillow."

"I'll get you one."

"Thanks. I'll take that Coke now."

"Caffeine free," I said.

"I'll take it."

I got it for him. He used it to wash down three pills he fished from a small plastic bottle.

"I'll resist telling you about the developmental history of tranquilizers," he said.

"Thank you."

"You remind me of your grandfather," I said.

"Is that an insult or a compliment?"

"Observation."

"Others have said the same. I long to be

away at the Duke campus, built and endowed by . . ."

I sat listening as he slowly talked himself down, drank two Cokes, used the bathroom twice, and finally, at a few minutes past midnight, took off his shoes. I got him a pillow. He took it and moved to what had been Victor's corner.

I turned off the lights and got into bed. It would not be the first night I slept without a pillow. I'd have to put the purchase of a guest pillow on my mental list of things I needed.

There was no problem. I lay in darkness in my T-shirt and shorts and let the thoughts of both Catherines, of Sally, and of what I had to do in the morning come. They came and went, and I slept well. I slept dreamlessly.

Greg was gone when I got up a few minutes before eight the next morning. The sleeping bag was rolled up with the pillow plumped on top of it. The cash I had laid out was still on the desk and there was a scribbled note I could barely read:

I have the feeling that what you will do today will be something other than what I would like. Consider the cash payment for your putting up with me last night. Greg

I called Ames and told him I would pick him up in half an hour.

"Did you get any sleep?" I asked.

"Some."

"Our shooter?"

"Didn't move."

"You have breakfast?"

"Not yet," he said. "Okay if we eat here?"

"Sure."

Half an hour later I was seated at a table in the Texas Bar and Grill and being served by Big Ed. We ate chili and eggs and didn't say much.

"Thanks," I said.

"For?"

"You fixed my car window last night," I said. "Or was it the car window fairy?"

"Me. Took a few hours off when our shooter was tucked in."

"You armed?"

Ames pulled his jacket open to reveal a small holstered gun.

"Leave it here," I said. "We won't need it where we're going."

I called Ettiene Viviase and he agreed to meet us at the jail just down the street when I told him what I wanted to do.

We could have walked to the jail from the

Texas, but I drove and we found a space with a two-hour meter. I dropped enough quarters into it and we met Viviase in the reception area in front of the bulletproof window, behind which sat a uniformed woman.

"She's here," Viviase said. "Make it good."

He took us through a door and into a small room where lawyers and clients, relatives and inmates, cops and criminals met to talk and lie and threaten and plead.

Torcelli, wearing an orange uniform, sat at the table.

He looked at me and said, "You've come to get me out."

"No," Viviase said. "He came to be sure you stay in here. You killed Philip Horvecki."

Torcelli's nose was covered by a wide bandage that didn't hide the spreading purple. The cavities of his eyes looked as if they had been painted black.

"I didn't . . . What? I didn't kill Horvecki. Tell him Fonesca."

"Go ahead," said Viviase. "Tell us."

I told my tale slowly and carefully so Torcelli wouldn't make any mistake about what he was hearing.

The first words from him when I finished talking were, "I want my lawyer."

"He withdrew from your case," said Viviase. "He has a bad cold."

"His feet are cold," said Torcelli. "Alana stopped paying him, didn't she? Find Rachel. Rachel will pay him."

"We're looking for her," Viviase said.

"This is a mistake," Torcelli said again, this time looking at Ames, who said, "Take it like a man."

"I didn't touch your daughter," Torcelli tried, turning to Viviase. "A kiss, maybe. What's the harm in that?"

"She's fifteen," Viviase answered.

"Fonesca, you were supposed to help me," Torcelli said, his voice dropping, his head in his hands.

"I guess I failed," I said.

19

"You sure?" Viviase asked.

"Sure," said Ames. "Followed the taxi right here."

The sky was almost black. Thunder from the north. Lightning flashes. The rain was light. It would, I was sure, turn heavy. It was a typical Florida rainstorm.

We had backup, two patrol cars running without sirens or lights, two armed police officers in each.

"Let's get it done," said Viviase, walking up the path to the door with one of the police officers, ringing the bell and stepping to the side.

Ames and I stood off to the side on the sidewalk, watching the other cops, two left, one right, circling around the building. Viviase rang again and then used a key to open the door and step in, his back against the doorjamb.

"You need a warrant," a voice came from

the darkness inside. "You have a warrant?"

"We don't need a warrant," Viviase said as a single small light came on, and Rachel Horvecki stepped forward inside the room. "This is a crime scene."

"I want him," I heard her say.

"Fonesca," called Viviase. "You want to step in here a minute? The lady wants to talk to you."

Ames and I stepped forward and through the door. The shades and curtains were all down and closed. The room was a funereal black.

Thunder rolled toward us. Then lightning, and in the flash we saw Rachel standing completely nude and carrying a shotgun that looked big and powerful enough to down a large, charging rhino.

We stood in darkness.

"Your husband confessed," Viviase said.

"To what?"

"To killing your father," Viviase said. "He says you helped him and it was all your idea so you could get your father's money."

"He didn't say that," she said.

"You're under arrest," Viviase said firmly. "Tell her, Fonesca."

Imperative. An order. Tell the naked woman in the dark with the shotgun how you figured out she and her husband murdered her father.

"I came here last night," I said. "You were out, looking for me. You were followed by Mr. McKinney. I found your father's collection of shotguns and rifles in the back room and some photographs on the wall of you and him. You were about thirteen and cradling a weapon almost as big as you were. Your father has his hand around your shoulder in all the photographs."

I could hear her move a little. I glanced at a shadow moving past the window to her right as she said, "If they shoot, I shoot."

"No one's shooting," said Viviase.

"I found some of your poetry in a drawer in your room," I said.

"You had no right," she shouted.

"Crime scene, remember?" said Viviase. "Your father died just about where I think you're standing."

I knew there were still bloodstains on the floor.

"You tried to kill me," I said.

"Why would I want to kill you? You were helping Ronnie."

"You were afraid I'd find out that your husband really did kill your father."

"Not true," she said.

"True," said Ames.

A slight *tink* of metal as I sensed the

421

shotgun moving toward Ames.

"Ronnie, or both of you, killed your father early that night," I went on. "You chose that night because you knew you had a nearly perfect witness. Essau Williams, a policeman or Jack Pepper, a minister, would be parked across the street watching your father's house, wanting to be watched as they returned to that spot across the street, like men punching into work. It was Pepper. And what did he see? Hours after your father was already dead, the Reverend Jack Pepper saw Ronnie enter the house just as a man in a coat and watch cap came through a side window and run down the street. Almost immediately, Ronnie came back out the door and looked both ways for the man in the watch cap. He looked around and he went back inside. You had already called 911 and said there'd been a murder. There was a car there almost immediately. A bloody Ronnie was kneeling by the body. The police didn't find you, because you were the man in the watch cap. There was only one problem."

"What?" she asked.

I was sure the shotgun was getting heavier. It was probably pointing down at the floor.

"Jack Pepper didn't immediately come forward about the man who came through the window and about seeing Ronnie in the house for only a few seconds. He didn't want to explain why he was sitting in his car in front of your house. There was a restraining order against him. You waited a while before coming forward with your story about seeing a man in a watch cap kill your father and go through the window. Your father was already dead. You were the one in the watch cap. When Pepper showed up, you talked loud enough for Pepper to hear a muffled voice and something thudding, probably you hitting the wall."

"Pepper should have come forward sooner," she said.

"He's come forward now," said Viviase.

"Want to give me that shotgun, miss, and go put on some clothes?" said Ames gently.

There was a sound of movement and she turned on a shaded table lamp.

She looked dazed.

"Ronnie said I killed my father?"

"He did," Ames said. "We heard him."

"It's on tape," said Viviase.

"Ronnie's not a bad man," she said. "He likes my poetry. He's so gentle in bed. I know he can't stay away from other women, from girls, but he always comes back to me."

And your father's millions, I thought.

"This is unfair," she said. "My father was

a monster. He did things to me I . . . it's
unfair. The police could never stop him —
him and his lawyers. He deserved to die."

The shotgun rose and pointed directly at
Viviase's chest.

"Could I have a glass of water?" Ames
said.

She looked at him.

"And could I maybe sit down?"

"Water?"

"Juice would be fine, too, but not grape-
fruit. Doesn't sit well in me."

"I like your poetry," I said.

"You're just saying that because you don't
want me to shoot you."

"That, too, but I like your poetry. None of
it is happy, is it?"

"No," she said. "Never was. Looks like it
never will be. I've got fresh orange juice.
Will that do?"

She handed the shotgun to Ames, who
said, "It'll do just fine."

"So," said Viviase while a policewoman
walked with Rachel to her room to dress.
"One down. Which one killed Berrigan and
why?"

Ames had removed the shells from the
shotgun and handed it to one of the police
officers who had come into the house from

424

all entryways.

"That's a mystery," I said.

"You didn't answer the question," he said.

"I don't have an answer."

"You have a pretty good idea," said Viviase.

I shrugged.

I drove to my place and let Ames out.

"Certain you want to do this yourself?" he asked.

"Certain."

"I'll be here," he said.

I knew the odds of reaching the person I had called were slight, and I was right. I left a message saying we had to meet at four at Selby Gardens.

"Walk along the path till you see me. I'll be sitting on a bench," I had said.

It was almost one when I got to the Dairy Queen on Clark Street. There was a huge photograph on the wall of the original DQ with old cars and long-gone people around it. I didn't order the Chocolate Covered Cherry Blizzard. I wasn't sure why. Instead I had a medium Banana Chocolate Oreo Blizzard. I also ordered a burger and a large fries. When my order came, I put the fries in a bag and worked on the blizzard and burger. It wasn't the DQ I had lived behind for almost four years. The owner was nice, but he wasn't Dave.

By three I was at Selby Gardens sitting on a bench facing the water. A white heron landed next to me, its wings flapping to a close, searching for something from the human on the bench. I did not disappoint. I placed three fries on the bench. He gobbled them up and was joined by two other small, brown, iridescent birds. After the fries were gone, the birds lingered, looking at me. They left only when they were certain I would give no more. The heron was the last to go. He flapped his wings and flew off over the bay.

At ten minutes to four, Winston Churchill Graeme sat next to me, right where the heron had been. He cleaned his glasses on his shirt and turned his eyes in the same direction mine were pointed.

"When I was sixteen, I thought about quitting school and joining the Navy."

"What stopped you?"

"The fact that my parents didn't object. They thought it was a pretty good idea. They thought going to college and becoming a lawyer was an even better idea."

"What happened?"

"I didn't become a sailor. If I had, I might

426

be out to sea instead of sitting here with you.

"Why are we here?" Winn asked.

"So you could tell me why you killed Blue Berrigan."

20

There was a single fry left. I had missed it, but I spotted it now as I was about to crumple up the bag and drop it in the nearby trash basket. I handed him the bag.

"For the birds," I said. "One left."

He nodded, adjusted his glasses, and threw the fry in the general direction of a pair of nearby pigeons.

"Why do you think I killed him?" he asked.

I reached into my pocket and pulled out the white and red golf tees.

"I found these in the backseat of Berrigan's jeep."

"So, he played golf."

"No, he didn't. I looked in his room and his closet and asked his landlady. He didn't play golf. You do."

"Maybe they didn't belong to whoever killed him. Maybe they had been there a long time," he tried.

"No," I said. "Both tees were on top of a splatter of blood. The killer lost them during the attack."

"I'm not the only one who plays golf," he said.

"No, you're not, but you're the only one who would kill Berrigan for blackmailing Greg. Greg told me that Berrigan tried to get more money out of him."

"Yes."

"And you told me you would do anything to protect your friend."

His hands were shaking now.

"What happened, Winn?" I said.

He paused, looked into the DQ bag as if there might be a miracle fry in it, and then spoke. "I was with Berrigan when he went to see you at that bar. I wanted to be sure he would go through with saying he had evidence to clear Ronnie. I stayed in the jeep."

"But?"

"He got frightened, panicked. You said something to him in the bar. He told me he wanted more money, a lot more money. He was hysterical. He said he'd tell you, tell the police that Greg had murdered Horvecki. He drove to his place and parked in front. He kept saying things like 'What am I doing? What am I the fuck doing?' He didn't get out of the jeep, just sat there looking over his shoulder down the street, hitting the steering wheel hard with the palms of both hands. I told him to get out. He wouldn't move. He kept saying he would tell the police that Greg killed Horvecki. I couldn't let that happen."

Winn closed his eyes.

"So you hit him with something in the backseat."

"Yes, one of Greg's grandfather's mallets."

"Then you got out of the jeep and ran before I got there."

"Yes."

"You went to Ronnie's apartment and put the mallet under his bookcase. He was in jail for one murder. Two wouldn't make a big difference, right?"

"You know, I could hit you with something and throw you in the bay," he said.

"No, you couldn't," I said.

"No, you're right. I couldn't. What are you going to do?"

"Nothing," I said. "You're going to go to Elisabeth Viviase's father and tell him what happened."

"I can't. My mother . . ."

"The odds are good that eventually, probably soon, a strand of hair, a string of cloth, a DNA trace is going to lead to you. You already left the two tees. What else did you leave?"

"I don't know."

"Turn yourself in, get a good lawyer. I'm sure Greg's grandfather will pay for one. You're still a minor. Think about it."

"Yeah," he said. "I'll think about it. Thanks. Will you turn me in if I don't do it?"

"You'll do it," I said. "Do you know who George Altman is?"

"Cardinals outfielder in the sixties?"

"And a Cub before that. Here."

I took the autographed baseball I had purchased out of my pocket and handed it to him. He took it and looked at me, puzzled.

"It's yours," I said.

"Why?"

"I don't know."

I got up.

Winn Graeme looked down at the ball cupped in his hands as if it were a small crystal ball.

"Mr. Fonesca," he said. "What will Greg do without me?"

At ten the next morning, I carried my tribute of coffee and biscotti into the office of Ann Hurwitz who motioned me into my usual seat. She was on the phone.

"I'm not investing in alchemy," she said patiently. "I want secure stocks and bonds. I do not want real estate, neither malls nor parking lots nor the foreclosed property of others."

There was a pause while she listened, accepted a bagged biscotti and coffee, nodded her thanks, and then spoke into the telephone as she jangled the heavy jeweled chain around her thin wrist:

"We've been through this many times, Jerome. You are forty-four years old. I am eighty-three years old. Depending on what chance and heredity bring your way, you will live about forty more years according to current actuarial projections. I, on the other hand, should have, at most, another seven to ten years. I am not interested in risking what my husband and I have saved. It is not because we intend to retire to Borneo on our savings. We wish to give to a set of charities, charities that support the continuation of human life. Get back to me when you've thought about this."

She hung up and looked at me.

"Lewis, you are the only one of my current clients who does not believe in God and does not want to live forever."

"If there is a God, I don't like him," I said.

"So you have indicated in the past. Almond or macadamia?" she asked, hoisting a biscotti.

"Almond."

"Tell me about your week," she said, "while I enjoy your gift."

I told her, talked for almost twenty minutes, and then stopped. She had finished her biscotti and coffee and my almond biscotti.

"Progress again," she said.

"Progress?"

"You made a commitment to Ames. You offered something resembling a commitment to Sally. After four years you are putting down tentative tendrils in Sarasota."

"Maybe."

"Have you done your homework?"

I reached into my pocket and came out with the stack of lined index cards on which people's favorite, or just remembered, first lines were. She took them.

"Why did I have you collect favorite first lines rather than jokes?"

"I don't know."

"I think it is time for you to have a new beginning," she said, quickly going through the cards, glasses perched on the end of her nose. "And now yours, Lewis, your book."

"Moby-Dick," I said.

433

"What do you think the book is about?" Ann asked.

"A lone survivor," I said. "I bought a copy of the book at Brant's and copied the line."

I took out my notebook.

"Is it that hard for you to remember? Almost everyone knows it. 'Call me Ishmael.' "

"Yes," I said. "Can I read what I have on the card?"

"All right," she said, lifting a hand in acceptance, "read."

" 'It was the devious-cruising *Rachel,* that in her retracing search after her missing children, only found another orphan.' "

"That's not the beginning of *Moby-Dick,* Lewis," she said.

"No," I said. "It's the end."

ABOUT THE AUTHOR

Stuart M. Kaminsky is the author of more than sixty novels and an Edgar Award winner who has been given the coveted Grand Master Award by the Mystery Writers of America. In addition to his Lew Fonesca series (for which the Sarasota Convention and Visitors Bureau has officially recognized him as "The Voice of Sarasota"), Kaminsky is also the creator of the critically acclaimed Inspector Rostnikov, Toby Peters, and Abe Lieberman mystery series. He resides with his family, naturally enough, in Florida.

The employees of Thorndike Press hope you have enjoyed this Large Print book. All our Thorndike, Wheeler, and Kennebec Large Print titles are designed for easy reading, and all our books are made to last. Other Thorndike Press Large Print books are available at your library, through selected bookstores, or directly from us.

For information about titles, please call:
  (800) 223-1244

or visit our Web site at:
  http://gale.cengage.com/thorndike

To share your comments, please write:
  Publisher
  Thorndike Press
  295 Kennedy Memorial Drive
  Waterville, ME 04901